Helen Phifer has ~~~~ rdresser, care assist~~ant and ~~~~~~~~~~~~~~~~ ~~~~, ~~m~~other of five and grandmother (although she still feels far too young to be the latter). For the last six years she has worked full time for Cumbria Constabulary as a PCSO and loves her job—well, mo~~~~~ ~~~~ ~~~~. She'll let y~~~~ into a little secret; she originally applied ~~~~ ~~~~ ~~~~ ~~~~ ~~~~ ~~~~ to help with her writing. She wanted to make it as ~~~~~~~ ~~tic as she could and never imagined she would be accepted!

She has loved to read and write since she discovered Enid Blyton as a young child. In her teens she was hooked on Stephen King—she loves reading books which make the hair on the back of her neck stand on end and he never lets her down. She started writing in her twenties. In her thirties she got an idea for a crime/ghost story that wouldn't go away. The fact that she couldn't find enough of the stories she loved persuaded her to get hers down on paper and she is so glad that she did. She started this book eight years ago and it has been a labour of love, but one of which she is very proud.

You can contact follow Helen on her blog at http://helenphifer. wordpress.com, her website at www.helenphifer.co.uk and on Twitter, @helenphifer1.

THE
GHOST HOUSE

HELEN PHIFER

CARINA™

This edition is published by arrangement with Harlequin Books S.A. CARINA is a trademark of Harlequin Enterprises Limited, used under licence.

Published in Great Britain 2015
by CARINA, an imprint of Harlequin (UK) Limited,
Eton House, 18-24 Paradise Road,
Richmond, Surrey, TW9 1SR

© 2013 Helen Phifer

ISBN 978-0-263-25400-6

98-0115

Harlequin (UK) Limited's policy is to use papers that are natural, renewable and recyclable products and made from wood grown in sustainable forests. The logging and manufacturing processes conform to the legal environmental regulations of the country of origin.

Printed and bound by
CPI Group (UK) Ltd, Croydon, CR0 4YY

For my brother Chris and my best friend Cathy,
two of the brightest stars in the sky

CHAPTER 1

Annie Graham studied the selection of keys on the rusty hook behind the kitchen door, looking for the one to the crumbling Victorian mansion. Recognising the white, plastic key ring she plucked it off the hook and pushed it into the bottom of her pocket. Earlier she had filled her rucksack with a torch, some rope, a bottle of water, a bag of Quavers and a bar of chocolate: all the things a girl couldn't live without. She felt like Indiana Jones, about to go on an adventure.

Her training as a police officer made her less inclined to fear the things most of her friends would. Through work she had been in some really sticky situations. She just hoped the inside of the house wasn't in as much of a state as her brother Ben had warned her about. Tess was whining to come but if she let her run loose and Tess got injured she'd be in big trouble or, in Jake's words, 'well and truly busted'.

She locked up then walked along the tiny overgrown path that skirted the outside of Ben's farmhouse and led through the woods to the mansion, which was a couple of minutes away. Soon the tall chimneys were visible, peeking above the tops of the oak trees. She pushed through a small gap in the bushes, fighting with the brambles, to find herself standing in front of the mansion.

It was magnificent; the walls were built from the same deep red sandstone as the Abbey ruins just below the entrance to the woods. It was remarkable to think that someone could actually afford to build such a stunning home and then abandon it. It had lain empty with no one to care for it for decades. The current owner was an elderly woman who lived in New York. As far as Annie was aware the woman had never even been to look at the house, which had been left to her by the last owner, a distant relative. Maybe if she had she would have done something with it; the potential was endless. Then again, if it had been developed her brother wouldn't have been able to afford to buy the farmhouse; there had been a clause in the contract that whoever owned the farm had to be the caretaker of the big house. Ben was a builder so it was perfect for him. Annie loved the peace and tranquillity that being up here brought to her bruised mind.

All the downstairs windows were boarded up to stop the local teenagers from going inside and breaking their necks. The upstairs windows were, surprisingly, all intact – hundreds of tiny panes of stained glass with the most intricate patterns of lead beading running through them. Annie didn't envy whoever once had the job of keeping those clean; they were grimy now with over sixty years of dirt. The front door was an amazing work of art. Set into a Gothic arch, the huge oak door had the biggest brass knocker she had seen. It was a scary goblin face with a mouth full of pointed teeth. Annie knew that if she had been a visitor to the house she would never have used that thing, it would probably clamp its teeth shut and swallow your hand whole.

Taking the key she pushed it into the lock and was relieved when it turned – at least Ben had sorted out one thing. Pushing the heavy door it let out a loud groan. Annie was apprehensive of going in alone. She heard Ben's warning in the back of her mind but he was out of the country and she was housesitting, so technically she was in charge. Her stomach was churning with nervous excitement at finally being able to explore the house. Stepping inside she shuddered; a mix of emotions overwhelmed her but the feeling that shocked her most was the warm surge of familiarity, which rushed through her veins. It was so strong that she wanted to shout, 'I'm back, I've finally come home.' *But why? Why do I feel like this and who am I telling it to?* The feeling of déjà vu confused her but she brushed it off as wishful thinking.

The house was amazing. The entrance hall was so large it alone could accommodate a party. The walls were covered in begrimed and dusty oak panelling, the air smelt damp and fusty, and Annie tried not to breathe through her nose because it was so overpowering. She tried to picture the house as it used to be and an image began to form in her mind of the house when it was a family home. Fearfully she pushed it away.

The house was dark and full of shadows so she decided to start at the top and work her way down. That way, if the floors were as rotten as her brother believed and she fell through the ceiling, she would have all day to try and contact someone to come and rescue her. As brave as she felt she didn't want to be lying in a heap on the floor when what little light there was began to fade: that was far too scary.

Cautiously she walked across the floor to the staircase, which was a sweeping, grand statement; it didn't seem too dangerous. Placing her hand on the ornately carved oak banister she tested the first step. It creaked loudly but held her weight. Placing both feet on it she bounced up and down to see if she would fall through; she didn't. Taking one step at a time she reached the first floor and grinned because the stairs hadn't collapsed on her. *Why are the men in my life such drama queens?* Treading carefully along the corridor she peered into the many rooms she passed; their doors were either wide open or missing. Each room was now an empty shell but she could picture exactly how they used to look, with ornately carved beds covered in sumptuous, richly coloured throws. The wardrobes and drawers all matched; small bedside tables with heavy brass lamps and delicate pieces of cut glass were on display along with pretty perfume bottles. The only thing left in them now was the beautiful marble mantelpieces and, in a couple of rooms, some discarded beer cans with faded logos – Annie didn't think you could still buy those brands.

At the far end of the long hallway was the only closed door on the whole floor; Annie found herself drawn towards it. Standing outside she closed her eyes to try and picture what was on the other side but her mind was blank. Her fingers reached out, wrapping themselves around the dull brass knob. She pulled her hand back sharply. The metal was so freezing cold the tips of her fingers felt numb. Her mother's voice spoke clearly in her mind, 'Curiosity killed the cat. When will you ever learn?' Annie, who had been at loggerheads with her mum since she could talk, whispered 'never' then gripped the knob and twisted it with all her strength until it gave a little and slowly turned. There was no sensible reason why she was so desperate to go in there but she knew she had to.

She was greeted by a schoolroom and gasped with pleasure to see two small, well-worn pine desks with matching chairs tucked neatly underneath them. A huge bookcase filled the back wall. It was laden with books and Annie, who loved to read, grinned with pleasure. The mantelpiece in this room was lined with a row of tin soldiers, all standing on guard ready for their next battle. Annie walked over and picked one up, murmuring with delight that they were real – it wasn't her imagination. How had this room stayed intact when the rest of the house was an empty shell? Turning back to the desks she pulled out a chair and sat down, her fingers tracing the lines and grooves in the soft wood. Lifting the top to peer inside she smiled to see a dusty, old, black leather book. Picking it up she blew away some of the dust.

From somewhere inside the house she became aware of the soft tinkling of a piano; the tune was vaguely familiar to her, comforting. She looked at the title of the book, which was written in elegant gold script: *Alice's Adventures in Wonderland*. A man's muffled voice called out; it was deep and sounded to Annie as if it was coming through a loudspeaker. A chill ran through her body. It sounded like someone she knew a long time ago but now couldn't quite remember.

'Alice, where are you? I want to come and play.'

Goosebumps broke out all over her arms; she knew she was the only person in the house.

'Alice, I'm coming to find you ready or not.'

Whoever the voice belonged to wasn't asking whoever Alice was to play the game, it was telling her she had no choice. Instinctively Annie looked around for somewhere to hide, her heart beating so hard she was afraid the steady thud of it would give her away. Then came footsteps climbing the stairs that were so loud they made the floor vibrate. Annie knew that it just wasn't possible, but they kept on coming. Soon they would be on the landing and heading straight towards her. Standing quickly she whacked her thigh on the sharp corner of the desk and bit her tongue so as not to cry out, 'I'm not ready, I don't want to play with you, whoever you are.' The footsteps got louder and she looked at the door, which had swung shut: there was nowhere to hide in this room.

The sudden silence was deafening. She knew that whoever had been calling out was now standing outside the door, listening. Annie backed away, putting some distance between herself and the door, adrenalin making every sense in her body alert. She had been in the police force for five years and was tough. Her self-defence training and regular Saturday night brawls with drunks had turned her into a competent fighter, but what really scared her was the thought that whoever was standing on the other side of the door may not be the sort of person that she could grapple with. *Do I believe in ghosts?* Her body taut, feet automatically taking up a fighter's stance, she raised her fists, which were clenched so hard her knuckles had gone white.

There was no light seeping under the door, it was blocked out by the black shadow standing on the other side, and the little light that had been in the room had faded. Her stomach muscles tightened; she was as ready as she could be. A huge bang exploded directly above the house and she shrieked, her legs wobbled, threatening to give way. Annie whipped her head around the room: it was empty. No tin soldiers or books, no desks. She squeezed her eyes shut then opened them: the room was empty just like the others. The door was now open just as she had left it and thankfully there was no crazy man standing on the other side waiting for her. But still an uneasy feeling of being watched settled over her. Forcing her feet to move she stepped forward and kicked something; she looked down to see a book on the floor. Too scared to read the title, although she had a pretty good idea what it was, she shoved it into her rucksack. Another crash of thunder echoed around the house making her shriek again.

Not caring any more about how safe the floors were she ran out onto the landing, along the hall to the staircase and took the stairs two at a time. Her heart was beating so fast she was positive she was about to have a heart attack right there in the big old house with only the ghost waiting and watching for her to come and join him.

Annie, never big on church or religion, began to hum the first hymn that came into her mind, 'All Things Bright and Beautiful', over and over again. In a matter of seconds she had crossed the great hall and the front door loomed in front of her. For a fleeting moment she envisioned it not opening, but with one almighty tug she was outside on the steps.

14

The smell of ozone filled the air. It hadn't started to rain but the sky was now a blanket of dirty yellow and grey. Slamming the heavy door shut behind her she fumbled to pull the key from her pocket. Gripping it tightly she rammed it into the lock. As she turned it she hoped that whatever or whoever was in that house was now locked in on the other side.

The last of the daylight had been obscured by the thunderclouds. Annie ran towards the tiny path as the first heavy drops of rain began to fall. The trees shielded her from the worst of it but it was the last place anyone should be in a thunderstorm. As if to confirm this, another huge crack echoed around the woods. Turning she took one last look at the house as a flash of brilliant white lightning lit up the sky above it. Her eyes searched for the window of the room she had just been in. Locating it she took a sharp intake of breath. At the last window was a blurry white shape of a woman staring back at her.

Annie turned and ran back to the farmhouse as fast as her shaky legs could carry her. Reaching the clearing her shoulders relaxed a little at the sight of the gate. She scrambled over it and pushed her way into the kitchen, slamming the door shut behind her. She leant against it but her legs gave way and she slid, in one big, dripping heap, down to the floor. Tess growled from the safety of her dog basket then, realising it was Annie, quietened and watched her warily. *Wow,*

Tess, what a guard dog you are. She began to take deep breaths to calm herself down and then, when she felt able, she pulled herself up and went into the living room to watch the storm, which was still raging.

The lightning illuminating the woods was the most beautiful yet terrifying thing she had ever seen, and it was centred over the big house. Trudging up the stairs she went to the only bedroom that overlooked the mansion for a better view. It fascinated her that the lightning was striking directly over it.

Annie was scared; she didn't want to be alone in the middle of the woods. What she would give to have her colleague and best friend Jake with her, his muscular arms wrapped around her. She couldn't get a phone signal on a good day up here. In a storm she was totally cut off. Jake would laugh at her and tell her she had lost the plot big time and maybe he wouldn't be that far wrong. He would be at work now, halfway through his shift, which is where she should be. At least then bad things happened to other people and not her.

Common sense told her the house wasn't haunted; there was no such thing as ghosts. But the other explanation scared her even more: her head injury could be worse than the doctor had thought. Then she remembered the book and went back downstairs to check her bag. If it wasn't there then she would go to the hospital tomorrow and tell them she was hallucinating.

Her bag was on the kitchen floor and for a moment Annie didn't know whether she wanted to open it or not. Eventually she unzipped it and rummaged around inside; her fingers caught the sharp corner of a leather bound book. *Oh crap.*

CHAPTER 2

By the time Will arrived at Jenna White's house the normally quiet street was thronging with people. Earlier, the arrival of Jake in the patrol car, after the call had come in for a missing teenager, had set a few curtains twitching. But now neighbours were standing in front gardens chatting away to each other, and several people had remembered that they had left something in the boot of their cars and were trying to look inconspicuous, but failing miserably, as they loitered at the rear of their vehicles.

A reporter from the local paper parked opposite Will, who growled under his breath at him: he was a right pain in the backside. His speciality was making every copper he interviewed look like an idiot. Will was well aware that some of his colleagues didn't really need much help in that department, but most of them came to work to help others – protect and serve the public and all that malarkey – so the papers should have been on their side. Will was just biding his time until the reporter stepped over the line and gave him a reason to arrest him, show him the hospitality of the custody suite and see how he liked bed and breakfast listening to the regulars: drunks wailing and being sick or drug addicts coming down from their highs.

A handful of youths, dressed as if they had starring roles in the Rocky Horror Picture Show, were hanging around by the gate of 9 Walton Path. Jake appeared at the front door and lifted his hand to wave at Will, who was out of his car and ducking inside the front garden before the reporter got the lens cap off his camera.

'Glad to see you mate, the word has spread like wildfire: bloody Facebook. And by the look of that lot over there they have her down as being abducted by a transvestite alien,' said Jake.

Will closed the front door behind him and followed Jake through to the kitchen. The house was neat and tidy and the sweet smell of vanilla filled the air from a reed diffuser on the hall table: it reminded him of his Nan's home. She had lived in the next street along and, as the queen of baking, her house had always smelt like this. Will felt his heartstrings tug at the sight of the crumpled woman staring at him expectantly.

'Mrs White, I'm Detective Sergeant Will Ashworth. I work in CID. Jake has told me about Jenna. You say she has never done anything like this before?'

'Never. She has never run away from home before or stayed out and not told me where she was staying. We did fall out because of her constantly arguing with her sister and I told her she was grounded until next weekend, but where would she go with no money? Something has happened to her, I just know it has. As soon as Sarah told me Jenna hadn't slept in her bed I knew then. She is such a kind girl, she wouldn't worry us like this.'

'I need to ask you some questions, and if you could give me as much information as you can it will help us search for Jenna and help Jake to fill out the missing persons report.' Will glanced at Jake who had found something interesting to look at on his boots. 'I know you told my colleague that Jenna hasn't got a boyfriend as such but you know kids, they don't always tell us adults what's going on.'

'She never mentions any particular boy. I know she has friends that are boys at college but they just hang around together.'

'Does she have any favourite places she likes to go?'

'The Abbey. She's doing an art project for college and has loved it there since she was a kid.' The woman sniffled into her handkerchief, then stood abruptly and left the room momentarily before returning with a glossy photograph, which she handed to Will.

He looked at the painted face staring back at him and passed it to Jake. He continued with his list of questions – 'Does Jenna keep a diary? Does she have a computer?' – to which Mrs White vigorously shook her head.

'I don't know about a diary, she may do because she was always writing things down. Her dad bought her a laptop for Christmas. It's in the dining room.'

Will smiled. 'That's great. Would you mind if we take it away to get examined and see if there is anything on it that could give us a clue where Jenna may be? Is it OK for me and Jake to go and take a look around Jenna's room?'

She whispered, 'Help yourself,' then stood and turned to go upstairs. Both Jake and Will followed her. She led them along the narrow landing to the last door, which had a picture of some movie star all the girls were crazy about stuck to it. Jake had no idea what he was called even though he'd watched the film a couple of times with Annie.

She opened the bedroom door and he stared at the assortment of posters on the wall; all were of the scariest people he had ever seen. They checked to make sure there was no sign of a struggle; nothing was out of place, there wasn't even an overturned cup and there were no bloodstains. The room was neat and tidy, for a teenager, and there was a black sparkly purse on top of the dressing table. Will opened it: there was a five pound note and a debit card. It was obvious that nothing untoward had happened in here, that Jenna hadn't been dragged from her bedroom fighting.

Walking out he nodded at Mrs White. 'Thank you. We'll go back to the station, see what we have and come up with a plan of action.

I'll be assigning you one of my family liaison officers, who will keep you up to date with our investigation and answer any questions you have. They will act as the go-between so you don't have to worry about trying to get hold of anyone at the station.'

Will nodded at Jake to follow him outside. He lowered his voice so the spectators couldn't hear. 'I hate to admit it but I think you're right to be worried. I'm forty percent she's shacked up with some boy or girl nursing off a hangover, but I'm sixty percent positive that something is wrong. It doesn't feel right. She isn't one of our usual missing persons, she isn't known to us, and I did some checks on *Intel* before I came here and there's no trace on the system for any of them. Until today the Whites were just your average family. Can you get an update from whoever is checking addresses and see where they are up to? I'll speak with the motley crew over there and see what they have to say.'

Jake smiled to himself as Will approached the crowd of Goths. Of all the jobs to get sent to today it had to be this one. He would bet a hundred quid that it wasn't going to be case closed in the next hour. He hoped that Jenna would turn up soon, tail between her legs and apologetic, but his instinct was telling him that it wasn't likely.

CHAPTER 3

He had no idea what was wrong with him; one minute he was happy with his rather ordinary existence, the next he couldn't bear it. The highlight of his life consisted of taking his elderly mother to the spiritualist church every Wednesday, where he would sit and listen to some phony pretend to pass on messages from the dead to the sad, desperate people sitting on the hard plastic chairs waiting for something that might mean it was their turn. His mother was just as bad. She held weekly séances for a couple of her friends and he was sure she made it up as she went along, but it gave him a couple of hours respite from her continual sniping at him.

It had been a month ago now that he had gone for a walk into town and spied the old tin box in the window of the junk shop. Melvyn, the owner, liked to call it an antique shop but more often than not it sold nothing but junk at extortionate prices. He had felt drawn to the box and before he knew it he'd gone into the shop and begun to wander around. He hadn't pointed out that he was interested in the box because then the price would go up by at least twenty quid, so he'd browsed for ten minutes and made to go out of the door when he stopped and looked at the box. He leant into the window and carefully extracted it from the rest of the rubbish that was in there. Melvyn had gone to put the kettle on so it gave him a chance to take a quick peek.

It had once been ornately painted with a golden pattern around it; now there was more rust than gold and it looked in such a poor state, but he felt his heart beat a little faster when he held it. Melvyn was talking very loudly on the phone to someone so he opened the box to look inside: there were some very old, grainy black and white photographs and a couple of letters. He tucked it under his arm and walked to the back of the shop. Melvyn was deep in conversation, the phone tucked under his ear as he stirred the tea bag around his chipped Charles and Diana royal wedding mug.

'How much do you want for this, Melvyn?' He was trying his best to look not in the least bothered so as not to arouse his suspicions.

'Fiver. It's an antique you know, Victorian.'

'A fiver? I only want it to keep some air rifle pellets in. I'll give you four quid.'

Whoever was on the phone took Melvyn's attention away and he nodded OK to him. He counted out four pound coins and put them on the counter. Melvyn nodded again then pocketed the money and turned back to pour the milk into his tea. He walked out of the shop with the box tucked under his arm and a big grin on his face: today was a good day for him. It wasn't often he got one over on old Melvyn. He went home and put the tin away in his wardrobe; safe until he had time to look at it properly.

***

He had been sitting here politely listening to his mother carping on about Edith's dead husband and thinking how fed up of his life he was. He was sick of being on his own and sick of his mother who was getting more irritating by the day. Then, out of nowhere, came the burning desire to kill someone. Inside, where he used to know nothing but calm, was now a violent torrent of bubbling horror. He didn't want to just smack someone over the head with a hammer or maybe run them over. He wanted to take a woman into the old mansion in the woods and slit her throat from ear to ear. He wanted to watch the rich crimson tide of warm, sticky blood flow across the pale, milky skin of his victim. She must have the whitest skin so the blood would contrast vividly against it and then he would slice and dice until the monster inside him was satiated and he felt like himself again.

'Are you listening to me? Edith wants a glass of water and judging by the look on your face you could do with one as well. What is the matter with you? Daydreaming like a fifteen-year-old boy! It doesn't matter, I'll get it myself.'

He blinked and looked around at the bunch of wrinkly old women staring at him.

'Sorry, Mother.'

She shook her head in disgust, and a vision of him slicing her throat into a permanent gaping smile made him jump up from the hard dining chair he was sitting on and knock the small card table she used for the séances onto the laps of the two women.

'Sorry, ladies.'

He left the room, brushing past his mother as she returned carrying a large glass of water. He bounded up the stairs and into his bedroom slamming his door shut; he then dragged the chair over and pushed it under the handle so the old bat couldn't walk in on him. Turning on his computer he waited for Google to load. He was a natural at internet grooming – it was so easy to be the perfect person to whoever you were talking to, and he'd surprised himself by the ease with which he had taken to it. He had always been a planner since he was at school, but he was also afraid of the black rage that had started to take over and knew that if the situation arose he might not be able to control it and it worried him. He logged into the dating site he had joined a month ago under a false name and typed 'single women in Cumbria', hitting the enter button hard. His tongue snaked from his mouth and he licked his top lip, as the pages began to load. He began to search for his next suitable victim to keep Jenna company in the cellar – he didn't want her to be lonely down there. He paused on a picture of a girl with the palest complexion. A green circle below it showed that she was online and could be messaged.

He typed: 'Would you like to visit a haunted house?'

Within seconds a reply flashed up on the screen: 'Yes, I would. Do you know of one?'

Oh yes I do, who would have thought it could be so easy.

***

Will returned to the station. He needed to speak to the DI and organise a search. One of the address checks had come up with a confirmed last sighting of Jenna White. The girl who lived there sometimes gave Jenna a lift into college and had driven past her last night at approximately twenty past eight as she turned into the approach road to Abbey Wood. She hadn't been seen since.

He pushed the numerical code on the keypad to open the door, hoping it was still the right one; they had a habit of changing it just as he would get used to it. He stopped off at the community office to speak to the sergeant and asked him for as many officers and police community support officers as he could spare so they could start searching the Abbey and doing the house-to-house enquiries at the few houses that were down there. It was a massive area and he was going to have to call in a few favours to get as many people as possible to help out. She could be lying injured somewhere. He hoped that she hadn't strayed onto the railway tracks that ran behind the Abbey and been hit by a train. There had been a few locals who had met their untimely death due to a high-speed Edinburgh-bound train passing through.

His head began to pound the same rhythm as his heart and he swallowed a couple of paracetamol before going up to the large room on the first floor, which was used to hold meetings and large-scale briefings. This shift was going to be a long one; he just hoped by the end of it Jenna White was reunited with her family one way or another.

***

The thunder was easing off with just an occasional rumble in the distance. Annie sat at the kitchen table with a mug of coffee in one hand and the other resting on the book. It had to be the book she had found inside the desk, but there was no way to explain how it got from the imaginary desk onto the floor. To say it was strange was a bit of an understatement. Pulling a tea towel off the back of a chair she rubbed at the thick layer of dust on the front cover. The book was bound in black leather which had softened and cracked with age; she expected the title to say *Alice's Adventures in*

28

Wonderland but instead it read *Diary*. She exhaled, unaware she had been holding her breath. Her hands trembling, she opened it and the read the inscription on the inside front cover: *This is the private diary of Alice Hughes*. A chill spread down the back of her neck: the man in the house had been shouting for Alice. The script was beautiful, elegant, and Annie wished that she could write like that. For a moment she felt a twinge of guilt that she was about to read someone's diary. How would she feel if it were the other way around? But it was obviously very old and she doubted very much that whoever it belonged to was still alive.

***

25th December 1886

My name is Alice Hughes. I am fifteen years old and work as a housemaid for Lord and Lady Heaton of Manor House, Abbey Wood, Barrow-in-Furness. I am very fortunate as I was given this journal as a gift from Lady Hannah who told me that, 'To write is a precious gift that should be used if one has been fortunate enough to be blessed with it.' It is thanks to Lady Hannah that I can write. She always gave me time away from my chores to sit in the schoolroom with Master Edward and learn whenever his tutor came to give him lessons. I did not like having to spend so much time in Edward's company for he is so horrid and hurtful to me for no reason, but I do so love to read and write and I suppose I should be grateful that I have been given such opportunities to learn, even if it did mean that Edward would pull my hair, or pinch my arms when the teacher was not looking.

Today has been such a busy day. Lord Robert and Lady Hannah had guests for Christmas dinner and I had to help Cook prepare and serve the food. Both Millie, the kitchen maid, and James, the footman, are ill which meant I had to do all of their chores as well as my own. Master Edward was not best pleased when his mother gave me a gift and he scowled at me all day. I am thankful that his Lordship kept an eye on him today for I overheard Cook telling Albert the butler that Edward had got into another fight yesterday. Edward is always so angry. I often wonder why he is that way when everyone is so nice to him.

I overheard Lady Hannah telling the vicar that Edward will be moving to London soon and will be attending a medical school there for he is so clever and bright and well advanced in his studies. I pray every night that he will leave soon and then I will not have to hide from him when he wants to play his silly games. I am writing this by the light of the candle, all tucked up in my bed. I must go now in case he is prowling around and sees the light from underneath my door for he will tease me mercilessly. He is not allowed into the servant's quarters but this does not stop him for he listens to no one.

30th December 1886

This morning I worked so hard I am exhausted. There is to be a party tomorrow night and Lady Hannah wants the house to sparkle from top to bottom. This is all very well but I feel as if I am the only one who is working, except of course for Cook who always works hard.

I do not understand why Edward dislikes me so. I wonder, if I were a boy would he still treat me the same way? A part of me thinks that he is jealous of me but why should that be so? He is rich and his parents love him dearly even though he acts like a spoilt, selfish brat and is so unhappy. He must be to carry on this way. I have nothing, why would he envy that? My mother died last year and I have no other family. I have been living in this house since I was nine years old. I was given plenty of tasks to complete despite my age but I did not mind for it passed the day.

I have been very fortunate that Lady Hannah likes me so otherwise I could have been sent to the workhouse when mother died. But she insisted I was to be kept on as a housemaid and paid a proper wage. I owe Lady Hannah so much I would never let her down in any way.

Today has been such a horrid day; I have never been so scared in all my life. Edward insisted I play a game of hide-and-seek with him. He told me if I did not he would tell his mother that I had stolen some of her jewellery. I would die of shame if Lady Hannah were to think me capable of such a thing for she is like my own mother to me. I had no choice even though I was scared and knew it would all end in tears. I tried to act brave even though I felt sick to the pit of my stomach.

He led me to the kitchen and stood outside the cellar door. He then ordered me to hide down in the dark, damp cellar. My knees began to tremble so much that I could barely take the first step down into the blackness. I looked around the brightly lit kitchen for Cook but she was nowhere to be seen. She was more than likely with her Ladyship discussing the menu for tomorrow night. Edward smiled at the look of fear on my face; he knew exactly what I was thinking. He knew that I wanted Cook to come in and save me from going down into the huge, dark cellar, which I so despise. I tried my best to put on a brave face for I did not want to show him how truly scared I was, because then he would tease me all the more.

I ran down the stairs into the blackness that waited for me at the bottom. I did not know which way to turn and bumped into something hard, hitting my shin and making me cry out in pain. My eyes began to water and I wanted to fall to the floor in a heap and wail. Now I have a big black bruise that hurts if I touch it. I could hear him laughing at the top of the stairs; finally he began to count. Edward must have heard me scrabbling around in the dark like a blind mouse. I had to keep biting my lip to stop myself from making a noise. I finally found a corner to crouch in and I tried to make myself as small as possible. My blood froze when he shouted, 'Coming, ready or not.' My heart was beating so loud I thought that it would give away my hiding place. My skin felt as if there were a thousand spiders crawling over it. I had to squeeze my eyes shut and I covered my ears with the palms of my hands, all the time waiting for him to jump out at me from the dark.

When I could no longer feel my feet I tried to straighten up; I do not know how long I had been waiting. I crept from my safe corner and felt my way around as my eyes began to adjust to the darkness. I knew in my heart he was waiting to scare me. I had lost all sense of direction in these vast rooms and did not know where the stairs were: I was lost. A strange noise came from somewhere not too far away and it was then that the tears began to fall as I brushed against something hard and cold. I cannot say if it was my imagination or not but I thought I heard a low, guttural growl and it was then that I started to scream.

Her Ladyship must have heard me because she sent Harold down into the cellar with a candle to light the way and find me. I was so relieved to see him I could not stop crying and I clung to him as he took my arm and led me to the steps and back upstairs to safety. When we reached the top I felt my legs sink from under me. Lady Hannah was standing there, her face a mask of concern.

The kitchen had never looked so cosy and bright. Edward was sitting at the table eating warm gingerbread, the smell made my stomach rumble. He smirked at me from behind his mother's back. Lady Hannah took my arm and led me upstairs to my room to lie down and rest. She told me Edward would be dealt with and as she turned to look at me I saw such sadness in her eyes. I cannot believe how someone so kind could give birth to such a monster.

5 th January 1887

Today I watched with great relief as Edward left. Alfie whose correct title is junior footman but also a bit of a jack of all trades like me when it comes to helping around the house helped him to load his luggage onto the horse and trap. Cook told me his Lordship had warned Edward to leave me alone or he would not be allowed home. I did not dare this to be true, since he scared me out of my wits in the cellar he has not even spoken to me. Two days ago I saw him in the garden beating a rabbit with a stick, the poor thing was squealing at the top of its voice like a baby. It was horrid, I wanted to run outside to help the poor creature but I was too scared of Edward for I know he would like to beat me with a stick. I ran to find Harold who was polishing the silver. Cook told me that Harold then went to tell his Lordship who went outside himself to put a stop to Edward's cruel torture but not before the rabbit was beaten to death and the frost which had turned the green grass white and crisp was turned blood red.

This house will be so much happier with him gone, I shall be able to carry out my chores without being afraid that Edward is spying on me and waiting to scare me. He has the devil inside him I am sure of it. On my way to bed I overheard his Lordship arguing with Lady Hannah and I know it was about Edward. I shall mention it to Cook but I know she will tell me to mind my own business and keep quiet. I think tonight will be the first night in weeks that I will sleep well.

*

Annie was totally engrossed until a loud knock at the door brought her back to reality. She looked out of the window to see a familiar flash of luminous yellow. Someone was looking around the barns. She pulled on the pale blue woollen beanie hat she bought last year, just in case it was someone she worked with, and then opened the door.

Jake was standing there grinning at her. He stepped forward and picked her up, lifting her off the ground. *How did he know where to find me? I never told anyone where I was staying.* Annie squirmed and glanced at the man behind Jake. She recognised Will. He had not long passed his sergeant's exam and just been promoted to detective sergeant in CID. He looked embarrassed by Jake's behaviour. When he finally put her down she felt guilty for not telling him where she was staying.

'So this is where you've been hiding from me. I leave messages on your voicemail because you never answer your phone. If I'm lucky I get a cryptic text message. Whatever happened to the art of conversation?'

Will looked at each of them.

'Jake, I'm fine, I told you I needed some time to myself. I just want to be lazy and not have to worry about anyone except me.' She felt the familiar flush as her cheeks began to burn at Will's reaction.

Will was trying his best to place her; she looked familiar. She only reached chest height on Jake, wasn't wearing any make up and was wearing a cute hat, even though she was inside the house, which puzzled him. He could hear Jake muttering and caught the shut-the-fuck-up-look on her face. He realised where he knew her from: she was one of the coppers in the community office who worked with Jake.

He coughed. 'Sorry to break up your lovers' tiff, but we have work to do, Jake.'

'We are not having a lovers' tiff, Jake is just overprotective and a pain.'

Jake threw his hands in the air in mock submission. 'Well, I'm sorry, Annie, but you can't be mad at me because I care. I've been so worried.'

She smiled and her whole face lit up. Will felt something inside his chest shift just a tiny bit. 'No,

I'm not mad but I have to get over this on my own, get myself together. You know how it is. He ruined my life for long enough.'

Will had to stop himself from giving the pair of them a round of applause. He felt as if he had stumbled into some bizarre scene from a soap opera. 'Right then, now you're both going to live happily ever after it's time to talk business.' He winked at Annie. 'A nineteen-year-old girl was reported missing a couple of hours ago and the alarm bells are ringing – we are very concerned for her welfare. We have a last confirmed sighting of her heading towards the Abbey last night so here is the million dollar question...'

Annie finished it for him, 'No, I'm sorry I haven't seen or heard anything unusual.' She opted to leave out the drama at the old house earlier.

'Is it OK to check all the outbuildings just in case she's hiding in one of them?'

Annie nodded, pulled her jacket from the back of the chair and followed them outside. Between the three of them they searched each barn in a matter of minutes.

'Sorry but it looks like there's nothing but junk in any of them.' She shrugged her shoulders by way of apology.

'Don't worry. I think you would have noticed someone creeping around anyway.'

Jake strode over to join them. 'What about the old house? It's huge. She could be hiding out in there.'

Annie's voice raised an octave, 'No, she's not in there.'

Jake arched his eyebrow. 'And you would know this because?'

'Because I was in there earlier and it was empty. My brother is the caretaker and I went to check it out. I don't think anyone has been in there since 1982.' She thought about the figure at the window but kept quiet.

Will picked up on her agitation and found himself intrigued: there was something she wasn't telling them. He didn't think for one minute that it had anything to do with their missing girl but something had put her on edge. 'I'll take your word for it but if we don't find her we may have to search the place just to cover our backs.'

'Well, let me know and I'll take you in because it's dangerous. I don't know how she would have got in though because the downstairs windows are all boarded up.' She ducked under a low beam but didn't go low enough and her hat caught on a nail.

Will was horrified to see the angry red wound and line of staples that ran along the back of her head. Her hair had been shaved to allow the doctors to patch it all back together but dark stubble was beginning to poke through.

Jake, not known for his tact, gasped, 'Jesus Christ, Annie, what a mess your head is. I'm surprised you haven't got brain damage.'

Her face bright red, she grabbed the hat and pulled it down over her head then turned and walked briskly back towards the safety of the house. Once she reached the kitchen door she turned to face them. 'If you need me, give me a ring.' With that she shut and bolted the kitchen door leaving them staring at each other.

'What the fuck is the matter with you, Jake? Why did you have to say that?'

Jake shrugged and Will was pleased to see that for once he actually looked remorseful. 'Ah, you know me, Will, I don't mean it. Before I can stop myself I've jumped straight in with my size twelve boots and the damage has been done.'

They walked in silence to the gate and Will couldn't help but turn around to take one last look. He caught a glimpse of Annie watching them from one of the downstairs windows; she looked so scared and vulnerable and he wanted to go back and give her a hug, tell her everything was going to be all right. *Bloody hell I'm going soft in my old age.*

They walked back to the main path, which ran through the woods, to meet up with some of the search team. Jake was subdued for a change and Will was thankful; his mind was working overtime wondering what had happened to Annie. But now was not the time or place because he needed to keep a clear head for Jenna White. On top of that he couldn't ask Jake about Annie because he'd never hear the end of it. He supposed he could ask around the station where, no doubt, someone would be all too willing to fill him in on every gory detail, but he didn't want that. He didn't want to violate her privacy, he wanted to hear it from her and he wondered how he could approach her if he saw her again. And he did want to see her again. Very much.

CHAPTER 4

Annie wasn't really angry with Jake. She was used to him opening his mouth and putting his foot in it. The number of scrapes at work she had got him out of was too many to count; it was because Will had been there she had felt humiliated. She only knew him well enough to say hello to in the corridor, up to now never having worked on any cases with him. The look of pity on his face had made her feel helpless.

She didn't want sympathy from anyone. It was her own fault she had stayed with Mike all those years when she should have done what she told the countless victims of domestic violence she dealt with through work: get out of there. But Mike could be so persuasive when he needed to be and a complete charmer. He would promise her he wouldn't do it again and tell her that he loved her so much, and every time she believed him, until the last six months when she had started to crack. She felt like a complete idiot.

41

As she had watched Jake and Will walk away she had wanted to run after them and offer them some coffee. It would be nice to have some company, especially after this morning's events. She knew all about Will's reputation around the station as a womanizer. According to Jake, who had been friends with him since they joined, his type was tall, blonde, stick-thin, the look of a starving supermodel. So why was the way he looked at her playing on her mind?

Jake, on the other hand, was the complete opposite. When, fresh from training school, she had been assigned a tutor on her first day in the station and had been introduced to him she had to breathe deeply to calm herself down. He was tall, dark and drop-dead gorgeous with muscles in all the right places. Every single job they went to the women practically threw themselves at him. He was always professional and never took them up on their offers of phone numbers or drinks, and Annie had found herself developing a major crush on her tutor.

Jake took to Annie and became her protector, to which she had not the slightest objection. After one particularly harrowing day at work – they had delivered two death messages in a row and been the first on scene at a fatal car crash – he invited her to his house for a bottle of wine and a takeaway. Annie couldn't have said no even if she had wanted to. Eager to have the chance to spend some time with him she had told Mike it was a girl's night out. He had moaned the whole time she was getting ready to go and she knew there would be a price to pay for it later.

She had arrived at the large Victorian semi in one of the nicest parts of town, which made her wonder exactly how he could afford it on his wages. Walking up the cobbled path bordered on either side by the most aromatic lavender and pink roses she had ever smelt, it occurred to her just how much she would like to live here with Jake.

Angry male voices filtered through the open sash window and then the front door opened, and out stormed an even better looking man than Jake. He slammed the door behind him, jumped over the lavender to the drive and got into a brand new Mercedes. The door flew open and Jake stood there, about to shout something, when he spotted Annie standing there with a bottle of wine in one hand and her mouth wide open.

'I hope you're not drooling after that. Because he is one spoilt, selfish bastard.'

Embarrassed, she shook her head. 'Is that your brother?'

Jake had laughed. 'Oh, how I wish he was, because then I could just punch him when he gets on my nerves. Come on, I'm starving. Get in here quick so I can order before he comes back.'

'He's coming back? Does he live here then?'

'Actually it's his house but we both pay the mortgage.'

She began to imagine how nice it would be to live in this lovely old house, which was decorated with a vintage shabby chic feel to it. It would be even better sharing it with two gorgeous men; she looked at Jake who was genuinely confused.

'Erm, I hope you're not fantasising about what you would like to do with my boyfriend?'

Annie had wanted the ground to open up and swallow her. Doing her best to look indifferent, she brushed it off. 'Well, it did include the two of you; I wouldn't leave you out, Jake.'

If Jake had been insulted he never let on.

Half an hour later the Greek God had turned up with two bottles of wine and a bunch of flowers. 'These are for you. I'm Alex. I was so rude earlier and I'm very sorry, but Jake can be such a tosser.'

Annie had accepted the flowers and smiled. 'You know him as well as I do then.' They had both laughed and Jake had tried to look insulted but failed miserably and joined in. That had been the start of a beautiful friendship.

When she was lying in casualty like a broken rag doll Jake had begged her to move in with them, but her pride had got the better of her and she had refused point blank. Although, if she didn't have something sorted out by the time Ben and his family arrived back in the country, she might have to take him up on his offer.

Ben was visiting their mother, who had moved to France six years ago. Annie had been out twice to see her and it was twice too much: they just didn't get on. Annie had never forgiven her for leaving her dad when they were young.

44

Annie had loved her dad so much. He had always been the one to tuck her in and read her bedtime stories, and then one day she had come home from school and her mum and Ben had been waiting in the hall for her with two large suitcases and three black bin bags of toys. Annie had begged her mum to let her stay with her dad but she wouldn't, insisting that Annie had to go with her. A black car had pulled up with a man she had never seen before driving, and her mum had loaded the cases, bags and then her children into the car with her and the mystery man and driven away.

Annie had never forgotten the look of hurt on her dad's face. He died not long after that and Annie blamed her mum for breaking his heart. Ben on the other hand was the golden child, or so she had nicknamed him. He would laugh it off but Annie knew he was their mother's favourite and it didn't bother her, well, not now she was an adult. It had when she was a kid because Ben could just about do whatever he wanted, yet whenever Annie asked it was always 'no'.

She had been so desperate to escape her family home that when Mike had asked her to move in with him she didn't even think about it. She packed her bags and that was it. And now look at how that had ended. She sat back down at the kitchen table to read some more of the diary; anything to take her mind off Jake and Will.

*

6th April 1887

Edward is coming home for the Easter holidays. The house has been so happy these last few months without him that I feel my stomach filling with butterflies at the thought of it. I have been able to practise my reading and writing in the schoolroom in solitude.

Lady Hannah came in one day when I was writing and told me that I was creating memories for the days when I am older and my memory may not serve me as well as it does now. I try to write every day but there is so much to do around this big house that I sometimes forget.

Today I feel as if a black cloud is descending upon me. I am so scared of Edward and what he may have been dreaming of to do to me whilst in London that I am finding it hard to concentrate on anything. I know that I am being foolish thinking this way and that Lady Hannah would not stand back and let him treat me so cruelly, but she is not always around and his Lordship is far too busy with work to notice what goes on in this house. I will just have to do my best to keep out of his way and hope for the best. I would tell Alfie how I feel but I fear he would step in to defend me and then he would lose his position in the house, and also his home, and I do not want anyone to suffer because of me. I know that Alfie likes me a lot, more than just as a friend, because he stole a kiss from me two days ago out in the woodshed, when he was helping me carry wood in for the fire. I pretended to be angry and pushed him away but I was not really and I think he knows this because he grinned at me and winked.

8th April 1887

So far Edward has been very polite and courteous towards me. He has not hidden in any dark corners to jump out and scare me yet. I think that London is changing him for the best. There must be lots of young ladies he can be mean to in the city. He has taken to wearing smart suits with a clean pressed handkerchief tucked into his pocket. Alfie told me that Edward insists on a clean one every day and he had to go into town to purchase some more to make sure Edward did not run out on his visit home.

Today I had to clean out all the fire grates. His Lordship took Edward to the town hall to a meeting leaving Alfie at a loose end. Harold told him he could help me. Alfie entertained me with tales of his family, which is huge: he has three sisters and two brothers. How I laughed when he told me of the mischief they all got into. He is very lucky, although he thought not and said he was so glad to escape from them when he got his job working here.

There was just mother and me until she died and she was always so busy we never got to spend much time together. I miss her so much and I often wonder what it would have been like not to have been an only child. I like Alfie very much. He is such a good friend to me. He has the palest blue eyes, which crinkle when he laughs, and a head full of wavy, blond hair.

By the time we had cleaned the last grate we looked like a pair of chimney sweeps and Cook ordered us to get washed and changed before her Ladyship caught sight of the pair of us and screamed with fright. Alfie nudged me in the side and we dashed up the servants stairs up to our quarters. Edward must have come back early because he was standing loitering at the top of the stairs and he glared at Alfie, who put his head down and excused himself. I continued walking up the stairs afraid that he would follow me but he didn't. I have no idea why he would be waiting around on our cramped staircase when he has the grand staircase at the front of the house to go up and down on. I have a horrible feeling that he was spying on me but maybe I am just being foolish.

12th April 1887

The house was empty this evening. Lord and Lady Heaton have gone to a party and we have all been given the night off. Cook and Millie have gone to visit old Mrs Blackley, who is very poorly. She used to work here before her retirement. Harold has taken them in the horse and trap and then he is going to meet Alfie at the tavern for a while before picking them back up again.

Alfie asked me if I wanted to go but the tavern is not the most suitable place for a young lady. I would be frowned upon by all within if I set foot in there. Cook wanted me to go with her and Millie but I could not face another dying person so soon after my own mother. I told her I felt ill and wanted to retire early. I ran up the grand staircase to turn her Ladyship's bed down and passed Edward on the first floor landing. He looked so dashing and handsome dressed in his best to go to the dance. He stared at me with his cold, black eyes but he carried on walking and I lowered my head. He ran along to the stairs and I found myself watching him through the balustrade. He looked up to where I was standing and fixed his cold eyes on me. My heart missed a beat and I was so scared because I remembered there was only me and him left in the house. He then lifted his hand to his lips and blew me a kiss. I was so horrified that I ran straight up to my room and shut the door, my cheeks burning bright with shame and, as much as I hate to admit it, I think I felt something other than hatred towards him because my stomach churned with butterflies at the thought of him blowing me a kiss.

It is my birthday tomorrow and I will be sixteen years old. I was nine when I first came to this house with my mother when she was offered the position of housekeeper. Tomorrow I will have no one to celebrate it with but it does not matter. I must remember I could be in a much worse place than Abbey Wood.

13th April 1887

I was awakened in the night by a stifled scream from outside my bedroom window. I got out of bed to look and see where it had come from. In the darkness I could make out two figures under the huge oak tree. I recognised Edward immediately. All the years I have spent hiding from him, I would know his silhouette anywhere. The other was a girl and I watched horrified as he pushed her to the ground, her petticoats and skirts tangled beneath her. I watched Edward lift his hand and strike her cruelly across the face and I whimpered out loud. He straddled her and turned to look directly up at my small attic bedroom window. I am positive he was smiling, as if he knew I was watching.

I should have run to awaken his Lordship. The girl was no longer struggling and lay still beneath him. Instead like a coward I ran to my bed and pulled the covers over my head. I was too afraid to move. I have heard about the things men and women get up to from Alfie so maybe Edward is in love with this girl. I tried not to remind myself that if you truly loved someone then you would not strike them. There were no more screams from outside and I stayed under my covers praying that Edward would not come looking for me.

In the morning there was no sign of Edward as breakfast was served and Alfie was sent up to his room with a tray. No one else said anything about what had happened last night so I kept quiet and made myself busy as far away from Edward's room as possible. I could not stop thinking about the woman and what had happened to her but I did not dare to ask anyone. I hope that she is safe somewhere but I know she has come to great harm. I would not dare to speak this out loud for fear of upsetting Lady Hannah or causing Cook to gossip.

*

It was intriguing. The handwriting was hard to understand at times and as much as she wanted to keep reading, concentrating so much was giving Annie a headache. Rain trickled down the kitchen window and Tess looked at her and whined.

'It's miserable out there, Tess, but I don't mind if you don't, and we may still be able to catch up with Jake. Who's a clever girl?' Annie bent down and scratched behind Tess's ears making her so excited that her tail began to thump against everything. Putting on one of the many waterproof jackets that were hanging on the coat rack and pulling on a pair of too big wellies, they set off into the woods.

She spotted flashes of Day-Glo yellow through the trees and headed in that direction, taking the path that skirted around the outside of the old house. She would never go back in there on her own; not after today. There was no rational explanation for what she had experienced earlier, but it had been so real.

It niggled at her that after all these years she had been the one to find Alice's diary. Surely there had been plenty of people in and out of the house to have found it and picked it up. She tried to picture what Alice would have looked like and an image began to form in her mind of a pretty young woman in a maid's uniform. This Edward sounded like he was made from the same stuff as most serial killers: cruelty to animals, no friends, cold and calculating. He probably murdered the girl under the tree. Annie shivered as she wondered if there was a grave in the woods containing the girl's remains. She needed to go to the library and do some investigation to see if there were any records about the family and servants that lived in the house. It could all be a fake; someone could be setting her up. But then again, up until thirty minutes ago no one knew where she was staying.

Jake's voice filtered through the trees and she headed towards it. It was typical of him to be so near to the house, but at least she would have his huge muscles to protect her. She wondered briefly if Will was still around, although she knew from experience that CID usually left the dirty work to uniformed officers. They would breeze into a crime scene looking like the men in black, make a few phone calls then disappear again: she doubted he would still be here.

Anyway, there was absolutely nothing he would see in her five-foot-six inch frame with a figure-not-to-die-for and a lifetime membership to Weight Watchers®. On the plus side, her eyes were a pretty green but she didn't even have a full head of hair thanks to Mike. Her black curls had been shaved off. How she had cried when she saw them lying on the cubicle floor in the hospital.

Up to now she had managed to avoid thinking about that night but suddenly it all came rushing back to her. She had been late finishing because of a fight outside one of the nightclubs on Cornwallis Street. Two of her colleagues had been smacked in the face by a group of drunken chavs who had not only been drunk but high on plant food or whatever fashionable crap it was they were snorting. Finally booking off-duty, she had gone to the car park across the road to her car, which wouldn't start. No money on her for a taxi, she had gone back into the station to find someone who could give her a lift home. Kav, her sergeant, had offered to take her as he was on his way out to pick up some food; he could drop her off first.

As he had driven up the street the house was in darkness, and she had hoped that Mike was either still in the pub or, even better, comatose on the sofa. He hated her working evenings but it infuriated him if she had to work late. It didn't matter to him that she had no choice. If a job came in ten minutes before the end of your shift you couldn't just stop what you were doing and go home like some other jobs. Most men would be proud to say their wife was a police officer but not him. For some reason he found it shameful.

She crept in through the kitchen door and closed it gently behind her. The kitchen light flickered into life and the familiar feeling of dread washed over her. She just wanted to crawl into bed but Mike was standing glaring at her.

'Where the hell have you been? You were supposed to finish at ten and it's nearly midnight. I heard you on the phone this morning making plans; did you really think you could just walk away like that?'

Annie recalled the phone call to Ben. She had been making plans but only to go and stay there to look after his animals while he was away. He had asked her again if she wanted a room permanently. This morning she had laughed off his offer, not sure what to say after he told her it was time she left the bully she was married to: 'I see the look in your eyes, Annie, not to mention the bruises under those long sleeved tops you wear when it's a hot day.' Those words had been playing on her mind all day. He knew, her brother knew that Mike was hitting her.

Suddenly she found the strength to tell him she was leaving him. 'Do you think I've been at the pub getting pissed or do you think I could have been working hard to earn the money for you to go and get pissed? We're through Mike; I've had enough of you. In fact, I can't remember a time when I could get enough of you. It's over.' She regretted the words instantly and knew what was about to happen was going to hurt.

His expression had gone from one of anger to rage. Striding towards her he drew back his fist and then slammed it hard into her stomach. Annie doubled over, winded. He was a dirty fighter. Her eyes watered and she struggled to breathe, but the feeling of indignity began to burn in her chest and the realisation that she would take no more hit her hard, forcing her to straighten up.

She curled her fingers into a fist and punched him square on the nose. The sound of the cartilage crunching beneath her knuckles had been the most deeply satisfying thing she had ever heard. The warmth of the blood which poured out added to the fire that was burning in her hand but she didn't care, she could cope with that. For the first time in years she couldn't stop grinning because she had given him a taste of his own medicine: it felt amazing. Turning to walk back out of the door and leave him, she grabbed the handle. Suddenly a whooshing sound cut through the air behind her and the empty champagne bottle that she had kept since their wedding day became the thing that ended their marriage for good. As it connected with the back of her skull, stopping her dead in her tracks, she collapsed onto the floor.

Annie wasn't sure what happened then but Mike must have walked out of the door, because he left her unconscious and bleeding all over her clean tiles. Kav had told her later that he'd got to the takeaway and noticed her handbag on the floor of the car. Knowing what women were like without them he'd turned around and driven back to drop it off for her. He'd strolled around to the back door because the kitchen light was on; the door was ajar and the handle was covered in blood. He peered through the crack and had been shocked to see Annie's lifeless figure lying on the floor.

The next thing she recalled was waking up to the smells and the sounds of the Accident and Emergency Department. There is nothing like twenty-six staples and multiple bruises to make you realise that your marriage is over: Annie wanted nothing more to do with Mike.

She thought about Ben and how he would be mortified if he knew what had happened. She remembered how he had asked her to dog-sit and made it seem as if she was helping him when really it was the complete opposite: he had been offering her a chance to escape, which was a good thing because now she needed it. There was no going back.

The worst thing about it all had been the fact that her secret was now public knowledge and the shame was burning inside her chest, adding to the pain and nausea she already felt. When she saw Jake heading towards her cubicle she had squeezed her eyes shut. He was followed in by the doctor.

'She's all right, Doc, isn't she? I mean she's not brain-damaged or anything?'

If Annie could have moved she would have squirmed. Jake watched far too much television. Next he would be asking if she was going to live; thankfully he hadn't. She had lain there waiting for them all to leave her alone.

At some point Kav had joined the party because she heard his deep voice whisper to Jake, 'I can't believe she was married to such a bloody wanker.' His boots squeaked on the highly polished floor as he stepped closer. 'Annie, can you hear me? Don't ignore me. We need to talk.'

She had whispered, 'Yes, Sarge.'

'You can drop the "Sarge" shit. How are you doing, kid?' Jake was hovering in the background and Kav turned to him. 'Can you go and find something useful to do, Jake? Mine's a tea with two sugars.'

Annie knew Jake would be insulted but he turned to go and find somewhere to get a brew: he knew better than to argue with Kav.

When Jake was out of earshot Kav lowered his voice. 'I need you to tell me exactly what happened. I won't gossip like our friend Jake but I want to know everything from start to finish.'

She had smiled at him, which, in turn, made her wince with pain. 'What is there to say? You know those women who stay with their partners even though they get battered senseless for no good reason, the ones we all berate saying how foolish they are and they'll end up dead? Well, that's me, the real Annie Graham is a stupid idiot who

57

should know better.' She watched as his huge fists clenched into tight balls.

'I'm so sorry, Annie, I had no idea. I better get to be the arresting officer because I intend to treat him with the respect that he deserves.'

'Thanks. I hope you do but I did manage to smack him one myself this time. I think I may have broken his nose.'

Kav laughed so loud the whole department turned to look their way. It was so inappropriate it made them both laugh even more.

'That's my girl. Now is there anyone you want me to contact for you?'

Annie declined his offer, not wanting anyone outside of work to know about what had happened. In fact, she would rather no one at work knew about it. Kav nodded and wrapped his hand gently around her left hand, which wasn't swollen, and squeezed it.

Jake rounded the corner carrying two plastic cups filled with steaming liquid. 'Bleeding hell I'm going to need that bed in a minute. I've got third-degree burns.'

Kav peered into the plastic cup. 'What's that shit? Don't tell me it's tea.' He took it from Jake, blew into the cup then sipped. 'I'll let you off, Constable. It tastes better than it looks.'

Jake offered the other cup to Annie. 'Hot chocolate?'

A passing nurse paused outside the cubicle then pulled the curtain to one side. 'Sorry, pet, she's nil by mouth until the consultant decides if he needs to operate on her hand.'

Both men looked at each other and Jake whispered, 'I'm glad it's not me you punched.'

A trio of doctors walked in and Kav stood up. 'You know where I am if you need me or want anything.' He stooped down and kissed the one spot on her forehead that wasn't coated with dried blood. He turned to Jake. 'Come on, let's go and assist in the hunt for Barrow's most wanted. He needs a lesson in extreme etiquette.'

Jake clapped like a big kid. 'Now you're talking, Sarge.' He blew Annie a kiss. 'I love you loads but I am not kissing you with all that dried blood and brain juice splattered all over.'

Kav's hand shot through the curtain and dragged Jake out by the shoulder. Annie shut her eyes as the doctor picked up her hand to begin to examine it again.

*

An outbreak of obscenities shattered her daydream and she walked straight into Jake, who was rubbing his hand vigorously.

He looked at her. 'These sodding nettles are everywhere. Oh look at you, Miss Nosey Parker, could you not take the suspense or are you just missing me already? I can't believe it doesn't freak you out living up here on your own. I'm scared and it's daytime.'

'Just remind me why you wanted to be a copper? Stop rubbing your hand and look for a dock leaf; it will take away the sting.'

'I told you why: I wanted a pair of handcuffs and I can't resist a man in a uniform. Look, I'm really sorry for embarrassing you before. I never meant to. It was such a shock seeing how bad the back of your head was. I had no idea.' He hugged her and she squeezed him back. 'Oh and I noticed the way you looked at Will. You were weighing him up, weren't you? How many marks out of ten would you give him? I'd give him a seven, possibly an eight? The only person I've ever given more than an eight to was that special constable with the bleached blond hair that joined last year. I was gutted he only lasted a month. Not that I'd ever cheat on Alex but it's nice to have something other than a bunch of hairy, sweaty coppers to look at.'

'You're awful, Jake. I wasn't weighing him up. Well, maybe a little. Anyway, I know he only fancies supermodel type girls and this, I'm afraid, is no supermodel.'

'You're wrong, Annie. Why do you have to be so down on yourself? If I wasn't into muscular rich men I'd shag you, even though you do look really scary with half of your hair shaved off and that massive scar. I suppose it would be a bit like shagging the bride of Frankenstein.'

She choked. 'Why thanks, Jake, that's good to know. It makes me feel so much better.'

Will walked up behind them and Annie pulled away from Jake, glaring at him, then punched him in the arm.

'Anything?'

'There is nothing here apart from these nettles. No sign of anyone being around here, Will.'

Annie began walking away. 'I'll see you later. If you want a coffee or somewhere to take a breather you are more than welcome to come back to the house. I promise I'll actually let you in this time.'

'Thanks. I might have to take you up on that offer. I'm getting the shakes through a distinct lack of caffeine.'

Jake rolled his eyes at her and mouthed, 'flirt'. Annie stuck her tongue out then turned and left them to it.

CHAPTER 5

He couldn't stop thinking about the girl. He kept replaying it over and over in his head. Had he really taken her to the big house and slit her throat? It felt as if it was all a dream and he was finding it hard to distinguish between his fantasy life and his real one. How had he turned into a stone cold killer?

He rooted around in the bottom of his wardrobe until he found his backpack. Placing it on top of the bed he unzipped it, his hands slick with sweat he fumbled to get it open. There, in the bottom of the bag, was the scarf his mother had given him last Christmas, which added to the ten others he had in his wardrobe. He took it out and rolled it across the bed until the knife appeared and he inhaled sharply. The long thin blade was covered in flecks of dark brown, dried blood.

It was a very old knife and he knew that by the worn, cracked wooden handle. It was hard to imagine this knife ever being used for anything other than to cut and slice pure white skin with such delicacy. He poked around in the small zip pocket at the front of the bag and felt the gold rope chain between his fingers. He pulled it out and held it up to the light. He had tugged it from Jenna's neck just before he sliced her throat open: his little piece of her.

He retrieved the tin box from the shelf and took out the photographs. They were mainly pictures of the servants but there was one photograph of Lord and Lady Heaton and their son Edward. It was this one that fascinated him so much; he was drawn towards Edward and had spent hours staring at him. He looked so aloof; there was quite a distance between him and his parents. There was something so compelling about him that he had begun to haunt his dreams.

That first time he had looked at the photographs he had recognised the huge house behind them and he knew he had to find out more about this man. He had spent a very enjoyable afternoon in the library going through the archives, researching the family, and all the time he had felt as if there was some bond between him and Edward, a bond that was growing stronger.

He knew that he had to find a way to open one of the doors to the house and go inside so he had gone there one wet, miserable morning when he knew there wouldn't be so many dog walkers around. He walked the perimeter of the building trying every door and had felt like crying when they were all locked up tight. He then began to wonder if the owners had ever left a spare key like his mother did: she left hers under a plant pot. He began to check the area, any plant pots and planters had long gone but around the back, near to a small door, was an overgrown rockery. He had spent the next ten minutes sweating and lifting up stones and rocks and had gasped when he saw a rusty piece of metal almost buried under one of them, the very tip sticking out. He brushed away the woodlice, dug his fingers into the moist soil and pulled out a rusted old key. He didn't dare breathe in case it was too good to be true.

Wiping the key along his trouser leg he walked over to the door and put it into the lock; the pleasure he felt when the key turned was indescribable. He was meant to be here. There was a reason he bought that tin box: he felt connected to Edward Heaton more than he ever felt connected to anyone in his entire life.

I'm sitting on an absolute fortune; some idiot would pay thousands for this knife. But he wouldn't part with it now for anything or any amount of money because it was a part of him and he still had so much work to do, work that he knew had never been finished over a hundred years ago. He wrapped it back up and hid the bag at the back of the wardrobe, pulling a blanket on top of it because if his mother found it she would phone the police in seconds. That he was her son wouldn't matter; there would be no loyalty. Then he kissed the gold chain and placed it into his tin box next to the picture of Edward, and put the box back on the shelf. He needed to play it cool for now, wait until all the fuss had died down. He knew it would take a while because missing girls were big news in this small town.

He sat down in his armchair and looked out of the bedroom window that faced onto the busy front street. He liked to watch the people going in and out of the newsagents across the road. There would be a steady flow of traffic until about seven o'clock and then it would slow to a trickle and become peaceful. If only they all knew that he was watching them and that, should he decide to do something about it, they would well and truly know. He felt invincible.

The young lad who had taken over running the shop for his grandad came out to put today's flyers on the billboard for the evening paper. He stared at the headline: LOCAL TEENAGE GIRL MISSING. They could search all they wanted. He doubted very much that they would find her. Even if they searched the house, that small room in the cellar had been hidden since the 1900s and no one knew of its existence except him.

***

The light was fading rapidly, the steady drizzle after the storm making the woods treacherous, so Will decided to call it a day. If the girl was here she was deep in the trees and bushes and it was too dangerous to send people in. The Abbey was surrounded by fields that went on for a couple of miles in each direction. There had been no dog handler available because there was a big drugs job on in Workington so, in other words, it was looking pretty hopeless for today. The area had no CCTV coverage except for one small camera on the corner of the house at the bottom of the track that led to the woods. Will doubted that it even worked; they never did when you really needed them to. He was frustrated. There were dead ends everywhere. Several roads led away from this area which made it possible to reach any number of villages or towns, and most of them were within walking distance. Jenna White could be anywhere. He hoped she was safe and staying somewhere of her own free will, but his gut instinct told him different and he had a feeling it would be a corpse they would find, if they were that lucky.

He had liaised with the Chief Inspector a couple of hours ago. He had been reluctant to call in air support for a missing teenager who had walked away from her home address on her own two feet: the budget cuts were playing heavily on his mind. Will couldn't blame him and his hunch wasn't going to be enough to convince him otherwise, at least not before the dogs had made a thorough search of the area.

He walked the perimeter of the crumbling mansion one last time; double-checking there was no way anyone could have gained entry. He found himself standing on the top step before the front door and shivered at the brass doorknocker: it was the freakiest thing he had ever seen. He still wanted to check the inside. If he didn't it would niggle away at him until he did, and at least it gave him an excuse to go back and talk to Annie.

Will wandered towards Jake. 'That's it for today. I'm going to see Annie, ask if she can show me around the house.'

Jake wolf whistled and winked.

Will growled, 'Get stuffed.'

'See you later, Detective Sergeant. Enjoy your coffee.'

Will walked away annoyed with Jake: he could be so childish at times. The rest of the search team headed on down the path that would take them back to the cars parked at the entrance to the woods. But he took the path that forked to the left and led to the farmhouse. He knew they were eager to leave the woods before it got dark, he was himself, but he wanted to see Annie again. She must be brave staying up here on her own; he doubted he would be able to.

He took out his phone and tried to ring the office to see if Laura had any updates for him. He had left her manning the phones and ringing around a list of Jenna's friends who hadn't been in when officers had called earlier. No signal: this place was a bloody nightmare. Following the narrow path that led to the farmhouse he felt the tiny hairs on the back of his neck begin to prickle: someone was watching him. He turned and stared into the trees but couldn't see anyone. Why did he feel so unnerved? A loud bark echoed through the trees and a big black dog came tearing towards him.

'Tess!' The dog stopped in her tracks, turned and raced back to Annie, who was standing by the gate.

'Hello again, I'm sorry to bother you but I need a favour.'

'Where's Jake?'

'The big guy went back to the station because he's too scared to be up here in the dark.'

Annie laughed. 'He's such a wimp. What can I do to help, Will?'

Will thought that Jake probably had the right idea because he couldn't shake the feeling he was being watched: he didn't like it. 'You did say you have a key for the mansion, didn't you?'

'I do, would you like it?'

'It's just, I'm thinking we need to cover all our bases. I know there is no way she could get in but I need to check all the same and besides, I've always wanted to go inside but it's been boarded up as long as I can remember.'

'Of course, but I really wouldn't suggest going in there tonight. It's a bit of a wreck and would be dangerous in the dark. Like I said, I didn't see anything when I was in there earlier.'

Will shivered as the temperature dropped along with the rest of the daylight. 'No, tomorrow is fine. What time is good for you?'

'I'm up at the crack of dawn so come as soon as you start work. You'll need some old clothes though, not fancy suits and Italian loafers.'

Will pretended to look hurt. 'Are you disrespecting my Tesco designer suits and Matalan shoes? What's wrong with this look?'

Annie giggled and he liked the way it transformed the mask of worry she had been wearing since he first saw her earlier.

'Nothing. They are very nice but you wouldn't want to ruin them, would you?'

He shrugged and turned to leave.

'Would you like a coffee?'

He told her he would love one and she opened the gate. Tess, who had decided that Will was OK, was running around his legs almost tripping him up. 'Is she being friendly or purposely trying to break my neck?'

'Both. She's a lovable pain in the arse.'

Will bent down to scratch behind her ears and she flopped down on her belly. 'Oh I see, one of those, are you? One stroke and you are anybody's?'

'So is her owner.'

Will's expression of mock horror soon put the colour back into Annie's cheeks and she stuttered, 'I'm not her owner. I meant my brother.'

'Oh, that's disappointing. I could have given you a really good scratch between your ears.'

Annie laughed. His sense of humour was making him more attractive by the minute: Mike had been

69

so miserable all of the time. Will followed her into the kitchen. 'Tea, coffee or, if you've finished for the day, would you like a glass of wine?'

'After today the wine would go down very well but I best stick with the coffee. I still need to go back, update the missing person's report and go over everything we have up to now, which isn't very much.'

Annie busied herself making a pot of fresh coffee and hoped the disappointment didn't show on her face. *Of course he can't drink wine on duty, you idiot. You of all people should know that.* For a brief moment she had imagined the pair of them getting drunk. She would give anything not to be alone tonight.

'I'd love to come up some other time though when I'm not working, if the offer is still open.'

'Anytime you're passing. If you're passing. I'm not sure how long I'll be staying here but it's at least the next two months.'

They drank their coffee and chatted about work and Jake. When Will stood up to leave it was completely dark outside.

'Thanks, Annie, that was really nice. Do I turn left at the bottom of this path? I've never been up here in the dark and I don't fancy getting lost. I'd never live it down.'

Annie wasn't sure whether he was joking or if he was just as scared as Jake had been but was too manly to say. 'I can drop you off at your car if you want. I need to go to shopping.'

'That would be great, I'd really appreciate it.'

Will climbed into her Mini with far more grace than she would have credited him for. She drove along the narrow lane and had a near miss with a dog walker who was dressed all in dark clothes with nothing remotely reflective on him apart from the handle of the dog lead.

'Bloody hell! Who in their right mind would want to walk a dog up here at this time of night?'

'Oh, you would be surprised. There are people up here all hours. It's usually teenagers who come camping in the woods but there are also the die-hard dog walkers. That was a bit close though. I never saw his dog; I hope I haven't already run it over.'

'I think we'd have felt the bump in this car – unless of course it was a Chihuahua.'

She stopped in front of the old wooden gates and Will offered to open them.

'It's OK but thank you, they are so awkward it's taken me two years to get used to them. Are you always such a gentleman?'

'Oh yes, you should see …' He stopped mid-sentence and Annie grinned; he had no idea how much she would like to see.

Getting out of the car she fiddled with the padlock and opened the gates, then got back in and drove the short distance along the road to the red Ford Focus: a typical unmarked police car. The only problem was that every criminal in Barrow knew they were police cars so they were technically useless.

71

'Thanks Annie, it's been a pleasure. I'm back in work at eight so by the time I've caught up on everything I should be here around nine. Unless Jenna turns up, but I'll let you know if she does.'

She waved goodbye to him and sped off. As soon as she reached the main road her phone began buzzing: she had three missed calls and two text messages and she didn't need to look closely to see that they were all from Jake, wanting to know the gossip. There wasn't any and she wondered to herself would she have liked it if there was, or was she being a fool? It was only ten days since Mike had almost killed her and she had walked out of their twelve-year marriage. She hadn't loved him for at least the last five years of it and had spent more time hating him than she ever had loving him. Her head was telling her to keep well clear of Will but her stomach got butterflies whenever she thought of him.

***

He swore but the car had been going too fast to take much notice of him. It was a good job he had been swinging the dog lead around. After reading the headlines on the billboard he couldn't settle. The taxi driver who lived next door had told his mother the Abbey was sealed off and there were search teams out there. He had been so careful, how could they know where to look? The last thing he wanted to do was draw attention to the

72

old house, but he needed to make sure everything was all right. And who exactly was driving along this track in the dark when the gates at the bottom had been locked. He knew the owner of the farm was out of the country, a friend of his mother's told her at the spiritualist church the other week. As far as he knew the police didn't drive Mini Cooper convertibles either. Someone must be keeping an eye on the place.

He needed to check out the farm. It hadn't even entered his head last night when he had led the girl up here to the house. Anyone could have seen him. He had thought he had every angle covered. This was an important lesson to learn: there are a million and one ways to fuck it all up. Still, no coppers had come knocking at his door and if they had found her body this place would still be swarming with them.

He followed the path that led to the farmhouse. A light was shining through the trees from a downstairs window. Maybe they were on a timer: you wouldn't go abroad and leave every light on in the house. Walking closer he climbed over the gate in case it made a noise when it opened. Keeping close to the house he reached the room that was lit and peered through the glass. On the table were two mugs and a black dog was asleep in the corner. A woman's handbag was on the chair: whoever it was must be coming back. He took a look around at the assortment of barns and outbuildings. He couldn't just leave. Not until he knew who was staying here. A door was ajar on one of the barns so he walked over and pushed it open with the tip of his boot. The smell of hay filled his nostrils and he had to lift a hand to his face to stifle a sneeze. He pulled a bale of hay from the stack and dragged it over to the tiny window that had a slight crack across the grimy glass: it gave a perfect view of the courtyard and the kitchen door. If he was lucky they would use this as the main way to go in and out. He was confident that whoever it was would have no reason to come in here at this time of night, and if they did he would say he was homeless and just dossing down for the night.

CHAPTER 6

Tesco was empty. Annie managed to do her shopping with no interruptions, which made a change. One of the things she disliked about her job was that everyone who lived in the town centre knew her both in and out of uniform. More often than not when she was doing her grocery shopping she would get stopped and told tales about what the next door neighbour was up to, or asked if she could do something about the smackheads over the road.

She filled the trolley with pizza, salad, pasta, chocolate and wine. She even picked up a packet of razors. *Time to shave those legs. You just never know.* She looked at her trolley, it was a lot different to shopping with Mike and she liked it.

On the stand near to the checkout was a single battered copy of the local paper. The front page had a picture of the missing girl staring back at her. Shivering, Annie hoped the poor girl wasn't lying dead somewhere near to the farmhouse.

Her journey home was uneventful. She didn't think twice about getting out of the car to unlock the gates. Usually she would feel a little scared because it was so lonely and dark at this time of night, and there were far too many stories of ghostly monks who wandered the area. Tonight she was too busy thinking about Will. She should really phone Jake and discreetly try and find out if Will had said anything about her, but he would second-guess what she was up to and then he'd tell Will: Jake could not keep his mouth shut.

She parked up and grabbed the bags of shopping from the boot of the car; the wine bottles clashed together. Unlatching the gate a feeling of being watched had settled over her and she felt uneasy again. Ever since she had gone into the mansion it had been there, hovering at the back of her mind. She had never experienced anything like it. Going into the kitchen she locked the door and dumped the shopping bags onto the table; her hands were trembling.

'I'm cracking up, Tess, and turning into an alcoholic, but you don't mind, do you? It will be our little secret.'

She picked up the half full bottle of wine and her glass then went into the snug to watch the television: anything to keep her mind occupied. Something funny was what she needed. She searched through the channels until she found a repeat of *Only Fools and Horses*. There was nothing like the antics of Del Boy, Rodney and a box of blow-up dolls to put a smile on your face.

Her back to the window, she didn't see the black figure sneak from the barn and skulk into the woods. Tess growled in the kitchen; she knew someone was out there.

*

Will arrived back at the police station and this time it was full of people; completely different to this morning. Everything was the wrong way round today. Usually at this time of night it was quiet, a couple of officers and the odd PCSO around. Everyone else would be out on patrol, waiting for the endless jobs to come in. He often thought it was a shame how much the taxpayer didn't know about the world of policing. Most calls to the police were absolute rubbish: reports of kids making a noise in the play park or playing football in the street. It drove him nuts. The parade room was full, the nightshift officers hanging around for the nine o'clock briefing to begin. He walked on to the community office and looked in, nodding at the two PCSOs, Claire and Sally, who were in there,

'Evening, ladies, anyone brewing up?' He gave them his best smile and they grinned back.

'We might be. What's it worth?'

He racked his brain for some juicy gossip to offer in exchange for some coffee. 'Oh, I know, have you heard about the shenanigans on the G shift night out? Wouldn't you like to know who ended up going back to a certain sergeant's house for a spot of picking car keys out of a dish?'

Both women stood at the same time, walking towards the kettle.

'Coffee nice and strong, and two sugars please.' He left and walked briskly through the maze of corridors to his office, a big grin on his face. He had known they wouldn't be able to resist. In less than five minutes they would be there, steaming mug of coffee and big smiles.

Will was tired. It had turned into a long day and as soon as he updated the duty inspector he was going home for a drink of something stronger than coffee. Right on cue the door opened and in they walked. Claire put the mug down on his desk.

'Right, Will, spill the beans. We want to know every gory detail.'

He paused for effect. 'Well, I got told by a very reliable source that Reece and Deana from custody went out and ended up going back to a custody sergeant's – mention no names but Jack escapes my lips – house, with a certain blonde officer who has a lilting Scottish accent, for a foursome.'

'Oh my god, are you having us on?' Sally squealed before they both collapsed into a screaming fit of the giggles.

Claire turned to Sally who was laughing so hard she had to hold onto her side. 'We really need to go on the next night out. Do you see what we're missing?'

They both blew him a kiss then turned to leave.

'Thanks for the coffee, girls.'

'You're welcome, darling. Thanks for the gossip.' Claire winked at him as Sally dragged her out into the corridor. Their laughter echoed all down the corridor, putting a smile on his face.

When the constabulary had announced it was taking on PCSOs it hadn't gone down too well with many of the officers. They had been concerned they would take their jobs from them for lesser pay, but that couldn't have been further from the truth. The first group that arrived from training up at headquarters had been like a breath of fresh air and Will thought they were amazing: he wouldn't have a bad word said about them. They often helped above and beyond their call of duty, which is more than could be said for some officers.

He sipped his coffee and updated the missing persons report then, tired and hungry, he set off to find the duty inspector to give an update. Climbing the stairs he phoned the local Chinese and the girl who answered rhymed off his order of beef chow mein and salt and pepper chips without him saying any more than his name. At the moment the woman who owned the takeaway knew him better than any of his last three girlfriends. *You sad bastard, Will Ashworth.*

He thought about Annie and what it was about her that had affected him so much. He had never before given her a second glance, but today she had looked so vulnerable and he had wanted so badly to hold her and tell her he'd protect her.

Maybe it was time to start acting his age. Most of his mates from school were married, some twice. All of them had families and what did he have? An amazing talent for not being able to keep his dick in his pants and a gay best friend. He chuckled because if he didn't he might just cry it was so pathetic.

*

Annie couldn't settle. Tess was continually growling at someone or something that she couldn't see and it was freaking her out. She stood up and pushed her face against the glass, peering out into the courtyard. But it was so dark she could only see the room behind her reflected in the glass and her own face, which she barely recognised. She looked so pale and there were big, black circles under her eyes, not to mention the world's worst haircut. She blinked away the tears that welled and let out a sob. *Stop it, Annie, your hair will grow back. You're alive and you're free. What more do you want?*

She wanted for her to be in a different situation; in a fun-filled loving relationship. She had never really liked being on her own and had always been a homebody. When she was younger, clubbing wasn't really her thing; nor was dating. The thought of having to start over filled her with fear. *Maybe I should buy some fake tan, get my nails done and see if the hairdresser can do*

31st October 1887

Edward returned from London yesterday. He is so much taller than I remember. I had finished my chores and was sitting near to the piano listening to Lady Hannah play a new piece of music she had learned especially for his coming home. Upon seeing me with his mother he stormed into the room and hugged her tight whilst pulling a face at me behind her back. I could not stop myself and stuck my tongue out at him like a sullen child. Realising my own insolence I stood up and hurried from the room, down to the kitchen, afraid to look back in case he was watching me. I wanted to be as far away from him as possible. I asked Cook if she needed some help and she pointed to a sink full of potatoes. She asked me to peel them so I did. I know she is grateful for the help because she is forever moaning that Millie cannot cut the slack. One of these days I will ask her exactly what she means.

The whole time I spent with my sleeves pushed up to my elbows, peeling dirty potatoes, I could not stop my mind from thinking about Edward. As much as I dislike him I have to admit he is so very handsome. I stared at the reflection staring back at me from the window. I still look like a girl although Cook made me blush two days ago by telling me that I was finally beginning to develop my womanly assets.

Lady Hannah took me for a trip into town last week to buy some suitable undergarments and new clothes as I have grown out of everything that I own. We had such an enjoyable morning together and she was very kind to me, she even took me for lunch in the new hotel that opened last week. She told me that his Lordship was supposed to take her but he was so busy with work that he still had not got around to it, so it was to be our secret and I was not to mention it to any of the other servants because she did not want them to get upset or jealous. I swore to her I would tell no one and it was very nice being treated like a lady instead of a servant.

I love Lady Hannah dearly. She has even begun to teach me to play the piano. One evening last week after his Lordship had retired and she had drunk three glasses of sherry after dinner, she told me that she had longed for a daughter of her own but it was not to be. She then said I was like the daughter she had always wanted but had never been blessed with.

A loud scream pierced my daydreams. It was followed by a horrible thud. I ran behind Cook from the kitchen to the hall where the noise came from and was greeted by the most horrific sight I have ever seen. Lady Hannah was lying at the bottom of the grand staircase and there was a huge pool of blood seeping from the back of her head. Edward appeared at the top of the stairs.

'Mother,' he shouted, and ran down them so fast I was afraid he would fall and land beside her.

Cook was crying into her apron. She ordered me to go and fetch Doctor Smith but I could not move. I felt as if my feet had been glued to the floor. I could not look away from the dark red blood that was staining the pretty white dress Lady Hannah was wearing; it was turning the soft silk crimson. Edward was bent over his mother sobbing.

'Alice,' screamed Cook.

I finally found my feet and ran as fast as I could. I turned to see Edward looking at me and I could have sworn that he was smiling that awful, wicked smile of his. I ran to find Alfie who saddled up the horse and trap and drove me through the bitter winter's night to the doctor's house. By the time we arrived back with the doctor, Edward and his Lordship had carried Lady Hannah to her bedroom. I will never forget the huge pool of blood that lay at the foot of the stairs: I had no idea a person could bleed so much.

Cook came downstairs and told me to get it cleaned up before his Lordship came back down and then everything went black. When I opened my eyes Edward was carrying me in his arms. He told me that he had caught me just before I hit the floor. He carried me into the nearest room, which was the library, where he gently laid me down onto the chaise longue. I was scared to be so close to him but at the same time it felt nice to have his strong arms wrapped around me. I looked into his eyes and for once they did not seem so black, just sad. I asked him how her Ladyship was and he told me the doctor and his father were with her. He spoke in hushed tones, not wanting anyone to overhear our conversation. He told me it was very serious. The doctor was worried because of the amount of blood she had lost and he said she had shattered a part of her skull. There was no way to move her to the hospital because it was far too dangerous with her head injury.

I began to sob uncontrollably and felt Edward's hands begin to stroke my hair and dab at my eyes with his handkerchief; I was taken aback that he was comforting me. As I write this I have come to realise that it was the first time I have known him to be nice. I like this kind Edward and I liked the feel of his hands as they smoothed my hair even more.

He stood to go and see his mother and I did not want him to leave me on my own, but he did and I carried on sobbing. I wanted to go and see her but I am too afraid of his Lordship. I stood on legs that wobbled and went to the door of the library. It was then that I heard his Lordship roar at the top of his voice. It was a dreadful sound full of pain and misery which echoed around the great hall. I looked up to see Cook running along the passage; the doctor walked down the stairs and shook his head at her. I knew then that Lady Hannah, the beautiful, kind woman, was dead – gone forever. I closed the door and stumbled back to the chair in a daze. Lying back down I cried until I fell asleep, where I would not have to face the awful truth.

I woke up in the dark. It was so cold. The fire I lit myself earlier had died down to a few glowing orange embers. The house was silent except for the ticking of the grandfather clock in the hall. Shivering, I stood up to go to my bedroom. I slipped from the library and ran along the corridor to the servants' stairs at the back of the house. I was too afraid to look into the hall in case I saw a vision of Lady Hannah crumpled and bleeding to death on the floor. I turned the corner and squealed to see Edward sitting on the bottom step; he was holding something in his hands that looked like a knife but it was so dark I couldn't be sure.

My heart began to race. I did not want to be alone with him. I mumbled my excuse and then dashed up the two flights of stairs until I reached the servants' bathroom and locked the door. My tear-stained face stared back at me from the small mirror above the sink and my eyes were huge with both sorrow and fright. I splashed cold water onto my face and then ran to the safety of my bedroom.

Undressing I slipped on the nightgown that Lady Hannah had only just bought for me and got into my freezing cold bed. I lay there trembling, waiting to get warm. A few minutes later a gentle knock on my door made my heart freeze.

He whispered through the door, 'Alice, it's me, Edward, please can I come in?'

I was terrified but my stomach began to flutter. I did not know what I should do. If Harold or Cook caught Edward in my room I would be in so much trouble. Before I could answer the doorknob began to turn and he crept in.

'Alice, are you still awake?'

I could barely whisper 'yes' but I did and he closed the door behind him. He walked across to where I lay and sat on the bed next to me: I felt sick with fear. I did not want Edward next to me but I could not send him away. He lifted a hand and began to stroke my hair and I felt myself shiver. He had been drinking because I could smell the sour whisky on his breath. I pulled away from his hand and then he slapped me across the face. Before I could do anything he was on top of me, his lips pressing down on my lips and his body pressed hard against mine. I am so ashamed of what happened next I cannot even write it down but I know it was wrong and it hurt so much that I cried in pain. After Edward was finished he stood up and walked out of the room, he did not even look back and I sobbed myself to sleep.

1st November 1887

I awoke early and spent a long time in the bath. Even after it had gone cold I stayed in there. I stayed until Millie hammered on the door demanding to come in. I was sore and did not know what to do with myself. I wanted to tell someone about what had happened because I did not know if it was right or wrong.

When I went back into my room Edward was standing by the window. He turned to me with tears rolling down his cheeks and told me how truly sorry he was and that he hoped he hadn't hurt me too much last night. He looked so sad and forlorn that I could not help myself and I told him I was sore but it was not too bad. He took hold of my hand and fell to his knees begging my forgiveness. He held onto my legs, his head pushing against my thighs, and I felt so sorry for him that I stroked his hair and told him I forgave him. When he finally stood up he took hold of me and kissed me. This time it was so gentle that I couldn't help but kiss him back.

5th November 1887

Today was Lady Hannah's funeral and it was so very sad for it reminded me of my mother's. Harold said that we should attend as a mark of respect. I did not really want to but I had no choice. I would rather have stayed at the house to make sure everything was prepared for the mourners. All the servants lined up at the back of the church, out of the way of the important people. I cried and cried. Edward was standing at the front next to his Lordship, with his head bowed. I was sandwiched between Cook and Alfie in the middle of the aisle where I had a direct view of the coffin and Edward.

Every time I see him I get butterflies and I am still not sure whether it is terror or indeed passion that makes me feel this way. Alfie squirmed throughout the entire service. I was so upset that he put his arm around my shoulders to try and give me some comfort. That was the only time I saw Edward lift his eyes from the ground. He turned and glared at Alfie. Edward's eyes were blacker than ever and he looked so angry I felt sorry for poor Alfie. I pulled away from his touch so as not to get him into any trouble.

After the funeral lots of mourners came back to the house and I spent the rest of the day rushing around serving drinks and food to them all. Cook said there is nothing like a funeral to give someone an appetite and she was right. They practically ate and drank his Lordship out of house and home. By the time the last one left I was exhausted. My poor feet were aching and my eyes stinging from the tears and vast clouds of cigar smoke which had turned the inside of the house into a haze.

His Lordship was in the drawing room and very drunk. I watched as Edward and Harold carried him up to his room. He has taken to sleeping in one of the guest rooms. He told Harold that he could no longer abide to be in the room where his beloved wife had died for she had taken his soul when she passed and he was nothing now but an empty shell.

Everyone retired to bed except myself and Edward, who had come to find me sitting at the piano, resting for a moment and thinking about Lady Hannah. He stood in front of me and I could not help but think how handsome he looked in his grief, and then I felt terrible for thinking such thoughts.

He pulled me into his arms and kissed me with so much passion; the heat from his body was so intense I feared we might set on fire. I know that what we are doing is wrong and I know full well that no good will come from it but I wanted him so badly. I wanted to feel those strong arms around me and his lips crushing against mine. He picked me up and carried me across the hall to the library, once again laying me down onto the chaise longue. My heart was beating so fast it was hard to breathe. I lay and watched him unbutton his shirt then he bent down towards me and I threw my arms around him, losing myself to him.

After a while an uncomfortable feeling that someone was watching made me lift my head and look to the doorway where I saw Alfie, his face white and such hurt in his eyes. As our eyes met he turned and ran. My cheeks burned with shame but Edward held me even tighter and I closed my eyes letting the heat wash over me.

11th November 1887

Edward is leaving today. He has important exams in London that he must not miss. I do not know how I will cope without him for he has become my rock. He has been there to give me comfort as I have him and we have spent hours talking each evening after I have finished my chores. The lovemaking between us has been so full of passion and pleasure that I never imagined it could ever be this way; he has never forced himself on me since that first time. According to Cook it was something that had to be done if you wanted to keep your husband happy and make babies.

I am ashamed of the way I have been behaving and I know it is not how a good girl should behave but it feels so right, for I think I am falling in love with Edward so deeply that I would not be able to stop myself if I tried. We have to keep our friendship a secret because I am a servant and it is not heard of for the master of the house to carry on as such. If his Lordship found out I would be sent away and I could not bear it; this house and the people in it are the only family that I know.

Alfie has not spoken a word to me since the night of the funeral and for that I am truly sad; he is my best friend and I miss him greatly. Once Edward leaves for London I will try and speak to him on his own and explain everything to him.

His Lordship has become so melancholy it breaks my heart to look at him. He is not eating his meals and stays in his room all day drinking nothing but whisky. He looks dreadful and Edward confessed to me that he is awfully worried about him.

I made myself busy and went to clean the schoolroom to keep my mind from missing Edward so much. He came to find me to say goodbye and I found myself wondering how we had gone from hating each other to loving each other in such a short space of time. He kissed me and I did not want him to stop. I wanted him to make love to me one last time before he left but I was being foolish and selfish. I held him tight and he told me he would be home as soon as he could to see me again. Then he turned and left and I wished that I could go with him.

13th November 1887

Alfie has managed to avoid me but today I crept away from polishing the silverware in the dining room and went to find him. I knew he would be in the greenhouse tending to the plants that Lady Hannah had planted herself from seed, for Cook told me he had done it every day since she died. That was Alfie all over, so kind and thoughtful he would not want to let the plants die: by keeping them alive he was keeping Lady Hannah alive.

When I walked in he turned away from me but I picked up a watering can and began to help him. He told me to go away and I told him that he simply must talk to me, that I did not want us to be enemies and that I missed him. I took his hand and dragged him to sit on the broken bench at the far end of the greenhouse. I told him how sorry I was that he saw me with Edward that night and that I was not proud of my behaviour but that I loved Edward. Alfie laughed loudly and told me that Edward was the most selfish, wicked person he had ever met. He told me that the only reason Edward was even interested in me was because he overheard a conversation that Alfie had with Harold about how much he really liked me. I jumped up. I was so angry with him for telling such lies and we had a terrible argument. Alfie tugged my arm and pulled me back down onto the bench, telling me to be quiet before someone heard us and we got in trouble.

I remembered all too well the Edward that would force me to play his horrid games, the Edward who would chase me with dead rabbits. But people change and I wanted to believe that he has outgrown all those childish pranks. Alfie shook his head and told me that a leopard never changes its spots. I do not believe him though; everyone deserves a second chance. But still he planted a tiny seed of doubt into my mind and each day I know that it will get a little stronger if I nurture it. I so want to believe that Edward truly loves me and that he may even one day ask me to become his wife.

Then Alfie shocked me and asked me to marry him. He told me that he loved me with all his heart in a way that Edward never would. I laughed and told him to stop being ridiculous. It was then that I hurt him in such a spiteful way that I don't think I will ever forgive myself, but I do not have feelings for him like I do for Edward. I told Alfie this and that I wanted to have lots of Edward's children, for them to run around and fill Abbey Wood with their laughter. This beautiful house would be a much better place with the sound of children echoing around the walls instead of the hushed tones of grief-stricken people.

Alfie stared at me in such a way that I almost began to cry. He got up and could barely stand; his entire body was shaking and I know that he wanted to cry. I never wanted to hurt him, but to me he is a very dear friend and not someone I want to share the rest of my life with. As he walked away I felt like the cruellest woman in the world and I prayed to God that Alfie would forgive me and find someone who would truly love him.

1st December 1887

His Lordship has not come out of his room for weeks and is refusing all visitors. Harold takes all his meals and drinks up to him. Cook told me and Millie that if he carries on this way he will die from a broken heart. I cannot imagine how sad he must be because I miss Lady Hannah's laughter and music every minute of every day. I used to dust whilst humming along and it would fill my heart with joy. Now I feel as if a part of me is missing so I cannot imagine how his Lordship feels.

Edward sent me a letter to tell me how much he misses me and how he is counting down the days until he is home for Christmas. I have it tucked under my pillow and read it every single night before I go to sleep. Cook has been teasing me, asking me who would be writing to me, and Alfie told her it was the master. I laughed when she clipped him around the back of the head and told him not to be so insolent for it served him right.

3rd December 1887

Today has been yet another terrible day of tragedy in this great house of sadness. I went outside to hang the billiard room rugs out to air and was greeted by the most dreadful sight. His Lordship was hanging from the big oak tree. His face was grey and his blue lips were parted with his tongue protruding through them. I screamed and screamed as loud as I could for I did not know what else to do. Alfie ran out of the scullery door followed by Harold, Cook and Millie. Cook fell to her knees and crossed herself. Once again I found myself frozen to the ground, unable to move, my eyes fixed on the terrible sight of his Lordship swinging like some huge marionette.

I have no idea how long we were like that, staring at the awful sight that we beheld, but the next thing I knew Doctor Smith and the policeman from the town appeared – Harold had sent for them. I overheard Alfie whisper to Cook that Harold had telephoned for Edward to come home immediately. Poor Edward, he has lost both of his parents in such a short space of time and in the most dreadful way. I feel guilty that I am excited he will be home sooner and I hope that I will be able to comfort him for I have nothing else to offer him.

4th December 1887

Edward arrived home to a house of silence and grief. His Lordship's body has been laid out in a solid oak coffin, with the shiniest brass handles, in the morning room so that people can come and pay their respects.

Harold asked me to do one final thing for his Lordship, to go in and make sure the room was presentable for visitors, not a speck of dust was to be seen. I was so scared, I did not dare to look into the coffin. I could not bear it. What if he opened his eyes? I placed a heavy book against the door to keep it open for I would have screamed the house down if the door had shut on me and I had been trapped in there with the cold, dead shell of my master's body. I have never worked so fast in all my life. I just hope that he and Lady Hannah have been reunited; I cannot bear to think of him wandering around a lost and lonely soul for all eternity.

Last night after supper Cook began her usual gossiping. Although it was far more subdued than usual but she took great pleasure in informing us about what happens to your soul when you take your own life. Millie was aghast to think that God would forsake someone because they were so desperate they felt they had no option but to take their own life. I told her later on that if a person was brave enough to carry out such a final task for whatever reason then surely God would not be so cruel as to turn his back on them.

Cook was also fussing about what would become of us now. She is convinced that Edward will want to sell the house, for it holds nothing but bad memories for him, and then we will all be out of a job and a home. I wanted to tell her that it must also hold some good memories but I kept quiet. Everyone would want to know exactly what I meant and I do not want to cause a fuss now: Edward has enough to deal with.

The whole time we were in the kitchen Alfie stared at me with the strangest look on his face. I do hope he is not coming down with some affliction.

5th December 1887

Edward found me in the schoolroom last night. I had come up to read and to keep out of everyone's way. I do not like being downstairs while his Lordship's body is in the house. I have been awake since the crack of dawn but I could not sleep. All the other servants were sitting in the kitchen around the hearth, drinking a bottle of wine that Harold had opened. I did not want to listen to any more of their idle gossip: I wanted to be alone.

Edward has been so busy with the police, then a visit from his uncle and the vicar, that he has not even acknowledged my existence and I have to admit it hurt me deep inside. The door opened and I looked up from my book to see Edward standing there. His face looked so much older than the last time I saw him. His eyes were black and for a fleeting moment I felt afraid; past memories rushed through my mind. It was such a pained smile that I stood from the chair and in three short strides he was across the room and sweeping me into his arms. I felt the warm rush begin in my stomach as his lips met mine. He held on to me so tight that I could not breathe when he kissed me and I had to pull away from him. He stroked my hair and took hold of my hand. I expected him to lead me up to my bedroom but instead he led me towards his. I paused at the door, afraid in case anyone should see me. Edward smiled and told me that he was the master of the house now and would do as he pleased. He told me that after his father's funeral he would tell the staff that I was no longer to be a housemaid. That we were courting and that I was to be treated like a lady. I could not speak I was so surprised. He laughed and pulled me into his bedroom, closing and locking the door behind me.

I had been in here countless times but never like this. His bed was huge compared to mine. We stood next to the roaring fire that I had built earlier. He began to undress me and before long we were on the bed. It was so soft and the silk sheets cooled my burning skin. I closed my eyes and hoped that the night would never end.

I awoke to the cold light of dawn and gasped: Cook would be furious with me if I were not downstairs in time to set the table. I untangled myself from Edward's warm embrace and picked my clothes up off the floor. I dressed quickly. There was not time to wash or brush my hair but I pinned it back up on top of my head as best as I could.

I crept out into the hallway only to be greeted by Alfie, who had just run down the servants' stairs. I knew that he had been sent to look for me and my cheeks flushed. He stared at me with contempt but there was also so much pain in his eyes. He told me that Cook had sent him to see if I was ill because I was late to rise. I pleaded with him not to tell her or anyone else but he did not say a word. Instead he turned his back on me and walked away, his shoulders slumped and his steps slow.

Once again I felt my heart tear a tiny bit more. If this keeps on I am afraid it will rip in two and I will die of a broken heart just like his Lordship.

CHAPTER 7

Derek Edmondson was sitting eating supper with his sister. He was there on a week long visit from Burnley. A practising medium since he was ten years old, he liked to travel around the North West to various spiritualist churches giving demonstrations of his psychic abilities. The pay was terrible but it was better than sitting at home with only the dead to keep him company.

Three names were whirling around in his head. They were like a tornado gathering speed and, quite frankly, it was making him ill. Beads of sweat formed on his forehead and he knew if he were to stand up it would make him feel dizzy. Unable to stop himself he began to mumble.

His sister turned to him. 'What did you just say? Oh Derek, you look awful. What's the matter? Are you ill?'

'Annie, Edward, Alice, Annie, Edward, Alice – no, stop this now, I command you.' He pulled himself from the chair onto unsteady feet. 'You have to stop this please.'

The whirlwind ceased and was replaced by a vision of a crumbling, Victorian mansion. He blinked twice to clear the image from his mind then slumped back down into the chair. His sister stooped, her hand pressing against his forehead to see if he had a temperature. He brushed it away, not wanting to be fussed over. She was anxious and he felt sorry he had caused her to feel that way, but something bad, maybe even catastrophic, was on the horizon and whoever this Alice, Annie and Edward were they were involved. Given the chance, Derek would have no intention of getting mixed up in whatever this was but he knew it was too late, and regardless of whether he wanted to be he was in it up to his neck.

'I'm fine, Joan, I just felt a bit peaky for a minute but I'm OK now. I do apologise if I scared you.'

Joan arched her eyebrows. 'Well, as long as you're sure. It's not like I'm not used to you acting a bit strange now, is it?'

Derek laughed then lay his head back against the chair and shut his eyes.

*

Annie stretched and yawned. Tess let out a loud snore. Annie pushed the diary to one side and got up to check the doors and windows were all secure. Her mind was buzzing. Had that house known anything but sadness? No wonder the atmosphere felt so oppressive in there. She had watched a programme once about past memories imprinting themselves into their surroundings. The old house would be the perfect place to test that theory out: two people had died in the house and gardens and she wondered how many more had suffered the same, if not a worse, fate.

Washing her face and rubbing some of her niece's moisturiser all over she then checked each of the bedrooms, making sure they were empty. The huge antique brass bed in the master bedroom looked so inviting: she could imagine collapsing onto it in a heap with Will. She carried on along the hallway to the smallest bedroom, which she had turned into a bombsite: tidiness had never been one of her better traits. Leaving the nightlight on and climbing into the single bed she pulled the duvet up around her head and tucked it tight under her legs. One of her greatest childhood fears had been the thought of invisible hands tugging off her blankets in the night, and she still felt that way whenever she slept in a strange place.

*

On his way out of the station Will called back into the community office to see if Claire and Sally were still there. As he walked in the pair of them erupted into a fit of giggles.

'Here, Will, what you told us before, well it put me right off my cheese and pickle sarnie.'

He nodded. 'Yep, I can see that it would. Sorry about that but it was good gossip. I can't believe you two didn't know anyway: you're losing your touch.' They both nodded in agreement and he coughed into his hand. 'I, erm, met Annie today. I haven't really spoken to her before – she seems kind of nice.' He felt his cheeks begin to burn as the words left his lips and they got hotter when he caught the look Sally gave to Claire.

'"Kind of nice", what's that supped to mean? Actually she is very nice, had a bit of a rough time lately though.'

'What happened to her? We haven't dealt with any assaults against one of our own. Was it an accident?'

'It never went to CID. Kav dealt with it kind of on a need-to-know basis and, basically, we are not supposed to know. Even Jake hasn't said anything and he is the super grass of the century. I think Kav has either sworn him to secrecy or threatened him with working the town centre.'

'Must be serious if Jake hasn't blabbed. Oh well, see you ladies tomorrow if you're in. Goodnight.'

This time it was Claire who looked at Sally; she shrugged. 'Will, I don't know the details, but all I know is that something happened to her at home.'

'Oh God, that's awful, I had no idea. I thought maybe she'd got into a fight at work or a car accident. Thanks, I promise I won't say anything.' He left the station with an overwhelming urge to go back and see her but what could he say? He wasn't supposed to know and he'd look stupid turning up this late unannounced. His stomach let out a loud growl and he realised the need for food and beer was the greater priority at the moment.

He sighed after eating a full Chinese and washing it down with two cans of Stella. His stomach felt like it was going to explode. He flicked through the channels until he found a Bruce Willis film: everyone loves a hero. But he couldn't concentrate. First he was thinking about Jenna White and then it was Annie. He stretched his legs, resting his feet on the pine blanket box he used as a coffee table. The thought occurred to him that Annie was down to earth and normal; she might even eat in front of him if he took her out for a meal. Not like his last girlfriend who would order a chicken salad and spend twenty minutes pushing it around her plate with a fork until he'd finished his steak and chips. He liked the thought of dinner with Annie and it made him want to phone Jake for her number. He lifted a hand to his forehead to check he wasn't coming down with something because he wasn't acting himself at all. He looked back at the screen. Kav was the hero in Annie's story and he felt his admiration for him increase: there weren't many supervisors who would deal with a crime and keep it so quiet that no one knew about it.

***

The woman looked vaguely familiar and, from what little he could see, she was quite attractive. In fact, he liked her a lot. When she had pulled off her hat inside the house he had gasped aloud at the sight of the back of her head. He wondered what had happened to her. He wanted to know exactly how alone this woman was because he felt an instant attraction to her: she looked like an older version of Jenna with her dark hair and pale skin – exactly his type – and he knew all too well what it was like to be lonely. He would keep an eye on her because he fancied her and if she played it right he might even show her his special room.

He had left the courtyard and made his way through the woods to the house, his mind overflowing with ideas. It would be nice to have a proper girlfriend. The things he could show her if she promised not to tell and if not – well, he had a safe place she could stay forever. As he walked around the mansion he realised just where he knew her from: she was the woman from the spiritualist church last week.

Satisfied that no one had been into his secret domain he made his way back to the farmhouse and turned the flash off on his phone. He was pleased to see her sitting at the kitchen table reading and he had managed to get close enough to take a couple of pictures; he doubted they would work but it was worth a try. The way she delicately sipped her wine turned him on and he snuck back into the hay barn to watch her a little longer. It didn't look as if there was a man around to lock up for her and he began to tingle with excitement at the possibilities. He watched as every single light in the house was turned on for a few seconds and then off again. The one that stayed on the longest was a small window at the side of the house and he felt himself go hard thinking about her alone, in the dark. *How easy do you scare pretty lady?* The urge to try and find a way into the house was overwhelming: he had to begin jogging to stop himself from doing something reckless and stupid. It would spoil his plans if he went in there on a whim. He needed to be practical. She could be his grand finale. If he wanted it to be perfect with her he needed to do a little more practice so it would be just as the voice in his head kept telling him it could be.

He arrived home out of breath and with ruddy cheeks. The house was still in darkness. Thank God for small mercies. She would be in bed snoring like a trooper so he could indulge in his fantasies without being disturbed by the voice from hell. How had he ended up with a mother who wouldn't die? She was going to live until she was a hundred. He could always kill her but that depended if he got away with everything else he had planned. If he got caught maybe the shock would give her a heart attack: it would be just his luck for her to drop dead when he was going to prison for the rest of his life. Smiling he checked the computer for an email from his next victim. Four more days and Jenna would no longer be alone: she would have another corpse for company. It was shocking to think of the number of teenage girls who were available at the click of a button and just ripe for the picking.

CHAPTER 8

Annie did not sleep well. Her dreams were filled with dead and dying people. By the time she got out of bed it was early morning and she couldn't shake the visions her dreams had left behind. They were as clear as photographs and had imprinted themselves onto her mind. Dragging the duvet from the bed she took it downstairs and lay on the sofa.

In no time, her eyes began to close and she drifted off. This time it was a handsome young man who haunted her dreams. His eyes were black and she had never seen eyes like them. He smiled at her and waved and she smiled back: he obviously knew her but she had no idea who he was. His expression changed to a sneer and he looked menacing. Annie knew that he wanted her to run and hide from him so that he could chase her. One of his arms hung down by his side and he was holding something that was dripping with a dark liquid. Terror took over and she began to run, pumping her short legs as hard as she could to put some distance between them. He was very fast though and catching up to her. His laughter sounded behind her so close that she felt his warm breath against her ear. His hand reached out to grab hold of her when a loud knocking on the door woke her from the nightmare.

She looked at the clock on the mantle and was horrified to see it was quarter past nine. Running her fingers over her head and rubbing her eyes she went to the kitchen door. She peered through the tiny pane of glass to see Will standing on the other side. He looked even better than yesterday, in a pair of faded jeans and a red Berghaus® jacket. *Oh bugger.* She unlocked the door and he grinned at her.

'Good morning, and a lovely one it is, bit of a nip in the air.'

Annie squeezed her eyes shut against the bright sunlight. 'Morning. Sorry, I didn't sleep too well last night and ended up on the sofa where I finally fell into a coma. Come in, I won't be long. Do you want to put the kettle on?'

'Of course. You get dressed and your coffee will be waiting.'

She ran for the stairs and realised she was wearing odd pyjamas and pink fluffy bed socks. *Nice one, Annie. This is certainly not like it is in the movies where you get to be in your best silk pyjamas with not a hair out of place. If this hasn't freaked him out you may be onto a winner.*

110

When she came back downstairs Will was putting her empty wine bottle into the recycling box. 'They're not all mine in case you're wondering. I only drink rosé, my brother drinks the red. I forgot to put them out for the bin men.'

'Don't worry. You should see mine, it's full of empty Stella cans and they are all mine.'

She laughed and tugged at the blue hat that was firmly back in place.

'You know it's driving me mad wondering what has happened to Jenna,' said Will. 'She couldn't vanish off the face of the earth with no trace. I'm worried in case she has gone and done something stupid. There are so many horror stories of teenagers falling out with their families then going and killing themselves. It makes me feel sick.'

Annie agreed with him. It wasn't that long ago she had been first on scene to a teenage girl who had hanged herself because she was being bullied. It had taken her weeks to get that image from her head.

She took a loaf of bread from the cupboard before turning back to him. 'Now, I'm warning you: toast I can usually manage but I'm not that good in the kitchen. For some reason I tend to burn everything.'

'That's OK, I'm used to it. My mum was an awful cook. I had to learn how to cook at school to stop my dad and me getting fatally poisoned. My dad had tears in his eyes the first time he had a roast dinner he didn't have to use a carving knife to eat the veg with. God bless her. He was more upset than my mum when I moved out. He said there was no way he could go back to the burnt offerings. But then he never had to because she went out shopping one day with her friends and collapsed in the street; she died instantly from a massive heart attack.'

'I'm so sorry. That must have been a terrible shock for you all.' She watched him fiddle with his mug then passed him a plate of toast.

His eyes lit up. 'Is that real butter?'

'Yep, not much point in eating toast covered in margarine: it tastes like plastic.'

'Annie, I'm impressed. I don't think I've ever met a girl who admitted to eating butter. My last girlfriend only bought that lower than low fat rubbish. I used to eat my toast dry it tasted so bad.'

Annie felt her cheeks turn red. 'Just don't tell my slimming club leader. It's one of the reasons I'll never be a size ten. I like my comfort food and wine far too much to be able to give it up.' Now she felt stupid as well as fat. *Way to go. You've just admitted you eat more than an elephant to a guy who thinks anorexia is in fashion.* She turned to the sink so he couldn't see her face and began to rinse the pots.

Will carried his plate over and put his hand on her arm. 'That was really nice, thanks. I'm sorry if I upset you, I didn't mean to.'

Annie turned to face him and felt fresh tears threaten to fall. 'It's not you, it's me. Since I hurt my head things have been affecting me in the strangest ways. I keep crying over nothing and talking utter crap.'

He stepped closer and pulled her towards him, holding her tight. She let her head rest against his chest. Will lifted his hand to stroke her head and she pulled away feeling self-conscious.

'I'm sorry. See what I mean? I keep acting weird.'

He stepped back to give her some space. 'Well, I'm not sure what my excuse is apart from the possibility the butter went straight to my head.'

They began to laugh and Annie felt her heart flutter. Damn, she really liked him even though she knew she shouldn't. 'Come on, let's go and check out the house before we get ourselves in trouble.'

She led him out to the tiny path she had run along yesterday. She was terrified to be going back into the old house so soon but she wouldn't tell him that. At least she wasn't alone this time. He followed behind her until they reached the house.

'Can you imagine living here? It must have been so amazing,' said Will.

'It is beautiful but I don't think that having this house and all the money brought them any happiness. From what I can gather they were afflicted by one tragedy after the other.' She didn't tell him how she knew this or mention the diary, wanting to keep it to herself.

They approached the front door and she pulled the key from her pocket, not realising how much her hands were trembling until she tried to insert it into the lock and missed twice. The third one hit home and she shoved against the door but it wouldn't move.

'The rain must have made it swell.'

Both of them leant against it and pushed hard. Annie hoped it wouldn't budge; it would save her the trauma of having to go back in and face her fears. But after a few attempts it gave a little and after a couple more it swung inwards. Her mouth went dry and her heart began to race as she followed Will inside; he was as mesmerised by the place as she had been yesterday.

They searched every room on the ground floor. All of them were empty, like she had said. The relief they hadn't found the missing girl lying dead in any of them made her heart slow just a little. The only door to the downstairs they had no key for was the cellar door, and for that she was thankful. Thinking about Alice lost down there in the dark made her skin prickle.

As they reached the stairs her stomach lurched and Will turned to her. 'Are they safe? I don't fancy falling through and breaking my leg – I'm far too busy.' He chuckled but she couldn't and struggled to smile back.

'No, they're fine. I was up there yesterday and everything is surprisingly solid. It's true what they say, they definitely don't build them like they used to.' She let him lead the way and she hesitated at the foot of the stairs feeling like a caged bird; her heart was flapping so hard inside her chest. A feeling of dread washed over her and she looked down to see a large dark stain underneath her feet. *Surely not. It can't be after all these years. Would blood still be visible to the naked eye?*

Will had made it to the top and was now watching her. 'Are you OK? You've gone white. You're not going to pass out on me, are you? Why don't you wait there and I'll check it out.'

'No!' Her voice was sharper than she intended. 'I'm fine. Wait for me.'

He held out his hand towards her. 'Come on, I'll pull you up.'

She ran up the stairs slapping his hand away. 'You are such a cheeky git, Will. I don't need your help, thank you. I managed to come up here all by myself yesterday.' All the same she followed behind him letting him, lead the way, as he checked every room: still no sign of Jenna.

At the far end of the hallway they found a narrow staircase tucked behind a partition wall. Annie knew where this led and felt safe walking up them to where the servants' quarters once were. Instinctively she knew which one belonged to Alice and stepped into the small, cosy room. A warm glow enveloped her. Will walked on checking out the other rooms along the small passage. Annie felt as if she were in a different time. Staring out of the window she could see the huge oak tree which towered above the overgrown garden below. The tree where Edward had attacked the girl and where his broken-hearted father had hanged himself.

Will's voice broke her trance. 'There's nothing up here.'

Annie whispered, 'No, not anymore.'

They went back down to the first floor. As they approached the schoolroom Annie thought she was going to be sick. She leant on the doorframe as he looked around the room.

Will had walked around the house oblivious to the atmosphere. Annie, on the other hand, was afraid of her own shadow.

'I'm sorry, you were right, but I suppose it was worth a try. I can't believe those mantelpieces have never been stolen. They must be worth a small fortune.'

'Ah, I can tell you why. There are too many scary stories about the woods and the Abbey and I doubt any burglar would be brave enough. Anyway there is no access for vehicles; it's a totally private road. Only my brother and the council have keys for the gates so no one could get a van up here.'

Will sighed. 'It's such a beautiful old place. I would have loved to have seen it when it was first built.'

Annie didn't mention that if she closed her eyes she could describe every room in vivid detail to him. Following him down the stairs she stopped as she felt a sudden change in the air as the temperature plummeted; goose bumps appeared on her arms. Exhaling, her breath came out in fine, white wisps. She sensed someone standing behind her on the top step and felt a pair of black eyes burning into the back of her frozen neck. Terrified, she couldn't have turned around if she wanted to so she continued to walk down the stairs and hurriedly crossed the hall to the front door. As she stepped outside she breathed out. Still afraid to look behind her she waited for Will to close the door and passed him the key to lock it, relieved to be out of the house.

'Are you sure you're OK?'

She nodded her head, trying to compose herself so that her voice didn't betray the fear that had taken over. Annie wanted to sound normal but she couldn't remember how being normal felt. 'I'm fine, really.'

They walked back to the farmhouse in silence. As they reached the gate she turned to him. 'Do you want a lift to your car? I need to go into town so I can drop you off.'

'That would be brilliant. You're a little star, do you know that?'

She laughed and felt her heart tug as she wondered if this was it now, if she had served her purpose.

'You know, if you fancy something nice to eat for a change I could come up and cook you a meal,' said Will. 'You provide the wine and I'll provide the ingredients and the personal chef.

Don't think I'm being pushy but judging by the contents of your fridge I think a good home-cooked meal wouldn't go amiss. The food will do you a world of good, not to mention my excellent company.'

Annie paused for effect. 'I'll have to check my diary.' Then she giggled. 'If you're willing to cook that's an offer I can't refuse. I would really like that.'

'How about tomorrow? It's my day off. I could come up then.'

She tried to contain the excitement that was bubbling under her cool exterior. 'Tomorrow it is then.' She winked at him. Even though she knew it was a hopeless situation it wouldn't hurt to just enjoy it for the moment. She needed cheering up and had never realised that underneath the reputation and the cool, calm exterior there was a man who was funny, kind and a bit of a gentleman. *Better stick a lucky dip on the lottery, maybe your luck is about to change.*

CHAPTER 9

The traffic was awful on the way back into town and getting parked was going to be a total nightmare. Next to the police station were the Social Services offices: they had a lovely big car park. Will drove in as if he worked there and parked in the last empty space, feeling momentarily guilty. He got out of the car and walked briskly along the narrow alley between the two buildings that led to the rear yard of the station. A van came whizzing out of the open gates, lights flashing; it almost took him out. He waved at the driver who mouthed 'sorry' then sped off, sirens wailing into the distance. The rear yard was pitiful compared to the one next door. There was just enough room to park roughly twelve assorted vans and cars depending on who parked them. Outside the back door two uniformed coppers were trying various door codes to get into the building.

'For Christ's sake, why do they change the code on a Monday morning when nobody has a clue what it is?'

Will stepped forward and typed in the four-digit code, releasing the lock and opening the door.

'Cheers, Will. We've been here five minutes and no one has got off their lazy arses to open the door.'

'Busy people, you know how it is. How many times have you bothered to open the door when someone has been knocking?'

Smithy looked at Will as if trying to work it out. 'Err, none.'

'See. Busy people or so I've heard.' Will left them to it and headed down to the CID office. As he walked in four heads turned to look at him and chorused, 'Morning, Sarge.'

'Yeah right, less of the "Sarge" and one of you get the kettle on. Any news on Jenna?' Four blank faces stared back at him. He walked across to the huge whiteboard. Jenna's picture stared defiantly back at him. He wondered why she needed to wear all that crap on her face. What was she hiding? Or who was she hiding from? He'd seen a picture of her two years before she'd discovered a love of pop stars that looked like corpses. She had been a pretty girl.

Underneath her picture was a list of all her family, friends and tutors. All of them had been spoken to except one. The rest had big red ticks next to them. Not one person on the list thought that Jenna was capable of running away, not that kind of girl. The name that was unchecked was that of her best friend who had been to Manchester all weekend. She needed speaking to this morning, sooner rather than later.

Laura handed him a chipped mug of coffee. He took it and sat down at his desk. He opened his emails. Scrolling through them he found one about a collection for Annie. It said that she was off ill and there was a card and collection in the community office. Before yesterday he wouldn't have even realised who she was. It was amazing how much your life could change in twenty-four hours. He finished his drink and stood up.

'Laura, are you on with anything?'

'No, I've just finished going through the list of Jenna's friends.'

'Good, you can come with me then.'

She grabbed her jacket off the back of the chair, grateful to get out of the office for a bit. Stu blew her a kiss and she stuck two fingers up behind her back. Will grabbed a set of keys from the whiteboard. He called into the patrol sergeant's office, where Kav was eating his way through a giant bacon and egg bun. He nodded at Will and gave him the thumbs-up. Will wanted to talk to him but not where there was an audience.

'Fancy a pint later?' asked Will.

'If you're buying, I'd love one.'

'I am, but only the first. You could drink a well dry.'

'I finish at six. Anything on our missing girl?'

'Stu is chasing up a mobile number with no registered owner. I'm hoping she might be hiding out with this mystery associate.'

'I hope so, mate, because Jake is convinced she's been abducted by little green men,' said Kav.

'Sounds like Jake. I'm off to speak to her best friend now.'

'Good luck. I'll see you in the Black Dog about quarter past for that pint.'

Will went back into the corridor and threw the car keys to Laura, who was leaning against the wall chewing on her thumbnail.

'You drive.'

They went in search of the car which, judging by the smudged numbers on the key ring, could be any one of the hundreds of cars parked on the massive public car park opposite the station.

'These bloody cars should have central locking. At least when you pressed the key fob you would see the lights flash.' She squinted trying to make out some of the numbers that had rubbed off. 'And how hard would it be to rewrite the call sign back on?'

'Found it.' Will was halfway across the car park and Laura had to jog to catch up with him. He got into the passenger seat, pulling the small blue file from the side pocket. 'There better be some petrol in it. I haven't got time to mess around.'

Laura turned the ignition key; relieved the gauge showed the tank was three quarters full. 'That's another thing which does my head in, filling out those books every time we use a car, it's like they don't trust us.'

'I hate to be the one to break it to you, Laura, but they don't.'

They drove to Lesh Lane in silence. Laura couldn't stop looking at Will and he wondered if he had something on his face or suit: she was freaking him out. She parked up outside the ex-council house. It had a neat garden and the windows were gleaming; he always noticed the small details. As they got out of the car he pulled his notebook from his pocket to check the girl's name. She was seventeen so it wouldn't matter if her parents weren't present. As Laura unlatched the gate the front door opened and a teary, red-eyed teenager stood waiting for them.

'Erin, my name is Will Ashworth. I'm a detective with the police.' He stepped forward and shook her hand. 'This is Laura Collins and she is a colleague of mine. We need to speak with you about Jenna, is it OK to come in?'

She stepped to one side to let them pass, pointing towards the kitchen at the back of the house. 'My mum told me this morning when I got back that Jenna is missing. I don't understand. It's really not like her.'

Laura glanced at Will. He continued to lead the questioning. 'Erin, I'm really worried about her. She didn't take any money or clothes with her and the only thing we can't find is her phone, which hasn't been used since she disappeared. Did she have any plans to go somewhere, maybe meet up with a boyfriend?'

123

Erin sniffed, rubbing her red eyes with the back of her hand. 'I promised I wouldn't tell anyone. Jenna will kill me.'

'Jenna hasn't spoken to anyone or been seen since Friday night, you're not grassing her up. What if she needs our help? Whatever it is you need to tell us, Jenna will thank you for it in the end.'

Erin paused and then the words that Will had been dreading came tumbling out. 'She met some guy off the internet.'

Both Will and Laura sat up straight. Laura flipped open her notebook ready to write every detail down.

'He's a lot older than her but Jenna said that he was cool and loaded.'

'Did you ever see him?'

She shook her head. 'No, Jenna was going to meet him for the first time on Friday. They'd only ever spoken on webcam before but she kept saying how he was so like her and he really got where she was coming from. She even said they were a match made in heaven, can you believe that?'

'Did she tell you his name, where he lived? Anything at all that may give us a clue where to find her.'

'No, she wouldn't tell me anything about him, said it was her little secret. He sent her two tickets for a Marilyn Manson concert in Manchester – he was going to take her there for the weekend. God, she was so happy when they arrived in the post and I was so mad with her. We always said we would go to our first Manson concert together and some old dude was going to take her while I sat at home twiddling my thumbs. That's why I went to see my brother this weekend. We had a big argument and I wanted to be as far away from here as possible.'

Tears were flowing freely down her cheeks and Will felt bad for her; he patted her hand. 'It's not your fault, Erin, Jenna would have gone to meet this man whether you were here or not and I'm sure she wouldn't have wanted you tagging along on a first date. Did she tell you where she was meeting him?'

'Something about a haunted house and ghost stories but I don't know where, she wouldn't tell me.'

She began sobbing again and Will knew he wouldn't get anything more out of her, so he pulled a business card out of his pocket and handed it to her. 'That's my contact card. If you remember anything or you're worried and need to speak to someone my mobile number is on there. You can ring me anytime.'

'Do you think she's dead?'

Will decided it was best to be honest. He didn't want to give her false hope when he didn't have a clue. 'I don't know, Erin. I hope that she is staying somewhere with him and she is OK, but the truth is we just don't know.'

Leaving Erin to her tears they walked back to the car.

'We need to find those tickets and trace who bought them. Even if they came off eBay we can trace the seller. I need you to get onto headquarters and tell them to hurry up with her computer; it's top priority now. If she met him on the internet it should be a goldmine full of clues. He could be anyone but he sounds like some fucking perv if you ask me,' snarled Will.

'I'll get it sorted as soon as we get back, boss.'

Will dropped Laura off at the station and drove back to Jenna White's house: he wouldn't leave until he found those tickets.

*

Annie couldn't remember the last time she'd visited a library, which was most likely something to do with the fact that she owed hundreds of pounds in overdue book fines from when she was younger. As a child she had spent hours in there, curled up reading everything she could get her hands on. Upstairs had been the reference library and the coolest museum she had ever been to, not that she had been to many. This one had stuffed birds and a huge moose head with big brown eyes that looked so sad. She'd probably look sad if someone had shot her, cut off her head and put it on public display for everyone to see. She used to make up scary stories about the flesh-eating moose that roamed the streets after dark looking for its body – it's no wonder she used to have terrible nightmares.

As she walked through the main doors she expected an alarm to sound and alert everyone she was here, but all that greeted her were the hushed tones of the staff and the few people in there. For the first time in a couple of days she felt relaxed, childhood memories soothing her anxious mind and reminding her of the time her life was far less complicated. Following the signs she found the records office tucked away at the back of the huge building. Annie was mystified when the assistant told her she had to put her bag into a locker and could only makes notes with a pencil.

The woman picked up on her expression. 'You wouldn't believe how many of our documents have been damaged or stolen. We have to take these precautions to make sure we have some left.'

'Oh that's awful. I only have a pen. Do you have a pencil I could use?'

'Yes, of course, dear, that's fifty pence please.'

Annie fished in her pocket for some change and handed it over.

The woman gave her a pencil. 'Do you have a reader's card, dear?'

For the second time Annie's face went blank.

'It's a membership card so you can look at the documents. You will need something with your address on to prove who you are.' The woman had the smuggest look on her face, clearly expecting Annie to have nothing with her.

Annie had to keep smiling to stop herself from grabbing hold of the woman and shaking her. 'I'll just look in my bag which you told me to put in the locker five minutes ago, I won't be a minute.' Inside her bag she found a crumpled bank statement and her police warrant card. She slammed the metal door shut and locked it, turning around to see the woman was now helping some man who wanted to trace his mother's parents. Annie thought she might actually scream in frustration when a voice from behind came to her rescue.

'Can I help you?'

She turned to see a young man in his late teens smiling at her. 'Yes please, that would be wonderful. I'm trying to look for some information on the old house in the woods behind the Abbey. But I needed a pencil and a reader's card and to be honest I haven't got a clue what she's on about: I'm confused.'

His name badge said Declan. Annie was relieved when he laughed. 'Hmm, Hilda tends to have that effect on everyone. Come on, I'll sort you out.'

She followed him to the desk and within two minutes had filled out a form which Declan took from her, along with her ID, to photocopy. She was now the proud owner of a brand new, blue and white reader's card.

'You take a seat and I'll bring over all the stuff we have on the manor house in Abbey Wood, that's the one you're talking about, isn't it?'

'Thank you. My brother is the caretaker for it and I'm interested in the history of the place.'

'Wow really? That is so cool. It's a big old scary place. You know he could make a fortune doing those ghost tours. I have loads of mates in college who would be interested.'

'That's not a bad idea, I'll tell him about it. Between you and me, though, I think he's too scared to even go in there.'

They both laughed too loud for Hilda's liking and she threw them a death stare. Declan disappeared and Annie made her way to a huge oak desk in the corner, which could easily fit four people around it working comfortably.

He returned with two large boxes. 'This is the best one. It has photo albums of the house when It was first built and the family who lived there. It really was a beautiful house. The other box has family letters from the son to his mum, he must have been sent to boarding school or something. I was reading them a while back until Hilda caught me and made me start filing all the newspaper clippings from the beginning of time into alphabetical order. There is also a ledger with a list of staff for the house when it was running at full capacity. That should keep you busy for a while. If you need anything else give me a shout.'

He walked away and Annie felt her faith in human nature restored. Hilda walked past; she was still glaring so Annie gave her the biggest smile she could muster. Picking up the heavy box with the photos the butterflies in her stomach began to flutter again. Normally such an easygoing person, the last few days were turning her into a nervous wreck.

Opening the first book she was greeted by photos of the house in all its splendor: it was breathtaking, it looked just as she had imagined it. The house was filled with fine art and beautifully crafted furniture. The worn sepia photographs would never do it justice but she took her time and studied each picture. Eventually she reached the last page and the schoolroom she had been in yesterday leapt out of the page at her – it was just the same: the books, the desks, everything. A chill spread over her as a voice whispered in her ear, 'I'm coming to get you ready or not.'

A different voice broke her trance. 'Are you OK?'

She looked up to see Declan standing over her, his face etched with concern. 'Oh yes, thanks, sorry I was just daydreaming.'

He winked at her. 'Hilda sent me over. She thought you were going to faint.'

He left her to it and she closed the book, placing it back in the box on top of the other one containing the family photos. She was terrified to look at them. She didn't want to know if Edward looked like the scary, young man with the black eyes from her dreams. Or Alice, what if she looked like her, then what? Replacing the lid on the box she pulled the other box to her. It contained bundles of letters and a red leather ledger. She picked up a letter and began to read.

Edward was telling his mum how much he missed her and Cook's homemade cakes and all about his new school. It felt wrong that someone's private letters should be available for the public to read. *Almost as wrong as reading someone's private diary, Annie?* She would hate it for her personal stuff to be put on display, not that she had anything worth reading, but the thought still made her feel uncomfortable. The Edward who had written these letters seemed like a caring, loving young man. She placed them back and lifted out the ledger.

Written in a column down the first page was a list of staff names. They were all there: Alice, Harold, Alfie, Millie, Thomas and a few more she hadn't heard of. Annie placed the book back into the box and stood up. She had seen enough evidence to prove to her the diary was not some fake. Everything in it was verified by the pictures and documents in front of her. She just wasn't sure what it all meant or exactly what she had become involved in.

Declan walked over to her. 'Did you find what you were looking for?'

Annie nodded. 'Yes, thanks, more than that, I think.'

'Well, now you have your very own reader's card you'll be able to come back anytime.'

She leant towards him and whispered, 'I don't think I'm brave enough to face Hilda again. But you have been fantastic, thank you so much for all your help.' Annie went to retrieve her bag from the lockers scratching her head as she did so.

Declan smiled at her.

He's probably wondering why you didn't take this stupid hat off your head.

CHAPTER 10

Will arrived at Jenna's house in minutes. Things were finally starting to pick up. If only someone had spoken to Erin on Saturday this whole thing could have been treated far more seriously. Mrs White answered the door and Will felt sorry for her. She looked exhausted, her eyes red and puffy from all the crying. *Where the hell was the family liaison officer? What if I'd been that vulture from the papers?*

'Mrs White, I've been speaking to Erin, can I come in?' He followed her back to the kitchen table, which was littered with crumpled tissues. There was a bright yellow teapot in the centre, which looked out of place in this house of gloom. He sat in the same chair as yesterday. 'Erin told me that Jenna met a man on the internet and had planned to meet him Friday night.'

A loud sob escaped from the woman who was trying to keep herself together.

'Do you have any idea who this man could be, anything, maybe a name you've only heard mentioned this week?'

Her head shook.

'Erin told me this man sent her tickets for a Marilyn Manson concert in Manchester. Did she ever mention this to you?' He knew he was clutching at straws. It was obvious Jenna had kept everything very close to her chest.

Mrs White held her head high and looked him straight in the eye. 'It's not that I'm a bad mother, Detective, it's just that all we seem to do is argue. She spends most of her time in her bedroom on the bloody computer. I knew it was a bad idea, you read of these horror stories in the papers, but you don't expect to wake up and be living one.'

Will reached out and took hold of her hand. 'I'm not for one minute saying you're a bad mum, Mrs White. Teenagers can be awful. I understand it's not an easy ride and I dread to think of the misery I caused my own parents. I just want to find Jenna and bring her home. Would you mind if I go and take another look for these tickets, they are really important?'

She squeezed his hand tight. 'I don't care if you tear the house apart if it will help you bring my baby back.'

The family liaison officer walked into the room carrying a bulging plastic carrier. 'Morning, Sarge. I've just been to stock up on some essentials. Would you like a coffee?'

Will shook his head. It wasn't like him to refuse a drink but he couldn't stand the oppressive atmosphere; he wanted to be outside in the fresh air. 'Make sure you're here to answer the door until Mr White comes home.' He let go of Mrs White's hand and excused himself. What a start to his new job.

He ran up the stairs and opened the door to Jenna's bedroom. The life-size poster on the wall was enough to give anyone nightmares. He took out his phone and rang Jake. 'When you checked Jenna's room did you find any concert tickets? No, OK thanks.' He stood still and looked around. All the usual places had been checked by Jake and then Debs from CSI. They must be here somewhere, and if she hadn't told her parents they had to be in the last place they would look.

He stared at the poster again. One corner was very slightly torn and a bit worn, as if it had been touched a lot. *Will, you are a bloody genius.* He pulled a pair of latex gloves from his trouser pocket and tugged them on. Carefully he peeled the poster away from the wall. He wanted to whoop with delight when he saw the plastic sleeve that was Blu-tacked to the wall underneath. Inside it were two pristine concert tickets.

His phone began to ring and he pulled it from his pocket, holding it to his ear with his shoulder. It was Laura. 'Sarge, there is a Marilyn Manson concert on the 1st October.'

Will continued the conversation. 'MEN Arena, doors open at six-thirty, thanks, Laura, I've found them. Have you spoken with IT yet?'

'It's not good news, they are short-staffed and in the middle of cataloguing the last pictures off some paedo's computer for a court case this week. They promise they will get onto it straight after that. I've given them your mobile and told them that you need it today and to ring you with an update as to where they are with it before any of them disappear home for tea.'

'OK, thanks.'

Will made it back to the station in record time without the luxury of blue lights or sirens. He headed straight to the large corner office that served as the CSI department and looked nothing like the shiny, exciting ones on the television. It was a large, square room with four desks in the middle and worktops around the sides with various pieces of equipment spread along them. It was always dark in here because the windows looked out onto a busy street so the blinds were kept shut: CSI Las Vegas it was not. Debs was sitting at the desk in the farthest corner staring at a computer screen. He flashed her a huge smile as he walked towards her and looked over her shoulder at the goriest photos he'd ever seen.

'Dear God, what's that, a family album?'

She dug him in the stomach with her elbow. 'How could you tell?'

'It's the partially severed head, it bears a striking resemblance to you.'

'Tell me, Will, did you come into my office to insult me or do you actually want something?'

'Both. No seriously, I need you to check these tickets for prints because you're the best CSI in the station.'

'You mean I'm the only CSI in the station. Let's have a look.' She pulled on a pair of latex gloves so fast if he'd blinked he would have missed it.

'Wow, you're quick with the old rubber. I bet our Stuart loves that.'

She laughed. 'You have a filthy mind, Will.'

'I found these in Jenna White's bedroom.'

She turned to look at him, her mouth open. 'Where? I searched in there yesterday.'

'They were stuck to the wall behind that freaky poster.' He was trying not to gloat but it was difficult. It was hard to get one over on Debs, she was always so precise.

'I'm impressed, that's a really good hiding place. I'll have to remember that one. Give me ten minutes and I'll see what I can find.'

Will leant down and kissed her on the cheek. 'You little darling.'

Back in the office everyone was busy: this was more like it. They finally had leads worth following up on and the atmosphere was charged.

Stuart came and sat on the edge of Will's desk. 'I've requested her mobile records and told them it's urgent. I've also tried to trace that number and it's coming back as an unregistered pay as you go.'

'Stu, you're not telling me what I want to hear.'

'Give me a chance. It came back as a Sony Ericsson which was part of a batch sent to the big Tesco last year. If you ask me, it's going to be impossible to trace.'

'Well, I'm not asking you, am I? Did they say when the phone first became active? It could narrow down our timeline. If it's only recently you could go to Tesco and search through the CCTV, ask them to check on the computer for dates they may have sold any.'

Stu grimaced. 'It's worth a try but I'd say it's a long shot and the crappiest job I've had in ages. It will probably come back as one of her mates.'

'I agree it's a long shot but it needs checking out and someone has to do it. Right now you're the man for the job. You can also ask the phone provider to ping her phone now we know it's more serious than a teenage tiff.'

Laura finished her conversation then slammed the phone down. 'Bastards won't give out any information about who bought the tickets unless they have my proof of identity. What a cheek.'

Will shrugged. 'I suppose it's data protection and all that crap. Give me the number. I'll tell them you're faxing through a copy of your warrant card.'

Stu was laughing at Laura who picked up the phone book and threw it at his head. 'Shut the fuck up, shouldn't you be on your way to Tesco?'

Will looked up at them. 'Now, now, behave yourselves, children. We wouldn't want either of you being investigated for being a pair of dicks now, would we?'

CHAPTER 11

He wondered what the parents did while their kids were telling complete strangers their life stories. The last girl he'd been chatting to told him she was eighteen and asked if he would like to see her on webcam. He didn't exactly know what this meant and when the message appeared on screen asking him to accept he pressed 'enter'. Curious to know what it was all about, he watched as the blurry image appeared on the screen. As it became clearer he could see the girl sitting on the edge of her bed wearing just her underwear. She asked him if he would like her to dance for him and he sat on his bed transfixed, watching her writhe around. She was so bold he had found himself getting turned on. There was no way he would ask her to meet him, she was far too outrageous. No, he preferred them quiet, a little different, girls that wouldn't put up much of a fight. Although if he needed some light relief he would certainly speak to this one again.

It was all arranged, he was meeting the next girl at the Abbey car park near to the café. This girl didn't want to walk up to the woods alone. She seemed far more timid than Jenna. She had even asked if she could bring a friend with her and he had considered it, but what if he couldn't kill both of them; one might get away and raise the alarm. Then again, where would she run to? The cellar was vast and he knew every nook and cranny. If she did escape she would be terrified in there alone in the dark and he had been very tempted to say yes.

***

Annie got home and collapsed on the sofa. Her head was itchy and sore. She threw the hat across the room, thankful that it wasn't summer. She cursed Mike. Why did she not leave him sooner, before it came to this? Her phone began to ring and the screen flashed that it was an unknown number, which meant it was probably someone from work. She answered it, pleased to hear Will's voice. 'How did you get my number?' Annie knew it was easy enough. He only had to ask Jake or someone in the office, she just wanted to tease him.

'Off an email you sent ages ago. Do you always put your phone number on emails you send to men you don't know?'

'Of course, don't you?'

'Not to men I don't; however, I would to a beautiful woman. I just wondered how you were and if you were missing me at all?'

She felt her heart skip a beat. 'Well, you know, I'm actually fine considering it's only been four hours since I last spoke to you.'

'You know I said I'd come up and cook for you tomorrow night?'

Annie felt the hot tears brim and began to blink. She hoped her voice wouldn't break deep down: she had known it had been too good to be true. 'It's fine, Will, I understand how busy you are, we can do it again some other time.'

'Oh, I was going to say that I might have something on tomorrow and wondered if I could come tonight instead?'

She hadn't expected that one. 'If you want to that's fine by me. I'm not busy tonight.' *Or any night, to be exact.*

Will laughed and sounded relieved. 'Good, I'm very glad you can fit me in. Is eight OK? I promised Kav I'd buy him a pint after work so I'll be free by then, maybe a bit sooner.'

'Eight is fine. I'll see you then.' She ended the call not wanting him to think she was desperate.

Laura sat scowling in the corner, staring at the computer screen. Stu smiled at her. 'Got yourself a date, boss?'

'You're nosey aren't you, Stu? Yes I have and, if you must know, it's with your wife.'

141

Stu laughed. 'Yeah right, she's got a real man at home. She wouldn't give you the time of day.'

The door opened and in walked Debs, who totally ignored her husband and headed straight for Will's desk. She sat on the corner close to Will who laughed so loud it even made Laura crack a smile. Stu frowned. 'I wish I'd bet you a tenner on that, Stu.'

Debs looked at her husband and winked, then turned and gave Will her full attention. 'Do you want the good or bad news first?'

'Either is fine by me.'

'Well, I have a couple of prints. I took comparison prints yesterday from Jenna's laptop before it got whisked away to headquarters. Two are a match for Jenna and there is one really good thumbprint in the corner that doesn't match. The bad news is it's not in the system.'

Will blew out a long breath. 'Thanks, Debs. I was just telling your husband what a star you are.'

CHAPTER 12

Annie turned the computer on in the study and stared at the screen, waiting for it to load. Her mind was overflowing with images of the house – her own personal slideshow – but there was one room it kept pausing on: the schoolroom. She had been inside that room and touched the things that were in the photograph. She had held the tin soldiers between her fingers and felt the cold metal they were made from. But how? It didn't make any sense. She looked at the diary she had put on the desk next to her. She was desperate to read some more yet at the same time terrified because she knew it was messing with her already battered mind. At least it was keeping thoughts of Mike at bay.

When Google finally loaded she typed in 'Abbey Wood'. Very little appeared. The first image was the one of the house just like the one she had seen in the records office. There were a couple of articles about the house and family but nothing like what she had expected. Surely the unfortunate happenings at the house had been a hotbed of gossip at the time. Annie began to think it was the most unpublicised haunted house in the world. Then a thought crossed her mind: what if it wasn't haunted and this was all a figment of her imagination?

Her mind began to spin and her eyes became so heavy it was a struggle to keep them open. She stood up and made her way to the snug and the sofa, which had become her temporary bed, and snuggled down into the duvet that she'd left there this morning. When she had spoken to the doctor he had told her to expect that her body would need to recuperate and she should rest whenever she needed to. She drifted off to sleep and found herself in the house. Annie knew she had come home and that this was the one place she truly belonged. It was hard to describe, but she felt as if she'd been away for a very long time and was glad to be back.

Her feet carried her from room to room; everything was as she remembered. The sumptuous velvet drapes that adorned each huge window still felt warm to her grasp. The richly coloured wallpapers brought the house to life. As she found herself in the library she picked up her favourite delicately hand painted vase. The heady perfume of the lilies that she used to arrange in it every week lingered in the air. The chair where Edward had held her brought memories rushing back and tears began to fall from her cheeks: she was so lonely.

Walking the long hallway to reach the kitchen her heart sank to see that Alfie and Cook weren't there to greet her: where was everyone? She had expected to see them sitting around the battered pine kitchen table with cups of tea in hand, nibbling on the freshly baked biscuits that Cook made every week. Her fingertips brushed the wood, feeling the surface that had worn smooth from so much use. The hours she had spent sitting around it eating and gossiping were too many to count.

The scullery door was ajar and a cold chill ran down her spine as her eyes settled on the cellar door. She was afraid of the terrible blackness down there and something else which was locked away at the back of her mind. She left the kitchen and walked back to the great hall and the foot of the staircase. Why was the house so empty? She felt like the mistress of the house but she knew that it was impossible because she wasn't Lady Hannah or Alice the housemaid. She looked down to see that she was wearing a beautiful dress of the palest blue silk. A gasp escaped her lips. Running her hand down the jewelled bodice she could feel the tiny pearls that had been painstakingly sewn on by hand. It was the kind of dress that Lady Hannah wore.

She found herself climbing the stairs to be greeted at the top by the most handsome young man she had ever seen.

She looked at him and then rushed up the last few steps towards him, falling into his arms.

Annie, in her dream-like state, was horrified but she was powerless to stop this vision of herself. Strong arms locked around her waist as he picked her up and whizzed her around. She looked into his cold, black eyes and a sickness in the pit of her stomach made her feel ill.

He grinned. 'I just knew you would come back to me.' Edward pulled her close to him, his lips brushing against her ear. 'I can see you Alice, pretending to be someone else, although I have to say it's quite a good hiding place. Definitely one of your better ones, but I know that you are there. Why don't you come out to play?'

Annie opened her eyes and sat bolt upright. Every nerve in her body was on edge. The voice had spoken directly into her ear it was so clear. She lifted a hand to feel her ear and shuddered; it was icy cold to her touch. She shivered more violently. The temperature in the room had dropped significantly and she buried her head into her hands and sobbed.

Later, when her tears had subsided, she noticed the fire was dying. Forcing herself to move she threw a couple of logs onto it and poked it around. She watched as it crackled, concentrating on nothing except the blue and orange wisps, finding some comfort in them. She thought about the spiritualist church she had visited last week after finding a flyer for it pinned to the noticeboard on the kitchen wall: it had seemed like a good idea at the time.

She couldn't remember the last time she had been to a church, any church. Sitting around the open circle she followed everyone else and bowed her head. The feeling she was being watched had made her look up to see a middle-aged man staring at her. She had felt her cheeks turn crimson and met his gaze, expecting him to look away: he didn't. Her hand reached up and tugged at her hat, making sure it covered the back of her head. He couldn't know about her, it was the best-kept secret in the police station. Her own mother didn't even know. Raising her head again she looked to see if he was still staring, and she was relieved that his attention had shifted to the guest speaker who had now taken up his position at the front of the open circle.

Then it had begun, every head looked up at the same time; anticipation and hope making the room fraught with tension. The majority were women who had an expression of desperation etched onto their faces. The speaker was a well-known medium from Burnley, it had said on the poster that had been tacked to the door. Annie smiled to herself; he looked like a sixty-year-old hippy with the greenest eyes she had ever seen. But they were kind eyes, which made up for his strange taste in clothes.

He smiled at Annie. 'Do you mind if I come to you first? It's very important.'

Her eyes widened with fear about what he was about to say but she nodded, he closed his eyes.

The atmosphere in the room was almost crackling it was so full of electricity.

'You attract danger.'

Annie didn't know whether to laugh or cry. Instead she forced a smile and looked to the old woman next to her.

'Something big is on the horizon and it's going to change your life, you might never be the same person again.' He opened his eyes and stared at her. 'Blood and death find you. All I can see are cold, dead people. You are standing in the middle of them, surrounded by them.'

Annie had stood abruptly; the chair scraped against the parquet floor, breaking the silence. One elderly lady gasped in shock. Bending down to pick up her bag, Annie briskly walked to the exit. She knew that every person in there was watching her but she didn't care, she let the church door slam behind her. That should give them something to talk about. *What a load of crap.*

The cold night air embraced her. A single flickering street lamp cast dark shadows across the empty car park. Jogging to her car she got in and locked the doors behind her. With trembling hands she gripped the steering wheel. Suddenly there was a knock on the car window and Annie almost jumped through the roof.

The medium shrugged his apology and she let the window down an inch. 'I'm so, so, sorry. I didn't mean to upset you. That has never happened to me before and I've been doing this a long time.

148

Whatever spirit was trying to talk to you was far stronger than I've ever encountered.'

Annie studied him. She was normally quite a good judge of character, but she couldn't decide if he was a total head case or a genuine medium. 'It's OK, I'm not having a good week, I'm not sure why but I thought coming here might help.'

'Sometimes we all need a bit of guidance. Listen, I do need to talk with you but not in front of an audience.' He passed a small, crumpled business card through the gap. 'You can ring me on that number. If I don't answer leave a message. I promise I will get back to you. We need to get to the bottom of this because I have a feeling it won't go away.'

She watched him walk back to the church. Could her life get any more bizarre?

Annie wondered if Derek was still in town. Maybe it wouldn't hurt to talk to him. At least he would believe her. She had thought it was all a load of rubbish but things were getting stranger. Picking up her car keys, she went to go and check the glove compartment to see if his card was still there where she had thrown it.

The early evening sun cast shadows everywhere so she didn't take any notice of the one in the hay barn window.

Picking up the card she felt comforted by it. *Oh Annie, what's the matter with you? What are you on? Derek of the healing powers?*

Her phone began to ring in the kitchen and she jogged back inside to answer it.

'Please can you open the gates for me? I'll be too knackered to walk up there all on my own,' said Will. 'Oh, and is there anything that you don't like to eat?'

'Not really, the only things I don't eat are faggots, black pudding, liver, you get the drift. I'll leave the gate open. Just snap the padlock shut once you drive through.'

'Jesus, Annie, do you think I'm some kind of cannibal? The most exotic things I cook are chicken enchiladas.'

'Sounds like heaven to me, and don't forget a pudding. I'm under strict doctor's orders not to diet until my head gets better.'

'Would I deprive a lady of a dessert? Never. But it will be out of a box.'

He hung up and she smiled: not everything was doom and gloom.

For the next hour the mansion and its ghosts were obliterated from her mind as she vacuumed like a maniac. Taking a towel from the laundry basket she quickly polished the downstairs and then filled the dishwasher. Satisfied, she ran upstairs to shower; at least she wouldn't need to spend ages on her hair. Make up, on the other hand, was a big job and would take some time. When she had done the best job possible she sprayed herself in Chanel No 5: if it was good enough for Marilyn Monroe then it was good enough for her. Looking at the clock she still had enough time to walk down through the woods to open the gates, exercising Tess at the same time.

*****

He watched her leave, taking the dog with her. He didn't quite believe it when she locked the kitchen door, but slid the key under a painted stone on the kitchen windowsill. He stood up, stretching out his arms and legs, then stepped out of the barn and listened for footsteps: it was all quiet. He walked over to the kitchen door and paused, did he dare to go inside? Maybe just a quick scout around to see what the layout of the house was. He pulled his sleeve down and lifted the key from under the stone, put it in the lock, turned it and pushed the handle. The door opened and he stepped inside.

He inhaled. Her perfume lingered in the air and, whatever it was, it was just right for her. The scarf she had been wearing yesterday was thrown over one of the dining chairs. Picking it up he held it to his nose: it smelt divine. If this was how good she smelt then he couldn't wait to get close to her. He was tempted to go upstairs and hide somewhere, maybe under the bed. He began to fantasise about what he could do with her and the scarf when the sound of a car engine in the distance brought him back to reality and he panicked.

He exited the house, locked the door and slipped the key back where he had got it from, then ran into the copse of trees at the front, heading for the tree with the thickest trunk. He stood as close to it as he could, not daring to move. The light was fading fast and the woods were already full of dark shadows; as long as the dog didn't come sniffing around he should be fine.

He held his breath as a car came into view. She was sitting in the passenger seat of a black BMW and the man from the other day was driving. Anger began to form a tight knot in his chest as he watched her throw back her head and laugh at something he'd said. His knuckles bunched into tight, white fists. Trembling, he had to take deep breaths to stop himself from marching over there and killing the pair of them: he knew he was capable of doing it. He looked down to see her scarf tightly clenched in his fist. Lifting it to his nose he sniffed once more – savouring the smell – and then wrapped it around his neck. He waited until they were inside the house then jogged back onto the main path. He pulled the dog lead from his pocket, just in case anyone saw him.

CHAPTER 13

As they entered the farmhouse Annie paused; something felt wrong but she couldn't quite put her finger on it. Her attention turned to Will who was emptying the contents of his carrier bag onto the worktop. It was like some bizarre scene from a cooking programme she used to watch on daytime TV before she joined the police. She half-expected Ainsley Harriott to walk in any second.

This was the first time in her life a man had offered to cook for her. Mike was so rubbish in the kitchen she used to have to make his tea and leave it in the microwave for him whenever she was on late shifts. She could get used to this. Opening the fridge she took out a bottle of her favourite rosé.

'I've got this or I can go to my brother's secret stash in the barn and get a nice bottle of red.'

'I'll try a glass of that pink girly stuff you refer to as wine. I noticed that you had plenty.'

She grinned and opened the bottle, pouring out two large glasses. 'You really are cheeky. Has anyone ever told you that apart from me?'

Will turned to face her and his smile reached all the way up to his cornflower blue eyes, which sparkled in the light. Annie did her best not to sigh: it was too good to be true. Here she was in her favourite place in the world, with a gorgeous man who could cook and even drink the same wine as her.

'Do you want to chop the salad?'

And just like that, her daydream was shattered. 'Have you never heard of ready-mix bags?'

'Yes, and now who is being cheeky? They don't taste as good as when you make it yourself. I'll have you know that I grew these tomatoes and cucumbers myself and, while it may not be up to the standard of The Ritz, you are still going to enjoy a decent, home-cooked meal.'

Annie gulped a mouthful of wine. 'Thanks, it's very kind of you but I'm doing OK on my own. It's not as if I'm starving or anything.'

Will turned back to the frying pan, adding chopped chillies and spices to the chicken and vegetables. It smelt amazing and her stomach began to rumble just to prove her wrong.

Will took a sip of the wine. 'You know, this isn't bad. In fact, it's much better than I imagined, but don't tell Jake that I drank it.'

Annie decided not to tell him that Jake had said almost the same thing: there was obviously some man thing going on. Taking some cutlery from the drawer she began to set the table. On the floor next to a chair were some pieces of dried straw.

Bending down to pick it up she wondered how it had got there when she had vacuumed earlier.

'Are you ready to have your taste buds tickled?' Will carried over a serving plate full of tortilla wraps and the bowl of salad. They sat down to eat. Annie forgot about the straw, she was too busy enjoying Will's cooking. They ate in silence and when they had finished Annie sat back and sighed.

'That was amazing, what's your recipe?'

Will finished his wine and refilled both glasses. 'If I tell you I'll have to kill you.'

Annie was so happy she thought this would be a good way to go.

'Come on, we should watch a film,' he suggested.

Annie led him into the snug and smiled at the look of wonder on his face: this room was probably the male equivalent of a walk-in wardrobe. There was a fifty-eight inch plasma television with every Sky channel, a wall that was lined with shelves holding hundreds of films, a roaring log fire and the biggest sofa in the world.

'Does your brother need a lodger? When can I move in?'

'He already has one, sorry. But if I ever sort out my sad, pathetic life he might just consider it.'

She looked beautiful and Will felt the blood pump around his heart faster than normal. Picking up the remote he began to flick through the channels to take his mind off her. He wanted to do all manner of things that weren't really appropriate for a first date, especially as he didn't even know if this was a date; he was struggling to work that one out.

His last girlfriend, now he had done things with her on their first date he didn't think should really be allowed on any date. The lust had been the only thing they had in common. After two months he couldn't stand that she was so clingy and cried every time he talked about anyone from work. When she left him for the window cleaner he had felt nothing but relief. Annie was so different; a survivor with a great sense of humour, not to mention she was gorgeous in an understated way, plus her cleavage was amazing. His last couple of girlfriends had been so thin there were men in the station with bigger breasts.

Annie came back in with another bottle of wine. 'I don't want you to get the wrong idea but I'm just a bit curious about how you're getting home. It's a long walk to anywhere from here. You can stay the night on the sofa, if you want. It's big enough for a rugby team to sit on and it's so comfy. In fact, I spend most nights sleeping on here. I don't sleep very well upstairs.'

Will liked the thought of her sprawled out on the sofa. 'I never really thought about it, I'm too lazy to walk home on my own so if you don't mind I'll stay here. I promise not to drool too much but I might snore.' He watched as her eyes filled with tears and she turned away from him. He stood up and put his hand on her shoulder. 'I'm sorry, was it something I said, are you all right?'

She nodded. 'I'm just being ridiculous again. I like the thought that maybe tonight would be normal and nightmare free.'

Will pulled her close and wrapped his arms around her, bending until his lips were pressing against hers. He briefly paused, pulling away, but she leant up to bridge the gap and their lips met. They kissed and he didn't want it to end, but he forced himself to break away.

'I'm sorry, Annie. I don't know what I was thinking.'

Annie looked down to the bulge in the front of his jeans. 'Oh, I know what you were thinking.'

He felt his cheeks burn and he grabbed her arm, pulling her down onto the sofa with him. 'You are such a bad influence on me, Annie, fancy wanting to take advantage of my body like that.'

She snuggled into his arms and Will thought that it might kill him, but he would show her that he could be a gentleman. For now he was happy to hold her close. He lifted his hand, careful not to knock the back of her head. 'It's OK, you can take the hat off when you're with me.'

'Will, it gives *me* nightmares, I don't want to put you off.'

He took hold of the hat and gently tugged it from her head; he bent down and tenderly kissed above the angry red cut and line of staples. 'I think it's kind of sexy, it makes you look well hard. I wouldn't mess with you.'

She turned her attention to the television but he caught the grin on her face.

CHAPTER 14

Emma didn't mind being in the Abbey museum after it was closed. The tombstones and selection of gargoyles on display around the room would give the average person nightmares, but she was used to it. She had been coming here since she was six with her gran who worked here, taking money and giving guided tours to anyone who was interested way before they got the audio taped ones. Emma had grown up around here. She knew every nook and cranny of the ruins. In all the years she had been coming here not one thing had happened that scared her enough to make her not want to come back. Granted it could get eerie, especially on foggy nights when the swirling mist made it easy to imagine a parade of ghostly monks passing through the old iron gates, chanting in Latin, but it had never actually happened. The other women who worked here wouldn't stay past dusk, locking up and leaving before sunset. Her gran would always say, 'It's not the dead that can harm you, it's the living you have to watch out for.'

So Emma found herself working the late shift and locking up most evenings. It was great because her computer had packed in and she couldn't afford to get it fixed. After she cashed up and quickly cleaned around she had the place to herself and, thanks to the newly installed coffee machine, a constant supply of fresh coffee. It helped her no end with her college work and her grades were excellent.

She checked the clock in the corner of the computer monitor: two minutes to eight. Damian was always late. If she told him to turn up for seven-thirty he would be here for eight. It was the one thing she really disliked about him. He should arrive at any minute, fingers crossed. She turned the computer off, checked the doors and windows were all secure then made her way to the front door to wait.

***

He had left his car in the small car park at the front of the museum; his was now the only car left. He was raging inside and he didn't know how to stop. It was burning so hot inside that his chest was actually hurting. A light turned on in the museum and he stepped to one side so whoever it was couldn't see him. He was curious to know who would still be in there at this time of night, especially with it being so dark outside. A young woman carrying some files came into view. A

160

terrible thought began to run through his mind: she looked a lot like Jenna, only slightly older.

He began fumbling with the dog lead as she came outside. She didn't check the car park, just turned to lock the door, unaware of him until he spoke. 'Hi, I'm sorry to bother you but I've lost my dog. You haven't seen him around here have you?'

'No, I haven't, sorry.'

He could sense her discomfort at being caught off guard. 'I was walking him in the woods and he ran off after a rabbit or something. That was two hours ago and I've been looking ever since. I daren't go home without him. My wife will kill me.'

'I've been working out in the back office so I haven't seen anything.'

He turned to get into his car and sensed her body relax. 'OK, thanks. Do you need a lift anywhere? You don't want to be hanging around here on your own in the dark. You never know who's out there.' He didn't expect her to say yes, but he could tell by the look on her face she was giving it some thought.

'Thank you, but my boyfriend is supposed to be picking me up. He's always late though.'

The clouds opened and heavy drops of rain began to fall. He smiled to himself. *Come on, you little beauty, you know you want to.* He got into the car and put the window down.

'Are you sure? It's not a problem, honestly. I can't go home yet anyway, not without the dog; my wife prefers it to me.'

The rain was torrential, soaking through her clothes and college books: all her work was going to be ruined. She was turning into a sodden mess; she dashed towards the car.

'Are you sure you don't mind?'

He smiled at her as she got into the car and slammed the door too hard, making him flinch.

'Oops, sorry, I'm used to my boyfriend's heap of junk.'

'It's fine, don't worry about it.'

She reached over to grab her seat belt and her phone slid from her wet grasp, falling to the floor. She bent down, struggling to find it. He reached out, grabbing a handful of her long dark brown hair. She screeched with shock. Before she could scream again his hand wrapped itself tightly into her hair, dragging her head back, before he pushed it forward with such force that her head slammed against the dashboard, dazing her. She reached up for his hands, scratching at them, but he held fast and slammed her head again and again until she was unconscious. When she stopped fighting, his hand reached under his seat for the knife that he'd tucked under there, away from his mother's prying eyes. He pulled her head back to expose her throat and he sliced her neck from ear to ear, a spray of blood coating him and the windscreen.

He pushed her head forward to try and slow it down. Part of him hadn't wanted to do it but he'd had no choice. If he let her go she would be able to describe him and his car to the police. The blood pumping from the open wound was warm and sticky and he watched, mesmerised, as the life bled from her.

In the distance, through the trees, he saw the beam of a car's headlights and the fear of being caught broke him from his trance. He pushed her down as far as he could into the footwell of the car, and rubbed his blood-soaked hand in her hair and on her coat. Then he started the engine and drove in the opposite direction to the lights: he had to get away from here.

His hands were still slick with blood and the strong coppery smell filled the car. He wiped them along the front of his trousers so he could grip the steering wheel better. That was another pair he would have to get rid of. His stomach began to churn; the smell in such an enclosed space was making him feel ill. He drove until he reached the playing fields on Rating Lane then parked his car along the lover's lane, which was deserted. Taking some tissues from the glove compartment he rubbed the specks of blood off the windscreen. The stench was awful, if the police pulled him now that would be it: game over. His hand reached out and caressed the blood-soaked hair of the dead girl. *Think, you idiot, think.*

CHAPTER 15

Two bottles of wine and almost the whole of Lost Boys and Annie was struggling to stay awake. She dragged herself away from Will's arms, which were wrapped tight around her. She needed to lock up.

He was fast asleep and looked so peaceful: there were no bad dreams for him. In the kitchen she grabbed her coat from the back of the chair. She couldn't find her scarf so she looked under the table to see if it had fallen to the floor and remembered the straw. She let Tess out of the back door, who quickly squatted and then came back inside. It had been raining heavily so she bent to wipe her paws with an old towel.

'How come you manage to walk through every puddle, Tess?' Annie shivered; something strange was going on. Surely no one had been into the house, Tess would have barked. She locked the door, relieved that she had Will for company.

He shuffled into the kitchen. 'Sorry, I'm terrible company.' He looked even more gorgeous all bleary eyed and with ruffled hair.

'I'm just locking up. Is there anything you need?'

'Only you. You're not going to leave me all alone on that big old sofa are you? We could put another film on. I promise to be a good boy.'

Annie preferred the thought of him being a bad boy but the thought of cuddling up to him was even better. She knew it was far too soon to even contemplate starting another relationship but she craved affection, and would hopefully get some sleep safe in his arms.

He took hold of her hand and led her back to the sofa where he'd fashioned a bed out of the duvet and pillows. Annie watched as he took off his pants to reveal a pair of lime green and black Calvin Kleins®. She sighed; how was she supposed to lie next to him all night and keep her hands to herself? Not wanting him to feel underdressed she went upstairs and put on her wonder woman pyjamas. But she felt self-conscious. If the sight of her in these shorts didn't send him running for the door she might just be onto a winner. It still niggled away at her why he was here, but she wasn't about to start interrogating him now. He held up the duvet and patted the space next to him and she climbed in, her, heart racing. This was bizarre even for her, but she wasn't complaining. Will's breathing slowed and got louder as he fell asleep, she closed her eyes and it wasn't long before she joined him.

***

It took every ounce of strength to manhandle the woman from the car. He decided to dump her body down by the dock near to the old paper mills. They were due to be demolished any time and the businesses that used to run from there had all relocated. He also knew there were no CCTV cameras in the area. There wasn't much point because all that was left was piles of rubble and crumbling buildings.

The blood made it hard to grip her properly and the stench was making him gag. He would have liked to have put her in the cellar with Jenna, an unexpected addition to his collection, but if he could barely carry her three hundred feet he wouldn't be able to carry her a mile uphill through woodland. He removed her clothes, knowing full well, along with the rest of the world, the basics in forensic science. The real challenge was getting her positioned. He didn't want to leave her lying on the floor as if she had just been abandoned; he wanted her sitting up on display. He placed her in a boarded up doorway but her head kept flopping to one side. Taking the scarf he had stolen earlier that evening he inhaled one last time, memorising the smell. Then he wrapped it around the girl's neck several times until it covered the dreadful, gaping wound. He wished he could be there to see the face of the person who unwrapped it. He attached the material to a rusted nail that was sticking out of the frame; it didn't look very sturdy but it worked. Hopefully rigor mortis would set in soon enough and then she wouldn't need her head holding up. He wondered why he had wanted to cover the wound on her neck when her forehead was grazed and dinted: it felt like the right thing to do, if there was a right thing in these situations.

Getting into his car he took one last look around to make sure there was no one lurking. His hands were trembling so much he could barely grip the steering wheel, and his stomach lurched every time he breathed in. If he was lucky his mother would still be at the church, giving him enough time to sort out the car and shower. Putting the windows down to hide the blood on them and let some fresh air inside, he drove home at the correct speeds, not wanting to draw attention to himself. He reached his house without passing a police car and drove straight into the garage. He shut the door and didn't turn on the light: none of the nosey neighbours could see in.

Stripping off his clothes until he was standing in his boxers he pulled a black plastic bin liner from the drawer and stuffed all his clothes into it. He would dump them behind the bins at the back of the druggie flats in the town centre. He began to clean the car, bleaching and scrubbing everything in sight. Tomorrow he would take it down to the Polish car wash and get it power washed on the outside as well, just in case any blood had got underneath: you could never be too sure.

He muttered to himself, 'This is all your fault, why did you make me so angry that I couldn't control the rage? I hope to God I haven't ruined everything.' He finished cleaning and turned the light off, then went upstairs to have a quick shower. Just as he was towelling himself dry he heard the taxi with his mother in pull up outside. Perfect timing. He dashed downstairs to put her cup of milk into the microwave and waited for it to beep. He slowly mixed the cocoa powder into the scalding milk and stirred again, careful not to crack the delicate porcelain cup. Then he took a deep breath to prepare himself for the interrogation that would begin in less than sixty seconds.

She walked in through the front door and locked it behind her. She came straight to the kitchen where she looked him up and down.

'Why is your car in the garage and what are you doing lounging around in your dressing gown? Are you ill?'

He envisioned taking the dog chain and choking her with it until her vicious tongue protruded from her mouth, all swollen and black. How nice it would be to permanently silence her. He knew that he would one of these days; it was just a matter of when.

She walked into the living room and sat on the sofa, turning on the television. She found a repeat of CSI and settled down to watch it. He placed the cup of cocoa next to her on the small oak table, then whispered 'goodnight' and turned to go upstairs. He knew she was staring at him, he could feel her eyes burning into his back and he knew she was wondering what was going on. He had a feeling she was beginning to feel a little bit scared of her wishy-washy son, but there was no way she would admit it to anyone. She was a tough old bird, he'd give her that.

***

Will's phone began vibrating in his trouser pocket against the wooden floorboards. Annie stirred but his eyes sprung wide open: it had to be work. He was used to calls like this; no one else would ring him at five-thirty in the morning. Extracting himself from Annie's legs he got off the sofa and picked up his trousers, tiptoeing into the kitchen. He fumbled to get the phone out of his pocket, finally grabbing hold of it.

'Hello, Will Ashworth speaking.'

Annie woke up and listened to the string of whispered swear words which came from the kitchen. Her stomach formed a tight knot; this wasn't good. He walked back in.

'Have they found that poor girl?' she asked.

He shook his head. 'No, another girl has gone missing. She was last seen at work in the Abbey museum last night. I have to go.' He bent down, kissing her on the lips. Then he slipped on his shoes and jacket and headed for the door.

'Wait, you need a key to get out of the gates.' She followed him into the kitchen and grabbed the spare key off the hook, throwing the pink, fluffy key ring at him.

'Thanks, for a minute I thought you were going to beg me to stay.'

She laughed and shrugged, closing the door behind him. She went back to the duvet, which was still warm, and Tess pattered in and took over watching her from where Will had left off.

CHAPTER 16

He woke early, needing to pee. He had slept well considering what he had done last night. He regretted it. He had almost ruined it all before he got to have some fun with the woman from the farm. *If I get caught I won't be able to finish what I've started.* The voice in his head, the one that had told him to watch her because she could be his downfall, echoed loudly. Wiping the seat, he flushed the chain.

As he washed his hands he glanced at his reflection in the mirror. When had his eyes got so dark? Maybe that was the result of being evil; it turned you rotten from the inside out. His face looked different too. His features seemed sharper, more chiselled. In fact, he felt as if the face staring back at him was someone entirely different, but that was ridiculous, it was impossible. Then he remembered the way his mother had looked at him last night. Had she seen how different he looked, could she sense he wasn't the same? Back in his bedroom he began wondering how he could get the woman out of the farm. If he waited patiently it would come to him, just as the plan for Jenna had. Somehow he would know what to do and when to do it.

***

Will found some chewing gum in the side pocket of his car. After blowing the fluff off two pieces he shoved them into his mouth and began to chew. There was no time to go home and shower and it was pointless anyway, seeing as how he was practically already on scene. He drove down the steep hill noticing the assortment of police cars in the distance; he headed towards them.

The whole area was sealed off. The blue and white tape stretched from the rusted black railings of the Abbey ruins across the road to a huge oak tree. Jake was standing on the inside of the cordon looking as miserable as Will felt. He rolled down his window.

'All right, lad, we need to stop meeting like this or people are going to talk.'

Jake grinned. 'They will indeed. Anyway, how did you get here so fast?'

Will cringed as he watched Jake figure it out and his expression turned to one of disbelief.

'Please tell me you didn't. The last thing Annie needs right now is a couple of quickies with the office Casanova. She's messed up enough as it is. Have you any idea what damage you could do if you mess her around?' Jake turned his back on Will and stomped across to the other side of the road. He turned his head. 'For God's sake, Will, I think I'm going to kill you. Bugger off and get out of my sight.'

He left Will no choice but to get out of the car and march over to him. Anger boiled inside his chest.

'What exactly do you take me for? I swear I went to see her after work last night. All I did was make her some dinner and offer her some company. That's it, nothing to it. We drank a couple of bottles of wine, watched a film and I slept on the sofa – end of.' Will thought it best not to add that he'd spent most of the night with an erection while lying next to Annie. It would probably tip Jake over the edge.

Jake glared at him. 'I'm telling you, Will, if you hurt her or treat her like one of those women you sleep with once and never speak to again, then it will be a crime scene containing the remains of your face that's being investigated. I'm not letting her get hurt again.' Jake's eyes filled with tears and Will was unsure what he should do, so he reached out and patted his arm.

'None of this was your fault, there wasn't anything you could have done. If she never told you what it was like at home how were you supposed to know? I don't want to hurt her, I just want to help.'

Jake grunted something which Will took as an agreement and he walked back to his car.

Running the last five minutes through his mind he wondered what had just happened. It was far too early for award-winning dramatics. He shook his head and continued to drive down to the car park where he saw a familiar figure standing in the distance barking out orders to some student officers. It was becoming a habit: how come serious shit only happened when Jake, Kav and Will were on duty? The whole town seemed to be falling apart. He parked up and sighed as Kav shook his head at him.

'Nothing, not diddly squat. There isn't much by way of forensics – no blood, no signs of a struggle – so it looks as if she went with whoever it was of her own free will.' He turned towards the white-suited CSI whose camera flash was illuminating the early morning sky. 'Debs said there are a couple of tyre impressions which she'll take a cast of and that's just about it.'

Will looked around the area. It was secluded here, and if it was last night there wouldn't be anyone around. There were two houses nearby but neither of them overlooked the car park.

'It's unreal. How can two girls disappear within the space of a few days with no trace? It just doesn't happen, well not around here.'

The sound of tyres crunching on gravel and the sight of Kav stiffening up made Will groan. He turned to see the newly appointed Detective Chief Inspector getting out of his shiny Land Rover™. Will had heard of his reputation as a stickler for perfection, and from the corner of his eye he watched every uniformed officer nearby checking they looked respectable. It was remarkable how straight they were standing: hands out of pockets or wherever else they had them tucked to keep them warm. Will and Kav both shared the same pained expression as he crunched his way along the gravel towards them.

Kav whispered, 'Bullshit baffles brains.' He then launched into an overzealous greeting, pumping the DCI's hand up and down. Will had no idea what Kav was talking about so he agreed and nodded along at what he deemed were appropriate moments until the DCI turned to him.

'I don't think we've met? DCI Stevens.' He stretched out his hand. Now it was Will's turn to talk crap and he did his best for a couple of minutes until Stevens yawned, obviously bored. Kav smirked, a student officer came shuffling over to them, his face drained of all colour; he coughed.

'Sorry to interrupt you, sir, but there's a reporter asking lots of questions, what should I tell him?'

Stevens beamed at the young officer. 'Ah the press, don't you just love how they get a whiff of a story quicker than the bloody sniffer dogs. Leave it to me, son.' With that he walked off, heading in the direction of the 'road closed' sign.

Kav laughed. 'Let him get on with it, that's what he gets paid lots of money for.'

Debs came to stand with them. 'Morning, gents. I hate to tell you this, but as you have already guessed there isn't much to go on. I've bagged up a couple of cigarette ends and an ice cream wrapper, but the shop shut at five and I don't really think our guy would have hung around for a couple of hours licking his ice lolly and then discarding his evidence. But you never know; not everyone watches CSI or the Discovery Chanel. There are some tyre tracks but same again. On an average day they get between five and thirty cars in and out of here. They could even be the boyfriend's.'

Kav answered Will's next question. 'He is at the station giving a statement as we speak. He was with friends at the Friars playing pool and was late to pick Emma up. He should have been here for seven-thirty but it was just gone eight when he got here. Said it was all in darkness and she was nowhere to be seen, so, being such a gentleman, he drove back to the pub to finish his game of pool. He did say he tried phoning her a couple of times but she wasn't answering him, which isn't uncommon for her when she's pissed off with him, as he so elegantly put it. Emma's sister rang him at ten-thirty to see if Emma had a key because she was going to bed. That's when he started to panic and phoned her friends. He then drove back down here with a couple of mates and began to look for her, and as you can tell he never found her and here we are.'

'So he has a good alibi but he could have killed her and dumped the body quick in some bushes.'

'True that, he could have, but his mates said he was gone for five minutes and it was raining hard, and he came back into the pub wearing the same clothes he left in, which were dry apart from a few spots of rain on his T-shirt.'

'Are we sure she isn't sulking somewhere, making him feel bad?' Kav pulled the folded-up incident log from his trouser pocket and began to read. 'Not according to her sister. Emma wouldn't worry her, they are very close and she would have told her she wasn't coming home. It's all wrong, Will. Two girls have gone and, as much as it pains me to say this, I don't think they are still breathing, if you get my drift. I reckon we have a serious problem and one I hoped I would never see in my career.'

Will did get his drift and he felt the same. Another van arrived and they turned to watch as the dog handler let Molly out of her cage. The dog was given one of Emma's blouses to smell and then told to go find. It did a couple of circles then headed towards the museum's entrance, where after a brief sniff around it came back and sat down, beginning to whine.

'Terrific,' muttered Will. 'The bloody dog hasn't got a clue either.'

There wasn't much more he could do here. They would keep the area closed for a while longer but at this moment they didn't know if it was a crime scene or not. He left by the other exit, not wanting to face Jake again, not until he'd calmed down. Will tried ringing Annie but it went straight to voicemail. He had to let her know something bad was happening around here and to keep the doors locked. He didn't want her getting caught up in it.

CHAPTER 17

Mary Grieve walked her dog every day at seven in the morning and seven at night, regular as clockwork. She had done for the last five years, since she had been given the puppy as an anniversary present from her late husband. Her grandson had bought her a shiny fuchsia pink iPod shuffle for Christmas and put all of her favourite songs onto it. He even had the words 'Best Nan xxx' engraved on the back of it. She didn't understand how it worked but all the same it was the best piece of modern technology she had ever been bought.

As she passed the old paper mill, dormant for at least forty years, she paused. Spot was acting strange this morning; his hackles rising he began to whine. Pulling her earphones out she looked around. Mary didn't get scared – well, very rarely. She had lived through World War II and a car crash in which her husband had been killed. No, she was a survivor and believed that when your time came that was it and there was nothing you

179

could do about it. She had studied the buildings over the years and had seen it all: smacked up druggies so off their heads that they were asleep in puddles of their own urine; drunken teenagers getting frisky and doing things which made her hair stand on end. And then she saw the girl inside the doorway to one of the buildings and gasped.

'Hello, lovey, are you OK? I'm going to call an ambulance, you hold on there.' The lifeless, naked body made Mary sob out loud. As she got nearer to it she knew there was nothing she could do to help this poor girl, but she had to keep talking as if there was, otherwise for the first time in sixty years she might lose control and that would never do. As she got closer she shuddered at the girl's open eyes, which stared straight at her. They were locked forever in the nightmare that had ended her life. Her forehead was a mess of grazes and dried blood. Mary took off her jacket and covered the girl as best as she could to give her some dignity. She couldn't let the poor thing be stared at by every Tom, Dick and Harry. Mary dialled 999. Not sure who to ask for, she asked for all three emergency services.

*

Will grinned as he squeezed his car into the last free parking space near to the station and then his phone rang. It was a control room operator to tell him that an emergency call had come in from Salthouse Mills reporting a dead body.

'Crap, I'll be there in a minute.' He pulled back out and followed the flashing lights of an ambulance and a fire engine to the crime scene, wondering who the hell had phoned the fire service; not much they could do. He parked behind the ambulance and watched the paramedics as they jumped out of it and made their way over to a uniformed officer, who must have been first on scene. Will got out and opened the boot to take a pair of blue paper overalls from his emergency stash. After fighting for a minute to get his arms and legs into the thing without bursting it at the seams, he slipped on some boot covers and a pair of latex gloves. He was relieved to see the officer had taped the area off and was actually holding a pale green scene log. He noticed an elderly lady sitting in the back of a patrol car. She had a small Shih Tzu on her lap. Will rustled his way over to the officer who was just signing the paramedics back out of the crime scene.

'Has death been pronounced?'

The paramedic nodded to confirm. 'We'll leave it in your capable hands, poor lass.' They went back to sit in the ambulance and complete their paperwork until they were told they could leave the scene.

'Sarge, I only went in there to lead the old lady who found her away from the scene and sit her in the back of the car. Nothing has been touched apart from Mary placing her coat over the body to give her some privacy, but she said she never physically touched her.'

'Excellent, well done, mate. It's nice to see that someone actually paid attention on their training.'

The officer, who looked about nineteen, smiled.

Will ducked under the tape. This wasn't how he had envisaged meeting Jenna White. As he got closer he focused on her face, it was hard to tell. Teenage girls change so much and she had no make-up on. He thought this girl looked a little bit too old to be Jenna but he couldn't be sure, he would need her parents to make a positive ID. It was then that he looked at the blood-soaked matted hair.

'Fuck.'

This girl had long brown hair; Jenna's was brown but shorter, more spiked. He stepped back feeling defeated. This thing was something bigger than he had ever dealt with. There was nothing he could do now until CSI arrived to work their magic. Debs was the only one on call for South Cumbria. Like every other department they were short-staffed, and she was tied up at the other scene so wouldn't be allowed to process this one for fear of cross-contamination. It would be at least an hour before they drafted someone in.

He looked around. There were no obvious signs of anything being left behind; just the body. He turned to walk back to the patrol car and to speak to the old lady while he waited. He opened the car door.

'Mrs Grieve, my name is Will, I'm a Detective Sergeant with the police. That must have been quite a shock for you. How are you doing? Do you need any medical assistance?'

'Just call me Mary. Mrs Grieve makes me sound ancient. To be honest with you, young man, I'm not actually sure how I'm doing. How could someone do that to such a pretty young thing? What is this world coming to?'

'I know, it makes me sick to my stomach. It's dreadful. Mary, can you tell me exactly what happened?' He listened as she described everything in minute detail; she was precise and straight to the point. 'Mary, when you were walking on your way here did you pass anyone in a car or a van, any cyclists?'

She shook her head. 'Not a soul. Usually there is the odd person around but this morning it was just me, Spot and that poor girl.'

'Thank you, Mary. I'm going to get someone to drive you home now. An officer will come and speak with you later and take a statement. Is that OK?'

'Yes that's fine, and thank you, officer, but I can walk. Spot needs his exercise and so do I. I will be in all day until I walk him again at seven.'

Will smiled at her and she nodded her head. 'If you're sure, it's up to you.' He watched her untangle some earphones and then push them into her ears.

'I'm positive, thank you. Just make sure you catch the monster who has done this because until you do I don't think I will sleep at night.' She stepped out of the car and walked off briskly, pulling the small dog behind her.

It took six long hours before the body could be removed from the scene and taken by the undertakers to the pathology lab at the hospital. Six long hours of the scene being guarded and processed. The officers left at the scene all bowed their heads as a mark of respect when the undertakers wheeled the gurney carrying the girl's body past them and loaded her into the back of a waiting black Mondeo estate.

In the last two hours quite a crowd had gathered, which meant more officers and PCSOs had to attend to keep the scene secure. The local press had arrived. The guy Will hated had been caught trying to sneak around the back and take photos of the body. For once Stu had used his initiative and arrested the prick for obstruction, and had him handcuffed in the back of a van where he was shouting about public interest and freedom of speech. No doubt the custody sergeant would have a hissy fit and let him go without charge but at least he was taken care of for now. When they had done what could be done they left the scene to be guarded by the PCSOs so they could go back to the station for a briefing. Will was angry, hungry and fed up. When they got out of the meeting and everyone had been given multiple tasks, Will and Stu headed back to their office.

'I'm starving, Will, should we go up to the hospital canteen for some breakfast before we have to go to the path lab for the post mortem?'

'Stu, that is a bloody brilliant idea. That's twice in one morning you've excelled yourself. Don't make a habit of it though, I can't take the excitement.'

Will had just come off the phone to the White family liaison officer to let them know that a body had been found but it did not match Jenna's description. He didn't want them hearing about it on Facebook or anywhere else. Laura and Paul, who had recently done their family liaison officer training, had been dispatched to prepare Emma's family for the worst, and to bring them up to the hospital to see if they could identify her. Will felt like crap, his head was banging and he wanted it all to be over.

*

Derek Edmondson was sitting at the table drinking his second cup of tea. *The Times* was laid out in front of him but he wasn't reading it. He needed to find the woman and the only thing he could think of was to go to the police station and ask for some help. He didn't really have a choice in the matter.

CHAPTER 18

Will and Stu had missed the all-day full English breakfast: the cook had just removed the last pieces of bacon as they joined the queue so they both opted for steak pie and chips.

'Glad to see you eating healthy, Stu. Debs hasn't managed to convert you to that eat no carbs for the rest of your life diet then?'

Stu laughed, spitting flakes of pastry all over the table. 'Come on, Will, seriously, do I look like I do everything my wife tells me to?'

Will took a moment to consider the question. 'Yes, actually you do but I'd never hold it against you.'

Shoving a huge forkful of chips into his mouth Stu mumbled, 'Get lost.'

They finished eating at the same time, stood up and wiped their mouths on some paper napkins. Carrying their trays over to the big trolley near to the counter, Will turned to thank the women behind it who all blushed simultaneously.

Once they were outside Stu lowered his voice. 'How do you do it? How come every woman you speak to goes red and gets their knickers in a twist? I don't think you're that fantastic, no offence and all that. I suppose you're not bad for your age. I even asked Debs the other night and she said she didn't know, there was just something about you.'

'What do you mean? Every woman I speak to does not get like that at all, you soft git.'

Stu rolled his eyes. 'All right then, tell me one who doesn't get all giggly around you.'

Will could think of one but couldn't say her name because Stu would tell Debs and she would tell someone else and within ten minutes the whole station would know, and he didn't want to cause Annie any embarrassment. He shook his head. 'None of them, do you daft bugger.'

Stu scrunched up his face. 'Unbelievable, you don't even care do you?'

They walked the rest of the way to the pathology lab in silence; Stu sulking and Will trying to think if every woman he spoke to turned into a gibbering wreck.

The Coroner's Officer, Lisa, and Matt, the Pathologist greeted them at the pathology lab. Lucky for them it was his day to be down here; he was normally based in Lancaster. Both of them looked grim. Will nodded at Matt and winked at Lisa, watching for her reaction. He was surprised when a faint redness appeared at the bottom of her throat and began working its way upwards, she let out a small laugh. Stu glared at Will who shrugged back at him. Matt broke the silence.

'The boyfriend and sister have just made a positive ID: it's Emma Harvey.' Matt led them into the male changing rooms to get scrubbed up. The strong smell of disinfectant hit Will's nostrils. It had been a while since he'd been in here, yet it felt like yesterday. Another dead girl, that time killed by a drunk driver.

When they walked through Dr. Frankenstein's lab, as Will referred to it, he positioned himself at the top end of the table where her head was, as far away from the stomach as possible. He could stand just about everything except the stench when they opened the stomach cavity and the smell of everything from faeces to puke filled the air. He smiled as Lisa took her position next to him; he left Stu to stand further down near to the stomach. Will knew how much Stu disliked post mortems and that Stu hadn't figured out what it was about them that he disliked so much, apart from the obvious. Will had been meaning to tell him about the stomach gases but he'd wound him up so much with his earlier comments he couldn't be arsed. It served him right.

Lisa was talking to him, but he was watching Matt as he pulled the sheet down and was making his initial observations. Lisa took some photographs and then Matt began to unwrap the brightly coloured scarf that looked out of place on the dead girl's body. Will thought it looked familiar; he'd seen one like it before but couldn't remember where – women's fashion wasn't really his thing. Lisa took a sharp intake of breath as she saw the gaping wound the scarf had been covering; it was crusted with dried blood.

'I think it's pretty obvious what the cause of death is, folks. That is one nasty cut.' Matt began to measure, photograph and record every injury on Emma's body. He occasionally looked to Lisa who was writing everything down.

She talked even though she was busy. 'I suppose it was going to happen one day, I mean, look at Bradford. It's inevitable with all the inbreeding around here. It's no surprise that some twisted sicko would eventually realise he wanted to live out his fantasies instead of dreaming about them in bed every night.'

Stu looked at her and Will. 'Are you having a laugh, a serial killer around here? No one is that clever, or that stupid, come to think of it, to want to start a killing spree around here. I mean, why would they? It doesn't make any sense.'

Lisa paused. 'We'll see. Girls just don't disappear and bodies turn up without there being some connection. Not in this town.'

Will agreed with her on that point.

Matt was carefully weighing the heart and looked over to Will. 'Shall we see what the results are first? And then we could set up a sweepstake for the number of victims we'll end up with before you and your shit-hot team manage to catch the killer.' He winked at Will. 'You can put me down for a fiver that this town has given birth to a serial killer, and I reckon we'll end up with four bodies before you catch him or he kills himself.'

Stu tutted. 'You're sick, you lot, you know that, don't you?'

Three heads nodded in agreement with him and Lisa smiled giving him her sweetest smile. 'Come on, Stu, you've got to laugh about it or you would go home and hit the bottle and end up a raging alcoholic. I suppose we are but we're not as sick as whoever did this, and besides, you won the last one we had so I don't know what you're complaining about. I'll go for five before he kills himself.'

Will shook his head. 'Thanks for the vote of confidence in my team of detectives. What are you two trying to say?'

Will felt his nostrils flare and his insides cramp as he got a whiff of the freshly opened stomach. He looked to Stu whose face had turned the same colour as the dead girl's.

'Urgh.'

Will smirked like an eight-year-old and continued breathing through his mouth, knowing he couldn't win. He would be able to taste the smell in the back of his throat all night. He thought about Annie to take his mind off it and wondered if she had received his last text message. If Lisa was right they were in trouble, because he'd already taken two girls in such a short space of time that he could already be planning his next one. He had a thing for the Abbey so it was likely that Jenna White was hidden there somewhere.

Will would get his posse of PCSOs to canvass the area again, revisit all the houses and search all the outbuildings and barns. Matt was talking fast and Lisa, head bent, was busy taking notes to type up later. The cities had state-of-the-art mortuaries but down here it was still good old-fashioned pen and paper.

CHAPTER 19

The cold woke Annie from her sleep. The room was freezing and her left hand, which was sticking out of the duvet, was so cold she could barely feel her fingers. It was dark. The room was full of shadows so she reached across to switch the lamp on. She pressed the button but nothing happened. Throwing the duvet back she stood up to try the main light switch, hoping there wasn't a power cut. Her teeth began to chatter and a feeling of dread settled over her; something was wrong. She opened the kitchen door and breathed out, watching her breath turn into a swirling white mist; it was even colder in here.

Sensing movement in the corner she looked to see dark shadows swirling around. They began to gather substance and formed a black mass, which began to swell. *I must be dreaming, I'll wake up now.* She pinched her arm and let out a yelp. *Nope, wide awake.* The shadow mass was getting denser. It was still in the corner but it was huge and looked more solid, not as transparent. It was forming into the shape of a man. Alarmed she backed into the snug, slamming the door shut behind her and pressed her back against it. She was unsure what good it would actually do but it was better than nothing. What she wanted to do was scream but who was going to hear her. Silent tears began to stream down her cheeks and she reached for her phone, which was on the side table. Her fingertips brushed against it and she clutched it tight, bringing it towards her. She dialled Jake's number: no signal. Who was she kidding? She had known there wouldn't be. Tess had backed herself into the far corner and was shaking more than Annie was. She closed her eyes and began reciting what she could remember of the Lord's Prayer; the rest she made up not knowing what else to do. She didn't even believe in this sort of stuff so what the hell was happening, and why to her?

She paused and felt the door move slightly. She pressed against the hard wood of the door. An image of a pair of ghostly arms reaching through the wood and wrapping themselves around her neck made her want to cry out in fear, but she couldn't make a noise. She had heard people say they were frozen in terror and wondered if this was how they felt. The blood in her veins felt as if it had turned to iced water she was so cold. Whatever was on the other side of the door was intelligent because it had been listening to her. She imagined a man standing on the other side, his head cocked to one side, waiting to make his move. It wanted to hurt her, she had no doubt about that: it felt evil. God, who was she kidding? What did she know?

Her heart was pumping the blood around her body so fast it was deafening inside her head. She was waiting for the door to be shoved with such force from the other side that she would be flung across the floor, but then a small ball of white light appeared by the window. There was a slight shift in the heavy atmosphere inside the room. It hovered, glowing brightly, and the panic in her chest began to subside a little. The light moved towards Annie, pausing directly in front of her for a brief moment, and then it moved through her body and, for a second, she felt different, not like herself. The feeling disappeared as quickly as it had arrived.

From the other side of the door she heard a woman's voice, it was gentle but firm. 'Edward, leave this place at once. You are not welcome here, ever. I forbid you forbid you to come back. Go back to the house, and the cellar if you must, but stay away from here.'

A growl so low and guttural made Annie begin to shake again, and she dug her heels in and pushed her back against the door as hard as she could. Instantly the heavy atmosphere dissipated and the temperature raised enough that her teeth stopped chattering. Her hand felt its way up the wall until she found the light switch with the tips of her fingers. Pressing it down she finally breathed out as the room was bathed with a warm glow. She didn't move, couldn't move, not yet. She needed to make sure whatever it was had gone. She pressed her ear against the wooden door. After a few minutes she pulled herself up then, making the sign of the cross, she took a deep breath and threw the door open. It was still dark inside the room but the shadow had gone.

The light in the kitchen wouldn't work but the atmosphere was no longer menacing. She stepped further in, ready to retreat if she had to. She was followed by Tess whose hackles were up and who was growling. Annie opened the fridge door to shed some light into the room. *Edward had been here in her house. Or had he? Am I going insane?* She sank to the floor, sitting next to Tess.

'Edward,' she whispered, afraid. Why would he come here, what had she ever done? He must have been dead for years. Confusion making her head spin she stroked Tess to calm them both down. She needed to speak to that medium guy. If he couldn't help her she'd have to try Most Haunted or Ghostbusters, but the most likely option would be the nearest mental asylum.

Once her shaky legs could bear her weight she went to get the card he had given her. Tess was whining to go outside so she opened the door and let her out. She ran straight to the gate and stared into the woods. Annie looked in the direction of the house and saw a flash of white darting between the trees and heading towards the mansion. She went back inside to dial Derek's number but it went straight to voicemail. She left him a message to call her back. He must know his stuff because he had told her this would happen, hadn't he, in his own strange way.

Tess needed a walk and as much as Annie didn't want to walk in the direction of the house she had no choice. She couldn't be sure who the white figure had been, so she needed to go and check no one had been, inside and that it was all still locked up tight. She wouldn't forgive herself if she found out those girls had been kept inside and she had been too cowardly to do anything about it.

Putting on her coat, hat and gloves she set off. There was a light drizzle falling now but it didn't stop Tess, who bounded off in the direction of the house. Annie followed but at a much slower pace. The paths were lethal in the rain and she didn't want to fall; she was aching enough already. Tess began to bark excitedly in the distance, shattering the peace and quiet. She must have found a rabbit or squirrel. She was obsessed with them. One of these days she was going to chase one too far and get stuck down a rabbit hole. The barking stopped, restoring the woods to their normal peacefulness; they didn't feel threatening like yesterday.

The outline of the mansion loomed in the distance and the déjà vu she felt was stronger with every visit. There were so many memories she could conjure up if she desired. Walking closer she felt as if she wanted to go inside. No, more like she needed to go inside. The feeling of belonging was so overpowering it must mean something. How did she know that Alfie had dirty blond hair, blue eyes and the cheekiest grin she had ever seen? He wasn't much taller than her and he radiated warmth. His big strong hands, which had tickled and stroked her hair, were kind and gentle. Alfie had been so heartbroken when he found her in the library with Edward. The hurt in his eyes so intense that even now, after all these years, it made her heart ache with regret. Things would have been so different if she had chosen Alfie and not Edward. They wouldn't have had much but they would have lived in a small house filled with love and laughter and, more importantly, children. How she had longed to have babies, but Edward's deceptive charms and dashing good looks had taken away her one chance of real happiness.

Tess began to whine, stirring Annie from her daydream. She was surprised to see she was standing in front of the Gothic front door, face to face with that awful knocker. Annie had no recollection of walking this far. She had been so absorbed in the memories that she hadn't realised. She had never believed in past lives, but since her head injury things were happening to her that she couldn't explain rationally. She needed to know what happened with Edward. It was something bad and whatever it was had changed Alice's life back then forever. *Or had it been my life?* Annie was convinced that deep down she already knew the whole story but couldn't unearth it from the depths of her mind. She hoped the diary would explain everything, but every time she read that small leather book scary things happened, and after this morning she didn't feel brave enough.

A wet nose nudged her hand. 'Tess, you bloody scared me.' She had a stick in her mouth and was wagging her tail. 'Come on, girl. Let's check the doors and then we're out of here.'

Tess followed, her tail still wagging. Annie shoved the front door hard: it was still locked up tight. Making her way around the perimeter she checked all the boards on the windows, none of them were loose. There were no corners that could be prised up to allow anyone to climb in either. But she couldn't shake the feeling of being watched and kept looking over her shoulder. This time it felt more inquisitive than anything else. She continued to walk around to the back of the huge house and came to the small scullery door, which was shut tight like the others. Her fingers reached out, touching the wood, and she snatched her hand back as a tremor ran through her body. The hairs on the back of her neck stood on end; she had no key for this door but there was something wrong with it, even Tess began to whine and back away. Why did this door feel as if it was the gateway to hell? Annie reached into her pocket for her phone, she wanted Will to come and see – *Come and see what exactly? It's a door you fool.*

Stepping back she studied it to see if there was anything to explain why her copper's instinct had gone into overdrive. There were no prise marks in the wood, no bloodstains. There was nothing other than an old, wooden door. She checked her phone: one missed call and a voicemail. She took one last look around before she began to walk as fast as she could away from the house, and before she got sucked into a whole different world. When she was a good distance away she felt compelled to turn around. She turned and caught sight of a misty, white figure waving at her from Alice's bedroom window; just a slight movement of hand. She blinked and looked again but the window was empty, desolate, like the rest of the house.

*

15th December 1887

Today was the reading of the will. It was such a different affair from when Lady Hannah's was read. Then there was only Edward, his Lordship and Mr Ernest the family lawyer. For his Lordship's all the staff had been informed by Mr Ernest that they were to be present. Edward was not happy about this, he told me so himself, because he said it was a private thing.

All morning he could not sit still and was agitated, pacing up and down the drawing room while waiting for the time to come. His Lordship's

199

brother arrived early and took him into the study where they spent the next hour talking in hushed tones. Cook was nervous and kept wringing her apron so much that Harold ordered her to go and put a fresh one on because she had creased it so. Twice I watched her whisper into Harold's ear and then stare my way. I am sure they must know about my illicit affair with Edward and if they did not then they soon will, because Edward told me last night when we were together in his bed that he would announce our engagement after the reading of the will. I am most nervous about this for I know that I am not and will never be good enough for him. I told him I have nothing to offer him but my love and he told me that was all he would ever want from me.

Last night he produced a small present wrapped in the most beautiful paper. I blushed and told him I did not want him to buy me anything, but he laughed and insisted I opened his gift. I unwrapped it and gasped when I opened the tiny box, for inside it was Lady Hannah's gold and diamond ring that she always wore on her wedding ring finger. It sparkled brightly in the candlelight and I felt tears begin to fall down my cheeks. Edward took the ring from the box and tenderly took hold of my hand, pushing it onto my finger and smiling at me: it fitted perfectly. I told him I could never accept it but he silenced my protests with a passionate kiss. He told me that his mother would not want anyone else in the world to wear it and then he asked me to be his wife. I feel as if I am floating on air. I am to be the Lady of the house. Those dreams of filling the house with the love and laughter of children may not be dreams for much longer. I told him I would only wear the ring after the reading tomorrow and he agreed that it would be best to wait until then.

I walked into the library where everyone was waiting. Not one person coughed, it was so quiet. Edward was the last to come in and he took his seat at the front of the room. Mr Ernest shuffled his papers, cleared his throat and then began to read. What he said next was such a shock I almost fainted and Harold had to sit me down on a chair. The house, land and money were to be divided in equal parts between Edward and myself. Cook gasped so loud it echoed around the room. I was so surprised I wanted to hide my face in shame. All eyes were on me and I wanted nothing more than to run from the room and hide in my tiny bedroom and shut the door on them all.

Edward was the worst. He turned to look at me and his eyes were the blackest I have ever seen. They were whirlpools of anger and hatred but then he smiled and congratulated me. He walked over and took hold of my hand and told everyone that today was truly Alice Hughes' day because we were to be married, and he slipped his mother's diamond ring onto my finger and kissed me on the lips in front of them all. I was horrified for this was not the time or the place.

My cheeks began to burn and the room began to swim, I felt my legs give way and then Edward scooped me into his arms and carried me into the drawing room, telling everyone to leave us alone. I kept my eyes shut for I had no idea what to say to him. How had this happened? How had I gone from being the housekeeper's daughter to the mistress of the house? Edward whispered into my ear that I should not worry and he would take care of everything. His lips brushed against my cheek and he left me alone while he went back to tell everyone about the changes that were to be made.

1st August 1888

Things have been so very different around the house. I have been so busy I forgot all about my diary and it was only when I was searching for something in my attic bedroom that I found it and lay on the bed to reread it. I have brought it down to the master bedroom and locked it away in my bedside drawer to continue writing in it when I get the time. So much has happened since my last entry. Edward and I were married in April, a year to the day we first made love. It was a small ceremony, for the only family I have are my once fellow servants.

In the space of a year I have known so much death and tragedy it can sometimes be too much to bear. They say death comes in threes and I fear they are not wrong. First there was my mother, then Lady Hannah and then his Lordship. Thank God for Edward. Although he spends more time in London at medical school than he does here I know that one day he will become a great doctor. He told me at the moment he is working on what is called a casual ward in the hospital, where the poor, unfortunate people can walk in to get treatment for any illnesses and ailments, even if they have no money to pay. On our last telephone call he told me he had his eyes opened on a daily basis and has never met so many women who were drunkards and who sell their bodies to men for the price of a cheap drink of gin.

It is my dream that he will return home when his studies are complete and we will be able to open up a place in town to treat all the poor people who are not as fortunate as ourselves. Edward has promised to take me to London soon to meet his doctor friends and see the hospital that he works so hard in.

Cook has a new kitchen maid, for Millie disappeared without a trace last time Edward was home to visit. She left no note and gave no indication she wanted to leave so it came as a great shock to us all. Millie was there when we said goodnight and was gone by the morning. It is most strange but Cook is adamant there is a young man involved and thinks that Millie may have eloped. I hope so because it seems a far more romantic outcome than the fear I have that something awful has happened to her.

Edward keeps insisting we should take on a new housekeeper but I have told him many times it is not necessary, and that I am quite capable of running this house without relying on outside help. I should also tell him that I don't want anyone to replace my mother but it seems it is never the right time.

Alfie left to go into the army after the wedding. I know it was all too much for him and that he could not bear to see Edward as my husband. How I wish he was here now because I miss him so much and Edward is rarely home to keep me company.

Edward was not in the best of moods last time he was home; he was very quiet and rather sullen. He went back to London in a terrible mood and I have not the slightest inkling why. I know he has endured so much in such a short space of time and that he misses his parents dearly. His lovemaking was so rough and not like him, he left me with bruises on my wrists and bite marks on my breasts, which smart. The morning after he saw the marks he had left and apologised profusely, crying and begging me for his forgiveness. I did forgive him because I do not want to be angry with him. I love him so much.

28th August 1888

Edward left for London today after a terrible argument. He came home two days ago to surprise me. He brought me the most beautiful bunch of white lilies, which are my favourite flowers, and a pearl necklace with a dainty diamond clasp. He carried me up to bed where we spent two days doing nothing but making love and talking. He was in such a good mood I thought it was now the right time to mention my longing for a baby; I have thought of nothing but since his last visit home and have been waiting for the right moment to tell him.

He exploded with fury when I mentioned it to him. He threw a vase at the wall and tore down one of Lady Hannah's favourite paintings. He then left the drawing room and went down into the cellar. Harold told me he had taken a decanter of whisky and a glass with him. I wanted to go and see him but decided I should let him be until he calmed down. I thought that he would be excited to be a father. How could I have been so wrong? Where has my charming Edward gone? Instead he has been replaced with the black-eyed, mean, hurtful Edward from two years ago.

When he finally came back up to see me he was so drunk he could hardly speak. His fists were not affected in any way for he struck me so hard across the face my eye swelled shut and I ran and spent the night in my old bedroom, praying he would not come looking for me.

He never spoke to me before he left but I hope once he gets back there and thinks about his appalling behaviour he will write and apologise for his outburst. Surely he must realise that for us to become parents will make our lives complete.

1st September 1888

As I took my breakfast in the dining room I read in *The Times* of a terrible murder that has occurred in a part of London called Whitechapel. The body of a woman named Polly Nichols was found and her throat had been cut from ear to ear. It said the woman also had terrible wounds to her abdomen and when she was found there was a clean white handkerchief placed across her throat. I am so glad that I live in such a beautiful, secluded house surrounded by our very own woodland and quite far from the nearest town. Nothing happens like that around here, thank the good Lord.

The newspaper described the woman as living the life of an 'unfortunate'. I will have to ask Edward exactly what that means. I have a good idea but would hate to be wrong. I could ask Cook but she would give me one of her looks and I cannot stand to be looked down upon by her.

Edward eventually telephoned me this afternoon to apologise about his dreadful behaviour when he was home last. He begged my forgiveness for hurting me so much after our last argument and asked if I was still angry with him. I laughed and told him I could not be angry with him for long. I mentioned the newspaper article and he told me not to worry about what happens down in London for it is a long way from Abbey Wood, and it is a big city full of strange people. He explained what an unfortunate was and I was right. He said they were the women he treated on a daily basis on the casual ward and that made me feel even sadder. The poor woman had led an awful life and it had ended in the most horrific way. Surely she must have gone on to a better place. When I said my prayers tonight I prayed for her soul. Before I got into bed for some reason I could not get the image of Polly Nichols out of my mind and it took a long time before I fell asleep.

9th September 1888

Once again, as I took my breakfast I read in the newspaper that another woman had been murdered in the most despicable way in Whitechapel. Annie Chapman had her throat cut just like the last one. The report went on describe her other injuries which were atrocious, and it made my blood run cold to think of the pain and suffering these poor women endured. I have no idea why it affects me so. Maybe it is because I know Edward is in London and has dealings with such poor women that it brings it home to me. This woman was also found with a clean white handkerchief placed on her throat. Did the killer feel guilty about what he had done and tried to cover it over? I will never know, thankfully. I will have to ask Edward if he lives anywhere near to this dreadful Whitechapel place. I hope he does not for it sounds as if the people who live in this place have very little money. Edward does not have to worry about that for he is fortunate enough to have plenty.

I have felt sick and tired all day but I don't know if it because these murders sicken me so and I cannot get them out of my mind or whether it is because I am coming down with something. I feel so drained and sick to the stomach all the time.

15th September 1888

Edwards's guilty conscience must have got the better of him for he arrived home unexpectedly today. I still feel no better and at dinner he wanted to know why I was picking at my food and not eating. He lectured me on the effects of a poor diet. I told him I had been feeling unwell and he insisted on me telling him my symptoms and checking my pulse and temperature. He did not think there was anything serious but insisted that we call out Doctor Smith first thing to confirm everything was fine. I told him to stop making a fuss but he would not listen.

As we sat in the library and talked about our plans for the future he told me he could not stop thinking about how cruel he had been on his last visit home. He apologised again but never mentioned my wanting a baby.

He had given the staff the evening off so we had the house to ourselves, which was a rare treat. For a time it was like it used to be and we made love so tenderly, just like all those months ago. Then he carried me upstairs where we lay in each other's arms until we fell asleep.

18th September 1888

Alfie came home on leave from the army today and I could not hide my excitement to see him again: I have missed him so dearly. I waited outside with Cook and Harold for him to arrive. When the horse and carriage pulled up in front of the house I ran down the steps and threw my arms around his neck and hugged him tight. He hugged me back for a short time and then stepped back as if I were burning him. I turned to see Edward watching from the billiard room window and I felt my cheeks flush. Edward was angry. I could tell by the way he was holding himself so stiff and upright. I felt my stomach clench.

Harold helped Alfie inside with his case and I retreated to go and find Edward. He was nowhere to be seen. Cook informed me he was in the cellar again. I reached the cellar door and then stopped myself. To this day I cannot bear to go down there, it still scares me so I left him to it. He told me the last time I asked him what it was he did down there that he was sorting through his parents belongings and did not want me to interrupt him. He said there were too many memories that belonged to him alone. I went back to the kitchen and sat down at the table. Cook placed a plate of freshly baked gingerbread on the table in front of me and for the first time in a week I felt my stomach growl with hunger. Gingerbread is Alfie's favourite although if you asked her if she had made it especially for him she would no doubt deny it. Next she placed the big tin teapot on the table and an assortment of cups and saucers. Alfie and Harold walked in and I was mother and poured the tea. We all listened to Alfie's tales of faraway places and laughed for he was so funny. Even Harold, who normally took notice of no one nor nothing, was intrigued.

I have no idea how long we had been sitting there when Edward came into the kitchen. He nodded at Alfie and told me to come with him to the morning room. I excused myself and followed him. I knew he was furious with me and I was terrified of what was about to follow. I always knew he was jealous of Alfie but I had no idea just how much. He slammed the door shut and demanded that I never go and sit in the kitchen again; he told me it was a place for servants and not the Lady of the House. He was pacing back and forth across the floor. Suddenly he stopped abruptly and turned to stare at me; his eyes were black. Then he told me that if he caught me talking to or touching Alfie again he would beat me until not one person on this earth would ever look at me again. I was scared because I knew that he meant every word he had just spoken. I apologised and tried to explain that Alfie was like a brother to me and we had grown up in this house with only each other for company. He struck me so hard that my head snapped back and my face began to burn. He grabbed my hair, which I had spent so long dressing this morning, and pulled it so hard the tears began to stream down my face. When he let go I ran out of the room and up the stairs to my attic bedroom and slammed the door shut. I threw myself onto the bed and cried myself to sleep. Edward never came looking for me and for that I was thankful.

28th September 1888

Edward has not spoken to me for over a week now. The atmosphere in the house is horrid. The doctor called this morning to tell me why the sickness has not improved. He told me that I am with child. I did not know whether to laugh or cry. I was so relieved that I wasn't seriously ill but I was also scared to tell Edward. Surely he would not still be angry with me when he finds out he is to be a father, for there is no greater gift than that of a child. I am hoping that this will bring back the Edward that I miss so much, the Edward who loves me and does not want to hurt me.

I could not stop myself and rushed to go and find him to tell him the good news. I found him in his study, head bent and writing a letter. He did not even look up at me, he was so absorbed in his writing. I coughed and startled him, for he looked up and slid the paper underneath the blotter. I walked in, closing the door behind me. He asked me what I wanted and I told him our wonderful news. I expected him to scoop me into his arms and kiss me. Instead he pushed himself up from his chair, the colour drained from his face leaving it a deathly white mask, his black eyes glared and he walked past me out of the room without speaking. I do not know what goes on in his mind. One moment he is happy and kind, the next he is cruel and violent.

I wondered how things would have been if it was Alfie I had married and was telling this news to. I know for a fact he would have picked me up and swung me around the room, whooping with joy. Dear happy Alfie who would no more lift a hand to swat a fly and rather die than hit me, unlike Edward, who I think takes great pleasure in hurting me.

I fear that the Edward I married was an illusion but I have no idea why. He is returning to London tomorrow so I busied myself packing his trunk and bags. I asked Harold if he knew where Edward was and he told me that he had gone down into the cellar. I smiled, thanking him, for I do not want anyone to know of the difficulties between Edward and myself, it is my problem and mine alone.

29th September 1888

How foolish I was thinking that becoming a father would put an end to his brutal outbursts. Last night he forced himself upon me and it hurt so much I was afraid I would lose my baby. He kept on biting me and holding my arms down so hard that today I am covered in bruises, the marks all down my arms and over my chest. I was so terrified for the child inside me that I did not struggle but lay there with silent tears of sadness rolling down my cheeks. He then went downstairs and drank so much of that awful whisky he likes so much that when he came back up he reeked of it. He was so drunk that he collapsed onto the bed fully clothed and fell asleep. His snores were so loud and he repulsed me enough that I crept from our marital bed up to my old bedroom.

How I longed to be a housemaid again. I used to think that I would never finish my chores and that I was so badly done to. Ha! How little did I know? Carrying heavy buckets of soapy water to scrub the stairs and spending all day on my hands and knees polishing floors until they sparkled, the thought of that life appeals to me so much more than being the beaten wife of the master of the house.

Edward got up this morning and never spoke a word to me; no apologies for his behaviour this time. Harold loaded the horse and carriage and I watched from the schoolroom window as Edward climbed in and did not even turn around to see if I was there.

I still catch my breath when I look at him for he is such a handsome man. Sometimes I have to pinch myself to make sure that my life is real. I think back to last year when everything was so perfect and he knew nothing but passion for me;

I miss it so much. Deep down in my heart I know that I love him even though at the moment I am also terrified of him. I understand that he may still be grieving and things are difficult for him. Despite everything that he keeps doing to me I still feel a sense of duty towards him for he is my husband.

I went downstairs to the kitchen knowing that it would be safe for me to do so now he had left. As I reached the door I overheard Cook gossiping to Alfie about things not being so perfect for the housekeeper's daughter now. I bowed my head and walked away, not wanting to hear any more of her spiteful gossip. I did not want to see the pity or even scorn on Alfie's face and I did not want to hear them say what they were all thinking: 'Who did you think you were, Alice Hughes?'

I have no idea what I am to do about my predicament and have no one that I can turn to. I just hope and pray that once Edward has time to think things over in London that he will calm down and beg my forgiveness.

I would give anything to confide in Alfie like I used to but he makes himself busy when I enter the room. Cook informed me he is returning to the army tomorrow.

Last night I dreamed about a life with Alfie. I know that he loves children because he talks about his sisters with great fondness. I am trapped in this most beautiful house with a man who does not love me and, in fact, I fear he loathes me more than anything else. I can only be thankful that Edward spends so much of his time in London for I dread to think what kind of life I should lead if he lived here all the time.

I could stand it no longer and went to find Alfie. He was outside in the greenhouse tending to the plants for Thomas the gardener. He looked at me for the first time in days and I could see the shock register on his face. I had not realised until this point exactly how dreadful I looked. He asked me what I was doing talking to him when it was obvious Edward – he almost spat the word out – had told me I was not allowed to. There was so much I wanted to say to him but instead I began to cry like a pitiful little girl. Alfie put down the watering can and walked over towards me. He paused, unsure what to do but then he wrapped his arms around me and held me tight. I felt foolish but I could not stop myself. Everything I had bottled up seemed to come out in those tears. I rested my head on his chest.

After a while he led me to our broken bench and once again we sat down on it and I poured out my heart to him. I told him of the beatings which Edward gave to me; he made me roll up my sleeves to look at the bruises on my arms. He was so angry at Edward but still his eyes stayed the calmest of blue. He kissed my bruised arms tenderly and my eyes filled with tears once more. I told him that I was with a child that Edward did not want and I told him of my longing to be in servitude once more. This made Alfie laugh and he told me that I was never cut out to be a servant in the first place. He told me how beautiful I was and how he had loved me from the very first day I had walked into the house when I was nine years old and he had been twelve. He said I had hid behind my mother's long skirts and had tears falling down my cheeks that day because I had fallen over onto the gravel drive and cut my knee. The long-forgotten memories rushed back and we sat there for hours talking until we were both ravenous and had to go back inside. Alfie told me that he had to go back to the army but when he was next home he would help me pack up my belongings and move away with him, somewhere as far away from Abbey Wood as possible. He told me he would love the child as if it were his own because it was part of me. We would tell the people where we moved that we were married and that no one would have to know any different because it was our secret.

For the first time in months I felt as if my life could have a happy ending, just like in the fairytale books I used to read. Alfie pulled me from the bench and kissed me. It was wonderful and it felt as if our lips were meant to be together, like two pieces of a puzzle. Horse's hooves in the distance made us pull apart and I feared that Edward had returned. I ran from the greenhouse back to the house, my stomach a tight knot. I waited in the library, watching to see who it was. Much to my relief it was the grocer making his weekly delivery for Cook. Much later on I found Alfie and made him promise never to speak of our plans to anyone, for I know that if Edward were to find out he would kill the both of us, of this I have no doubt. Alfie took my hand and lifted it to his lips. Kissing it tenderly he promised it would be our secret until the day we left and never came back.

As I write this, my heart feels so much lighter. Now that I have unburdened my soul, I know that Alfie will take care of us both and I will not have to fear for my unborn baby's life with him. I am making plans and for the first time I feel that there is hope. I will gather only the important things that I need and store them in my mother's old trunk in my attic room. I will have to ask Mr Ernest how I withdraw the money that was left to me but I will not do this until I know the date that Alfie is coming home to fetch me in case he alerts Edward, although I feel I will be able to buy his silence for he is a strange little man.

30th September 1888

Alfie left this morning and with him he took all of my heart, not just the small piece that has always belonged to him. I watched him from the schoolroom window as I did not want Cook to see me waving him goodbye, for she cannot help herself from making idle gossip. How ironic; this was the parting that should have been between

Edward and myself yesterday. Instead there had only been relief that I would suffer no more pain until his next visit home.

As the carriage moved away Alfie turned to look up at the window. He blew me a kiss which I caught and blew straight back. He gave me that boyish grin that I love so much, and my heart filled with joy. I am so fortunate that he is still willing to love me even though I let Edward into my life when all along it should have been him. I am so thankful that he has found it in his heart to forgive me. I will make him the happiest man on earth and take care of him as he deserves. I have not once seen Alfie's eyes turn black with anger and hatred. They always remain the purest of blue; so still and gentle like the calmest sea.

CHAPTER 20

Derek drove into town to the police station with butterflies in his stomach. He parked in the public car park opposite and fed his money into the machine for a ticket. It could be a while before he got to speak to someone. He walked to the main entrance and plucked up the courage to go inside the building. There was a row of bright blue plastic chairs bolted to the floor. Sitting on them were two young girls who were bickering over a lost phone. He stepped close to the glass counter and pressed the bell. A woman came through immediately with a smile on her face, her name badge said 'Lena'. Derek smiled back.

'Hello, my dear, I wonder if I could speak to a police officer in private please. I'm very sorry I can't disclose what the matter is to you.'

She nodded. 'That's fine, don't worry about that, can I take your name and I'll get someone to come and speak to you.' He told her his name and she asked him to take a seat. He sat down as far away from the two girls as possible; they were still arguing. After only ten minutes a young woman opened the heavy wooden door next to him and said his name. Derek stood up and smiled at her, then followed her through the door into a small interview room with a table, four chairs and a tiny window.

'Mr Edmondson, my name is Sally. I'm a community support officer. Would you like to tell me what the problem is?'

'Well, this is going to sound as if I'm mad, and believe me I'm embarrassed to have to come here and say it, but I am not mad and I really need to tell someone about it, and you, my dear, have drawn the short straw. There is a woman I met who needs help, and I don't know anything about her except her name is probably Annie. You see, I'm a psychic medium and she came to a meeting at a spiritualist church last week. I got a message from my spirit guide about her and it was a serious one.'

Sally wrote it all down on a scrap of paper. 'Go on, Mr Edmondson, I'm listening.'

'Well, I can't get her out of my mind and I know something terrible is going to happen. I need to find her so I can help her. I think I have her car registration or at least part of it. If I gave it to you would you be able to trace her and check that she is all right and pass a message on from me? I understand I'm asking a lot but I can't stress how important this is; her life may be in danger.'

'I can do a check on the registration which will give me her name and address, but I'm afraid I

220

can't give that information out to you, sir, it's confidential. But I can ask the area officer to call and pass your contact details on to her. Would that be OK? I'm sorry but it's the best I can do.'

The tightness that had been gripping his chest the last few days subsided a little. 'She drives a red mini with a black soft top, it has two racing stripes on the bonnet and the registration is something like ANN 1E.'

The officer stood abruptly. 'If you could just bear with me, sir, I'll go and make some enquiries. It won't take long.'

Sally left the interview room and ran straight around to the CID office, bursting through the door with such force it nearly knocked Will, who was standing on the other side, off his feet.

'Jesus, Sal, what are you trying to do? Finish me off?'

'Sorry, Will, there's a strange guy in interview A. He came in to ask us to trace a woman from a spiritualist church he met last week, reckons she's in grave danger.'

'Bollocks, it sounds like just the job for you, Sal. I'm up to my neck in it with missing and dead girls and all that.'

She cut him off. 'Will, he just gave me a description of Annie Graham's car and number plate, it's a private one she bought herself last year.'

Will felt the pie and chips he'd eaten earlier try to force their way back up. He pushed past Sally and dashed around to the interview room; it was empty. He went out into the front office. There were two girls sitting glaring at each other but no one else. He went out onto the front street to look around but it was mid-afternoon and it was busy, plus he didn't have a clue what the man looked like.

'Shit, shit, shit.'

Both girls looked his way and grinned. Sally was holding the internal door open for Will to get back in.

'I only left him for a minute, he can't have got far.'

'I need you to get the CCTV from the front office and get CSI to print the pictures out; this could be our guy. We need to identify him and fast. It's a bit of a coincidence we have one missing girl, one dead girl and he comes in to find out where one of our officers lives.'

'Will, he said he feared for her safety, that she was in grave danger. He seemed like a decent guy, just a bit strange.'

'Yeah, well, so did Ted Bundy and he killed at least twenty-eight women.'

They both walked around to the front office where Lena had rewound the CCTV footage of the man sitting on the chair. She paused it and Will screwed up his eyes.

'Nope, never seen him before in my life. But we need to find him, and quick.' He began dialling Annie's number but it went straight to voicemail again and he had to stop himself from throwing his phone at the wall and smashing it into pieces; it was bloody useless.

Derek was back at his car. As soon as the officer had left the room his phone had begun to vibrate in his pocket and he knew it was Annie. Not wanting to waste any more of the nice police woman's time he had left the station and walked back to the car park; oblivious to the world around him he listened to the voicemail. Her voice was so quiet he had to concentrate to hear what she said. A chill went through his body. Whatever it was had started.

CHAPTER 21

Alice knew the house from the outside was a decaying wreck. The exterior looked unloved, making the house look sad. Inside, however, was a different story. There was an atmosphere building more and more each day. It was as if an unseen electrical charge was running throughout it. The shadows that walked the house were getting blacker, denser. Noises could be heard, if you were listening, and they came from the cellar.

Upstairs Alice's solitary white mist wandered the corridors, trying her best to console the recently departed soul of the girl who had been taken from her life so abruptly and without reason. Alice had to make Annie see what was going on in here. When she had first come into the house Alice had felt such a strong connection to her. She had tried her best to show her how the house used to be: in the schoolroom she had placed her diary, which had been hidden for over a hundred years, in plain view. Alice wasn't strong enough to stop the monster a second time around and it tormented her that evil was so much stronger than good. All Alice had ever wanted from her life was to be happy and to help others. Instead she had married a maniac, a killer. When she had found the strength to put an end to his murderous ways it had plagued her mind for the rest of her life, and she had never truly found the happiness she deserved.

Deep inside, Alice had known from the very beginning that there had been something wrong with Edward. She had loved him so completely but it hadn't been enough for him. She knew that he had planned everything with incredible precision. In the days after his death things had become much clearer to her. The dawning realisation that he had used her because she had been left half of the estate caused her great pain. Instead of turning against her he had fooled her for his gain. She realised that Lady Hannah had not fallen but that her loving son Edward had pushed her to her death. He had engineered the downfall of everyone. Alice had nothing but regrets for her lifetime but hopefully she would be able to change things this time. There was no way she would let Edward loose to torment and kill again and again; he had to be stopped.

Annie was so much like Alice but she had no idea what was at stake. It would be her that would put an end to it all for good. Alice felt herself draining. It was strange, she had never thought about ghosts when she was alive but here she was, trapped in the house where she had died forever, with Edward's evil spirit always lurking around. He kept to the cellar, in the shadows, rarely summoning up the courage to come upstairs into the light. He liked to dwell in the dark, reliving his evil deeds. Alice wasn't afraid of him any more but he made her uncomfortable, and she would disappear as far as possible when she sensed him nearby. He had a thing for the woman as well; he lurked and watched her. She supposed that if she felt connected to her then he was bound to feel threatened by her. Alice had managed to stop him from doing any real harm to her but it was exhausting and she needed help. She needed someone to come and banish Edward for good and send his soul to hell where he belonged. He should not be roaming around causing heartache and havoc. If her connection to Edward was finally severed maybe she would be reunited with Alfie. Alice sighed and her image faded as a whisper of air rippled through the house.

CHAPTER 22

Annie got back to the farmhouse; her stupid phone had no signal and she desperately wanted to hear Will's voice, anybody's voice would do – even Jake. She needed someone to tell her she wasn't going mad, not just yet. All her life she believed that things happen for a reason, she just needed to know what that reason was at this moment in time. She was tempted to ring Ben but he'd get worried and come home and, selfishly, she didn't want him to. It wasn't like he could actually do anything about it.

Going into the kitchen she heaved off her wellies then, taking the milk out of the fridge, she made herself a mug of hot chocolate; it was comfort food weather out there. Her plan was to find one of the Mars bars she'd hidden for emergencies at the back of the cupboard, take the diary and read it until she finished it. See if there were any clues in it as to what was happening, and maybe Derek would ring back and she would be able to put an end to it all and live happily ever after. As she sank into the sofa her phone began to ring. She answered and wasn't disappointed to hear Will's voice.

'It's me, I'm just ringing to make sure you're OK.'

'I think so, why?'

'I'm worried about you. Bad things are happening. The girl who went missing last night, her body was found this morning. I've just left the post mortem. And you know all about Jenna so I think our guy has a thing for the Abbey. No brownie points for guessing who is up there on her own.'

Annie decided to come clean and tell him about what had been going on. 'Will, something strange is happening up here but it's nothing to do with those girls and I don't know how to explain it without sounding like I've lost the plot. I'll tell you more when you get a chance to come up, but I've been trying to get in touch with some medium bloke I met a few nights ago.'

'Is he called Derek Edmondson?'

'How do you know that?'

'He came into the station earlier asking Sally to check on you and to pass a message on.'

'How did he know who I was? He doesn't know my name. Oh wait, he might, I left him a voicemail earlier.'

'He described your car and registration. Look, I need to find him, Annie. It's a bit of a coincidence that he is from out of town and we suddenly have a maniac on the loose killing girls. Do me a favour, will you? Please come into town, I'll meet you outside the station and take you to my house or Jake's, if you prefer. If you're too stubborn to do that then lock the doors, check the house and wait for me or Jake to come to you. Whatever you do don't answer the door to anyone. Personally I'd prefer it if you came to stay at mine for a bit, until we catch this guy.'

'I can't leave, Will. I have to look after Tess and the chickens; I need to be here. I'll be fine. I'll stay inside and if I so much as see a dog walker heading this way I'll ring you.'

Will sighed. 'You are so stubborn, you know that, don't you? I'll be up as soon as I can but it could be a while yet.'

'Yes, I am stubborn but if it's any consolation I can't wait to see you.'

'Don't go outside, I mean it. And lock up.'

She ended the call with a smile on her face. Little did Will know but she doubted things could get any worse. She systematically checked every door and window, the nagging doubt that it wouldn't make one bit of difference to whatever she was experiencing at the back of her mind. In fact, she was scared she might be locking whatever it was in with her. Upstairs was freezing cold, just as downstairs had been this morning, and she shivered. *Aw come on Annie. What you need is a doctor's appointment, the sooner the better.* But just in case she filled her holdall with everything she might need in an emergency and dragged it down the stairs, shoving it into a cupboard at the bottom. Even after this morning it still felt safer down here, because if anything happened up there it would be much harder to escape. There was a lock on the stair door and she slipped the bolt across.

In the kitchen she searched the drawers for a torch and found two. She tested them, making sure they worked. There was no way she was getting caught out again. She tucked one under a cushion on the sofa and placed the other one on the coffee table. She then she took a box of light bulbs from the pantry and set about flicking switches and changing any bulbs that didn't work. When the whole of the downstairs was bathed in light she felt much better. She thought about going out to the shed to fetch a couple of hammers just in case, or was that going over the top? It was better to use a household item than a knife if you ever had to, that's what she told all those battered women she dealt with on a daily basis. It would stand up much better in court – self-defence, your honour. But she didn't care, she wouldn't be bitten twice; if she needed to use a knife she would. There was also the heavy brass poker by the fire if she had to defend herself from whoever was killing around here. It occurred to her that she would probably be fine, because at the ripe old age of thirty-two she was out of the age bracket for the victims by at least ten years.

Sitting down she picked up her hot chocolate, which was no longer hot, and put it back down.

She decided to wait for Will to arrive and then find the biggest wine glass in the cupboard and fill it to the brim.

Tess began to bark and she jumped up to peer out of the window. Like a knight in shining armour, there was Derek walking along the path towards her car. She was not sure how she knew it but she felt inside her that he was one of the good guys, and he was probably too old to go around killing and running rings around the police. Besides, what choice did she have? She didn't know any other mediums who were willing to help her. In fact, she didn't know any at all. Ignoring all Will's earlier advice she unlocked the door and stepped outside.

'Hiya, you got my message then? How did you know where to find me?'

Derek walked forward and held out his hand. 'To be honest, I'm not entirely sure. Can we please start again? Derek Edmondson. I think I'm very pleased to meet you. And you are?'

'Annie Graham.' She reached out and took hold of his hand, shaking it as if they were old friends.

'I can't really explain, but after I listened to your message I got an urge to come for a walk in these woods – it happens sometimes – so I did, and here I am. I saw the car through the trees and ventured up the path.'

Annie was amazed but grateful that he had found her. She invited him in. 'Would you like a cup of tea?'

'I would love one, thank you. There are some things we need to clear up. Do you want to tell me exactly what has been happening from start to finish?'

'Where do I start?' She filled him in on everything that had happened. 'To be frank with you I think I'm losing my mind. I have a head injury and I think the doctors haven't realised just how serious the brain damage is.'

Derek laughed. 'Aha, that would explain it then. Sometimes a serious head injury can result in an awakening of the dormant part of your mind, which is far more susceptible to things that happen on a different level. A lot of folk call it a sixth sense.'

For the first time in days Annie's shoulders relaxed and she breathed a sigh of relief. 'Oh, thank God for that. It all started when I walked into the empty mansion not too far away from here. When I walked inside I had the most amazing feeling of déjà vu. I felt as if I had lived there a very long time ago. This morning I woke up to a freezing cold room and a huge black mass in the kitchen which formed into the shape of a man. I feel as if I'm being watched all the time, and sometimes it feels all right but other times it feels downright scary.'

'Oh dear, that's not good, that's not good at all. Did the black mass speak or do anything?'

'Well, it tried to open the door I was holding, but then an orb of brilliant white light appeared

232

and a woman's voice told it to leave, so it growled at her but it went. I think I know who this woman is, but then sometimes I feel as if I am this woman from the past. I'm confused and you're the first person I've told about this in case they put me in a straightjacket and cart me away.'

Derek smiled and his crinkly green eyes lit up. 'No, my dear, you're not going mad. It sounds as if you are experiencing a variety of things, all of which are proven to be in existence, although I have never met anyone who in such a short space of time has seen so much. Welcome to the world of a psychic. Now sometimes it can be a gift, which will stay with you for the rest of your life: I have been speaking to dead people since I was nine years old. Or it can be a temporary thing. Whichever it is your life won't be quite the same again, I can guarantee that.'

Annie wanted to believe every word that he said, it all made so much sense, but the cynical part of her thought he was talking a load of rubbish. She was tempted to tell him about the diary but a voice inside her head told her different. *It's for your eyes only. When the time is right you may do as you wish but for now keep it close to your heart.*

Derek was watching her. 'Keep what close to your heart?'

'You heard that as well?'

He nodded and began to explain about the wonders of being gifted. For the next thirty minutes Annie listened to him transfixed until, from the corner of her eye, she saw a streak of luminous yellow walking through the trees towards the path. Jake was waving at her. She turned to face Derek and watched the colour drain from his face at the sight of the big, burly policeman.

He stood up. 'Well, it was nice to meet you properly this time. I think I should get going now, I've taken up enough of your time.'

'I know that he looks scary but honestly he's a big pussy cat and my best friend who has been sent to check on me.'

Derek relaxed a little as Jake walked into the kitchen.

'Knock, knock. Did you know your new BF Will has sent me up here to be your personal bodyguard until he finishes work? Mind you, I'm not complaining as long as you get the kettle on: I'm dying of thirst and starving. Have you got any food you can cook that you won't burn until it's unfit for human consumption?'

Annie laughed. She was so glad to see Jake and threw her arms around him. He hugged her back, squeezing far too tight but she didn't care; it felt safe and warm.

Derek walked towards the door. 'I should get going now. We could meet up at the church tomorrow if you're free and try to do a session together. It may help to get to the bottom of everything.'

Annie didn't dare look at Jake. She thanked Derek and shook his hand again. 'I'll ring you in the morning and let you know.'

He walked out into the courtyard. 'I'll look forward to it, and please don't hesitate to ring if you need to speak to me. Be careful, Annie.'

She watched him walk along the path and disappear into the trees. Jake's loud laughter filled the kitchen and filtered out of the door. She went back inside to see him doubled over.

'What's so funny?'

His face turning many shades of red, he spluttered, 'Who was that? Why would you even want to go to a church and what did he mean by a session? I don't think Will would be too impressed if you're having sessions with strange old men so soon into your relationship, especially in churches. Annie, I'm shocked. What has got into you?'

She shoved him hard in the chest. 'I'm not going to a church to have sex with him, you moron. Oh, forget it, I can't explain it to you, you'd never understand: it's complicated.'

'Why don't you try me. It's not like I have anything else to do but babysit you all afternoon and I could do with a good laugh.'

CHAPTER 23

He was obsessed with the woman from the farm. He couldn't get her out of his head; day and night she was in there. It didn't help that she looked a little bit like Julie, the only woman he had got close to marrying until his mother had messed that up as well. She had been such a quiet pretty thing and he had loved her so much. Unable to buy a house of their own she had moved in with him and his mother, but had to sleep in the spare room because his mother wouldn't let anything sinful go on under her roof. His mother had picked and picked until she had worn Julie down to a nervous wreck and then she left him. She just packed her bags and left; no note or anything, not even a goodbye. He had first thought about killing his mother that night. His heartbreak got so bad he couldn't function for months.

When the medium had spoken to the woman so bluntly he had been shocked. In all the years he'd sat there like the dutiful son, listening to the drivel they usually spouted, he'd never heard one that

236

didn't say anything that wasn't wrapped in cotton wool and sugarcoated. He had been glued to his seat while watching the exchange between them. When the medium dashed out of the door after the woman he was scared to death. He had excused himself and went upstairs to watch from the small window which overlooked the car park. He had taken a couple of photos on his phone, intrigued by the pretty woman in the blue hat, and then gone back downstairs to sit next to his mother. The guy had come back inside and tried to continue with his session but it was different, the atmosphere had changed from one fraught with tension to one of deflated energy, as if someone had cut the power cable. The medium had passed a few messages onto some old dears but couldn't concentrate, and after thirty minutes of stumbling along the guy had excused himself saying he felt ill, and left.

He had gone into the kitchen to help make the tea, just like he did every week, and to listen to the snatches of conversation to see if anyone knew who the mystery woman was. He heard one woman say she recognised her and his heart had begun to beat faster. His trembling hands managed to pour scalding water all over the worktop, narrowly missing Edith who had walked away, shaking her head. He cleaned up the spillage before his mother came in and embarrassed him with her harsh comments.

When he had realised the woman from the farm was the woman from the church he had been ecstatic; fate was finally shining his way. He decided to go to the supermarket, where it would be busy, and try and print out the pictures from his phone. He had to queue to use the photo machine. When it came to his turn he stood at the kiosk fumbling around it, he had never used one before and didn't have a clue how it worked. A teenage girl came and used the kiosk next to him and within two minutes had printed off her pictures and was ready to go.

'Excuse me, would you be able to help me? I'm not very good with this stuff and haven't got a clue.'

She didn't speak, just smiled at him, and then transferred his pictures onto the screen. If she thought it was odd that they were all a bit blurry and of the same woman in different situations she never said anything.

'There you go, just press that "print" button and that's it. You can pay for them at the kiosk over there or at one of the checkouts when you pay for your shopping. You just give them that receipt. Or if you're skint like me you can just walk out with them. They never know if you've paid or not, no alarms go off or anything.'

He thanked her for helping him and went to queue at the cigarette counter. He had never stolen anything apart from the scarf the other day, and he hadn't meant to do that. He watched as the girl walked out of the shop clutching her stolen pictures. She was right, not one person had so much as given her a second glance. He paid for his pictures and left the building holding a copy of the local paper under his arm. The headline KILLER ON THE LOOSE made the paper feel so hot it felt as if it were burning into his skin. He smiled. For the first time in his insignificant life he had made the headlines. He was untouchable.

Walking home he thought about the woman at the farm and exactly what he would like to do to her.

CHAPTER 24

Annie wasn't about to explain to Jake that she was having a psychic episode. He would find it hilarious and tell her it was more like a psychotic episode and that she needed medical help. She made two mugs of coffee and got a packet of chocolate fingers out of the cupboard. Jake had stripped off his body armour, followed by a waterproof jacket and then a black fleece jacket. All he had left on was a skintight black polo shirt and a pair of combat pants.

'God, you look hot in black. I like the new shirts.'

He flexed his bulging biceps. 'You like, Miss Graham? Well, you can have a feel but don't get too excited. I wouldn't want Will to think he had some serious competition.'

She ran her fingers up his arms and across his chest. 'Alex is one lucky guy.'

He laughed and turned, shaking his bum in his best Beyoncé style at her. 'I do sometimes wonder myself. You know I did try and get it on with girls for years but it just didn't work.'

'Yeah, but that was before you met me.'

He snorted. 'Bless you, I do love you, Annie, and you are really special and all that and just maybe if I didn't live with a hot, rich man I would be tempted.'

She punched him in the arm. 'You're such a gentleman, Jake. I like it when you let me down gently. Will said they found a body but it wasn't Jenna's.'

Jake collapsed onto the sofa. 'It's shite, the poor girl earlier was left dead and naked apart from a purple scarf which was wrapped around her neck, which, according to Will, was holding her head onto her body, and Jenna White is still missing. I hope I catch the sick bastard first because I won't be giving him a caution then cuffing him, I'll be kicking seven bells of shit out of him and then cuffing him.' She flopped down next to him and he put his arm around her. 'I've missed you. You're like an annoying little sister but then again maybe not. I don't think a little sister would get the hots for her brother every time he took his coat off.'

They both laughed and Annie felt her eyes getting heavy. Knowing she was safe she let them close and drifted off to sleep.

Jake managed to reach the controls and turn the television on. He was getting paid to look after her and couldn't think of another job he'd rather do. She looked worn out, her head was a mess and she had big black rings under her eyes but, contrary to what would have been expected of him, he had managed to keep those observations to himself.

His radio began to ring as he got a private call. Will's collar number flashed on the screen.

'All right, Will, what can I do for you?'

There was a slight pause. 'Did you manage to get up to Annie's?'

'Yep, I'm sat on the sofa with my arms wrapped around her and she has her head buried in my lap.' Jake smiled at the sharp intake of breath on the other end of the radio.

'Cool, as long as she's OK. Please can you stay with her until I get up there to take over. Do you mind?'

'I told you it's fine. Take as long as you want. Oh God, she's good, you don't know what you're missing mate.' With that Jake ended the call.

***

He sat in the chair in his bedroom, staring out of the window, until he heard his mother turn off the television downstairs and lock the front door. Lifting his arm he checked his watch. It was still early; she must be tired. Her nightly ritual involved rattling every door and window to make sure they were secure. Once she had made the slow trudge up the stairs and spent her five minutes in the bathroom she would go past his door and shout 'goodnight, God bless', making him cringe every time. Somehow he didn't think that God was ever going to bless him again, not after the terrible things he had done.

The fire had started inside him two hours ago. Determined not to give into it he had sat glued to the chair. Images of such sickness and depravity raged through his brain and they made him feel both repulsed and excited. He didn't understand how something so sick and disgusting to him could make him so aroused. He had stared at the metal sign outside the newsagents, watching it sway in the breeze. The hypnotic effect had cleared his mind for a little while but then the owner had come out and pulled the metal shutters down, dragging the sign back inside the shop, and now he had nothing to focus on.

He wanted the woman from the farm.

The computer screen glowed on the desk and he thought about logging on and watching the little whore for a while to see if she could take his mind off the blood and death that he so craved. He pictured Jenna's smiling face and it made him feel even worse. He was in such turmoil he stood up and caught his reflection in the mirror and stared. He didn't remember having such a hard face.

The voice whispered to him, 'Why don't you pay our friend a visit – you know you want to?'

He shuddered. Unable to stop himself he got dressed and crept out of his room. The loud snores coming from his mother's bedroom masked the sound of the front door opening. He drove to the small car park across from the ruins and parked next to the public toilet; his was the only car there. Taking the dog lead out of the glove compartment –

243

who would have thought something from the pound shop would be so useful? – he took his backpack from the front seat and slipped the knife inside with the rest of his carefully assembled kit: a torch, rope and some duct tape.

He thought about the room in the cellar of the mansion; his room. The first time he discovered it he had found himself drawn to the rocking chair in the corner. He had sat there for a long time; happy to be there. After a while he began to dig with his hands in the soil underneath the chair and found the knife. Its worn wooden handle had felt so right in the palm of his hand, as if it had been made to measure, just for him. He had known instinctively that this room belonged to the young man on the photo and now it was his. Jenna had made a nice addition to it. He wanted to show the woman from the farm the room but needed to lure her there somehow. It was just a matter of biding his time. He knew the opportunity would arise and he began to feel a tingle of excitement as he reached the old trail with the steep sandstone steps that, after quite a climb, would lead into the woods.

***

Jake extracted himself from Annie, whose head was almost resting in his lap. He slid a cushion underneath her and went to find something to eat. He was halfway through eating a mountainous sandwich, which contained one of everything

244

edible from the fridge and cupboards, when the beam of a car's headlights lit up the kitchen. Jake opened the door and watched Will make the effort to get out of the car.

'When was the last time you had something to eat? You look like crap, mate.' He handed over half of his sandwich to Will.

'Erm, thanks but it depends what's in it.'

'Trust me, it's better that you don't know. Just eat, it tastes fine.'

Will took it from him and bit into it. 'How's Annie?'

'Sleeping Beauty is fast asleep on the sofa. I had to move in case she got the wrong idea and thought I was you when she woke up.'

Will was too tired to take the bait this time. 'Thanks, Jake. There's still nothing on Jenna. I had the PCSOs canvass every house and farm building in the area: everything within a three-mile radius has been searched.'

'She'll turn up eventually, one way or the other. I'll get off now. I officially finished three hours ago.' Jake began the ordeal of getting dressed again. 'Oh, and I'm sorry about this morning, it was way too early for that kind of shit.'

'No, you were right. I have got a lousy track record with women, but there is something about Annie that makes me want to wrap her up in bubble wrap and keep her safe.'

Jake laughed. 'Oh well, good luck with that one, she isn't your typical girlie girl. Although I think even girls as tough as old boots dream about being swept off their feet. Just don't mess her around.' He went out into the courtyard and began the walk down the path, back to the car he'd left parked near the big wooden gates at the entrance to the woods.

Annie sauntered into the kitchen rubbing her eyes. 'Where's Jake?'

'He had to go and change his pants. He said that you drooled all over his crotch.' He winked at her and she smiled.

'Oops. Hi, how are you doing?'

'I'm fed up and starving. Jake gave me half a sandwich he'd made but I was too scared to look inside. It was edible though.'

Annie set about pulling pots and pans from the cupboard. 'I can cook pasta without too much trauma. Is that OK?'

'Perfect.' Will slumped onto the kitchen chair and relayed the day's events to Annie while she cooked.

***

He had a close call as he came up the last of the steep steps that led onto the main path through the woods. The biggest policeman he'd ever seen was walking along the path, talking loudly on his phone about what to have for tea. He stepped to the side behind a holly bush, not daring to breathe. After ten minutes he summoned up the courage to move. There weren't any more police around so he relaxed a little as he made his way along the path. When he reached the house he took his familiar route to the hay barn to watch. The woman was busy cooking in the kitchen, occasionally turning to speak to the man who was sitting at the table. She wasn't wearing the blue hat and when she turned her back to the window he saw the terrible wound running across the back of her head.

He shivered, feeling guilty for wanting to cause her any more pain than she had already suffered. This was more like his normal self, and for a moment he realised that he didn't want to be a killer. So what was he doing stalking some woman he didn't know? It was wrong; he knew it was. And then, like snapping his fingers, his mood changed and he no longer cared what was right or wrong.

He watched her take a bottle of wine from the fridge, pour out two glasses. He felt a prickle of hope. If they got drunk it would be easier to overcome them. The man would be the problem; if he went for him first and knocked him out cold he should be able to handle her. One hit over the head would wipe her out and that would be the pair of them sorted.

He began to hum some strange song from a long time ago, a song that he couldn't remember the words to but knew the music all the same.

***

247

They ate in silence and then carried their glasses through to sit on the sofa. Will groaned when he sank down into it, afraid he would go into a coma for the next twelve hours. Annie sat next to him. She could still smell his aftershave but very faintly. Mike never used it even though she bought him some every Christmas.

If anyone asked her how she felt right now she wouldn't be able to explain how, in such a short space of time, she was completely head over heels for Will.

He nudged her. 'Tell me to mind my own business but I can't stand it anymore. What did happen to your head?'

She sucked in her breath and took a moment to exhale. 'You mean you haven't heard the gossip around the station? I find that hard to believe. It must be the hot topic of the year.'

'Yes, you would think so but, surprisingly, it's been the best-kept secret of the year. I think Kav must have threatened everyone involved with working everyone's favourite council estate for the next ten years. I did try to quiz Sally but she only told me she had been sworn into the secret society of keeping Annie's secrets safe, and even good old Jake has contained himself, so it seems as if you have some very loyal friends and colleagues.'

Annie blinked away more tears; she was turning into a right softie. 'Well, seeing as how you asked me so nicely I'll start at the beginning.'

CHAPTER 25

Mike didn't want to stay in this place full of skanks any longer. He'd never been in a bail hostel before and didn't want to go in one ever again. Yes, he'd hit his wife over the head with a bottle but it had been her own fault and she'd broken his nose. It wasn't like it was the crime of the century, and if it wasn't for the fact that she was a copper he wouldn't even be in here. He went upstairs to his room, which was so tiny their garden shed at home was bigger. He filled his holdall with what few belongings he had and threw it out of the window onto the grass below. Then he walked downstairs and out of the front door, as if this was just the moment he was supposed to leave.

He wasn't familiar with Carlisle but he managed to find his way to the train station easily enough. He spent the journey from there to Lancaster in the toilet to avoid the guard. From Lancaster he scraped enough change together to buy a ticket, and an hour later was sitting in his garden shed waiting to make sure she wasn't at home or likely to come home soon. She would be staying with those two gay men whom she preferred spending time with than him. Well, he would show her he had changed. How after almost losing her he couldn't live without her, and he would treat her like she deserved. He was lonely without her and if he was lucky she might just drop the charges and they could start again, maybe go on a holiday abroad somewhere.

After a while he took the spare door key off the hook in the shed and was now sitting on his own sofa drinking a can of cheap beer, which contained more water than alcohol. When he'd opened the door the air had smelt stale so she hadn't been home for a while.

Because of the nature of the assault he wasn't even allowed in the same town as her. Why should he have to stay in a dump full of paedophiles? He didn't see why he should be the one banished from his own home. Once the staff at the bail hostel reported him missing the first place they would check would be here, but if he kept the lights off and the curtains closed he should be fine. They needed a good reason to knock a door down and he didn't think that his wife was that important.

As he walked into the kitchen he wondered who had cleaned up the blood; there had been a lot. He picked up the carrier bag of beer he'd left by the back door and carried it into the living room, for once not bothering to kick off his shoes. Instead he took pleasure in walking on the new carpet in them. None of that crap mattered now. He sat back on the sofa and sipped at the can of the worst lager he had ever tasted.

His eyes adjusted to the dark and he could see the outline of the frame that contained the photo of them on their first holiday to Hawaii. Getting up he walked across and picked it up, then smashed it against the corner of the fireplace. Fragments of glass crunched under his foot and he dropped the frame to the floor and used his foot to grind them into her smiling, happy face. Tiny cuts appeared on the picture and it wasn't long before she was nothing more than an outline. He wished the picture in his mind could be erased that easy.

Instantly he regretted it. If he wanted to win her back he would need to learn to control his temper. He couldn't stand the thought of her being single. The blokes in the station were like dogs on heat; he knew the reputation that coppers had. Taking his phone out of his pocket he dialled her number. It didn't even ring, just went straight to voicemail and her soft voice told him to leave a message. He paused, about to speak, but instead ended the call.

He grimaced as he drained the last drops of lager from the can, but still he reached for the plastic bag and pulled out another. Tonight he would sleep in his own bed for the first time in days. He dialled her number again and again until his finger was numb and his brain was sick of hearing her voice.

*

Annie went in the kitchen to get a glass of water; the wine was going straight to her head. Her phone lit up on the table, flashing to say she had a missed call. Curious to see who would phone so late her heart skipped a beat and bile rose in the back of her throat. There were seventeen missed calls from Mike. Her legs wobbled and she held onto the corner of the table to steady herself. She didn't see Will until she turned around.

'Annie what's the matter? You look as if you've seen a ghost.'

She slipped the phone into her pocket. 'Nothing. I just feel a bit queasy. Wine and painkillers aren't the best combination. I'll stick to water for the time being.'

Will believed her, which made her feel even worse. She didn't want to cause him any more bother than she already had, and she knew she would have to face up to Mike sooner or later, but she wanted to do it on her terms. Mike had terrified and bullied her so much in the last five years she was amazed she had stayed with him so long. She didn't need anyone fighting her battles, this was one she would take care of herself, one she should have taken care of before it got to this.

The phone began vibrating in her pocket so she took it out and switched it off. It never occurred to her exactly how Mike had got hold of his phone from the kitchen drawer, even though Jake had informed her that after he was arrested he was released to live at the bail hostel in Carlisle.

CHAPTER 26

He watched and waited until he could stand it no longer. The bolt had slid across the kitchen door over an hour ago and the lights had dimmed. It looked as if he would have to wait for another time. He was a cold-blooded killer and he didn't have a clue how to get into a locked house – not exactly a hard core criminal then. Creeping past the barn he decided to go home. It was probably the best idea he'd had in the last twelve hours. He was cold and kept shivering but his head was burning and hot to the touch; he must be coming down with something. Better to go home and dose himself up with some paracetamol and go to bed.

It was a beautiful night. The moon was full and bright, illuminating the path. In the distance he saw a flash of white dart between the trees and felt as if he wasn't alone. He shivered again. His mind was playing tricks on him, making him see things. There were no noises coming from the woods and it would be impossible for someone to walk through the undergrowth in the middle of the night without making a noise. He never passed anyone on the path which led back to the road and, not far from the car park, he pushed the dog lead in his pocket: there was no need for an excuse when everyone was tucked up in bed.

As he drove into his street his bedroom light shone through the crack in the curtains. He knew that he had turned it off when he'd left. Opening the front door slowly so as not to make a noise he stepped inside. A creak above his head told him everything he needed to know: his mother was in his bedroom.

Slipping off his shoes he crept up the stairs avoiding the third step from the top, it squeaked. He paused on the top step. All clear thought had left his mind and had been replaced by a swirling black mist. This time she had gone too far.

The door to his room was pulled to. His hands bunched into fists as he pushed it open. His mother turned to look at him, accusation in her eyes. In her bony fingers she clutched his photographs and it was obvious that she remembered the woman in them. His computer, which he had forgotten to shut down, jerked into life as his leg hit the corner of the desk. The image that appeared on-screen was one of the teenage slut with her legs wide open and wearing no knickers. His mother flinched, the disgust on her face taking him to the edge.

He strode to where she was standing, stretched out his arms and wrapped his fingers around her bony throat, squeezing as hard as he could. It didn't take much before her eyes began to bulge from their sockets. She clawed at his hands in a pitiful attempt to fight him off but she was too frail to make a difference; he was too strong. Her lips moved as she began to recite the Lord's Prayer and he felt the anger inside him swell. His entire body shaking, he squeezed so hard he felt the hyoid bone in her neck snap. Her body went limp and it was over. He'd finally done it, yet tears of frustration rolled down his cheeks and landed on the wrinkled cheeks of his dead mother. Her eyes were open and she stared at him; she was still watching him from the grave – what a mess. The black mist subsided and every bit of strength drained from his body. He laid her on his bed as his knees gave way and he sank to the floor, his eyes fixed onto the computer screen.

He sat like that for hours until the moon disappeared and the body next to him cooled. There was no going back. The police would come for him sooner or later. His hand had been forced and now he would have to make his move. Whatever it was that had taken over his soul wouldn't let him stop now. He stood and looked down at the woman who had wiped his tears as a child whenever he had hurt himself, and she had died terrified, knowing she had given birth to a monster.

He pushed the guilty thoughts away. He had no time for emotion now; he switched it off and didn't think he would ever turn it back on.

Bending over he picked her up in a clumsy fireman's lift. For a frail old woman she was a lot heavier than he'd expected. He managed to manoeuvre her down the stairs and through the narrow kitchen. He opened the utility room door; as he squeezed through a hollow sound echoed in the small room as her head hit the doorframe. He smiled, the chest freezer was the only place he could think of to put her for now. The miserable cow had never filled it with food. At least now he had a reason for it until he could figure out what to do with her.

He lifted the lid and pulled the sliding tray out from the top. He took hold of the packet of cheese and onion pies, which were the only things in there, and put them on the side. He then began to lower her inside, which was much harder than he had imagined. After ten minutes of struggling to get her to fit he finally shut the lid.

Humming to himself he picked up the pies and took them into the kitchen. Shutting the door he wedged a chair under the handle for good measure; he didn't want to risk her coming back to life and escaping. He turned the cooker on and put the pies on a tray and placed them inside. Sitting at the table he waited for them to cook. It was funny how much of an appetite he had considering he'd murdered his mother.

The house was truly silent for the first time in his life; he could get used to this. The timer on the cooker pinged and he took out his pies. Yes, he really should have done this a long time ago, it had improved the taste of his food no end. He finished a second pie then rummaged around in the kitchen drawer until he found some paracetamol. He swallowed four with a gulp of the whisky his mother kept hidden at the back of her baking cupboard. Then he took a black bin bag from the cupboard under the sink and went upstairs to strip his bed. He placed all the bedding into the black bag and re-made the bed with some fresh. He then picked up his stash of photos, which had fallen to the floor, and began sticking them onto his bedroom walls, saving the best for last.

A few days ago he had ordered a giant poster of his favourite picture of the woman from a website. He had hidden it on the top shelf of his wardrobe. He took it out, unrolled it, and stood on his bed to pin it to the ceiling. His work done, he lay on top of the bed fully clothed and stared at his pretty woman until the morning sun began to filter through the clouds and his breath slowed, until his eyes closed and he fell into a deep sleep.

CHAPTER 27

Mike woke up feeling refreshed for the first time since he'd been arrested. It's true what they say, there really is no place like home. He showered, shaved and got dressed, picking out the new shirt that Annie had bought him for Christmas, but which he hadn't worn, and his best jeans. He opened one of the many bottles of aftershave she had also bought him and sprayed himself. It was nice and he hoped that she would like it.

The first place he rang was the hospital, who told him she'd been discharged six days ago. Now he just had to find out where she was staying. He looked through the address book she kept by the phone. Her brother's number was written in red pen on the inside front cover. Of course, she had mentioned that he'd asked her to look after his animals. He picked up the house phone and dialled Ben's number and let it ring. On the tenth one she answered and he heard her voice, she sounded groggy. He put the phone down then swore at himself. What if she dialled 1471? She would know it was him; no one else would be ringing from their house. He could have kicked himself. He waited to see if the phone would ring but it didn't. Hopefully she was too tired to care about the caller, and if she did it didn't really matter because he was going to be paying her a visit very soon. He wanted to surprise her and show her how much of an effort he'd made.

*

Now she was awake Annie filled the kettle; she needed coffee. Will followed her into the kitchen.

'Did I tell you how sexy you look in those shorts.'

Her face flushed red and she turned away from him. He walked over and kissed her on the back of the head, below the line of staples. 'In fact, you are the sexiest woman that I've ever woken up next to and not had sex with.'

She pulled away from him, opening the fridge to take out the milk. 'Thanks Will. You mean I'm the only woman you've never had sex with. You know you don't have to lie all the time, it's fine. I know I'm not your usual cup of tea and you don't have to keep treating me like a damsel in distress. I'm not going to crack or shrivel up and die. You don't owe me anything and I don't want a babysitter. I can look after myself.'

Will took hold of her elbow and turned her to face him. Annie felt stupid after that little tantrum

259

but it needed to be said. She didn't get what the attraction was for him. He moved closer and bent his head towards hers, his lips brushed against her soft, pink mouth. Annie tried to pull away but couldn't – she didn't want to. Her insides felt as if they were on fire. Frantic hands began to pull at each other and she sighed as Will scooped her up into his arms and carried her back to the sofa and lay her down. He paused, unsure whether to continue, but she reached up her arms, wrapped them around his neck and drew him down towards her.

Annie looked to the window and screamed. There was a man's face pressed up against the glass. Will jumped up and ran to the kitchen door to see who was outside; there was no one around. He hadn't actually seen the face but Annie appeared behind him, all the colour drained from her face. She couldn't swear on it but she thought it looked an awful lot like Mike. But that couldn't be because he wasn't allowed to set foot in Barrow.

*

1st October 1888

I was so busy this morning sorting out my things that I did not sit down until mid-afternoon to take some tea and read the newspaper. I picked up *The Times* and the headline made me distraught.

There had been not one but two more murders in the East End of London. Both Elizabeth Stride and Catherine Eddowes had been found with their throats sliced open and other unspeakable atrocities committed against them. It read that the first victim's body was still warm when it was discovered and that the murderer must have been disturbed doing the dreadful deed. I felt my heart miss a beat when I read the next line; it described how a red handkerchief had been found across the victim's throat this time. Edward always insists on new handkerchiefs and I had packed into his trunk some brand new red ones I had bought from the haberdashery shop that had opened in town. I was horrified but continued to read. Because the killer had been disturbed this had resulted in the death of another unfortunate woman. She had been mutilated in a way that was not so dissimilar to an earlier victim.

I reminded myself that Edward would not be the only man in England to own some red handkerchiefs and he told me himself that London was a very big place. I should thank my lucky stars that I only have Edward to contend with and not some murderous madman. Although, selfishly, I have to admit that he is hideous enough. I still have the bruises and marks from his last visit home. I am counting the days until Alfie comes to rescue me – my very own knight in shining armour – and then we can begin a life filled with love and laughter instead of one filled with fear and loathing.

I cannot think of anything that these women may have done which would deserve such a dreadful fate. How sad and lonely to have lived such a desolate life and then die in such a way. I do not understand why but I feel as if I have a connection to these women. Maybe it is because I know all too well the hardships of a working class life. I feel as if there is something just out of my reach. I am going to church tomorrow and will light candles for each and every one of these four women, and while I am there I will pray for their souls as well as my own.

10th November 1888

The Times once again is full of stories of yet another horrific murder of an unfortunate woman: poor Mary Jane Kelly.

Edward did not come home this weekend as he promised when he finally telephoned me last week and I was grateful that he did not. I kept my voice polite because I do not want to arouse his suspicions that I am planning to leave. He telephoned again at lunchtime and I asked him what he thought about the murders, and he began to rant most vehemently about a man called George Lusk who had formed a vigilante committee and was in every newspaper. He told me that the man had nothing better to do and was probably trying to mask the fact that he was indeed the man responsible for these murders. It was all so very strange but I listened to him and just agreed when I thought he would expect me to.

When he finished ranting about Mr Lusk, he then informed me that I was ruining his life and that I was nothing more than a spoilt servant, and he wished he had let me rot in the cellar when he had the chance. My hands were trembling when I replaced the receiver back onto the cradle. Why does he behave like a madman? He is getting worse and I am so very grateful he is not coming home. I have decided that if I never see that man again it would not bother me in the slightest.

All day my mind was plagued by thoughts of Edward as well as the terrified faces of all the murdered women who had been so savagely attacked. I could not get them out of my head, they were etched into my memory. I went into the drawing room where I had left a pile of newspapers with all their dreadful stories on the sideboard. What was it that kept drawing me back to them again and again? I laid all the newspapers out onto the huge dining table and then took a pair of scissors from the drawer, and began to cut out each article and place them next to each other. There were so many it took me a long time but I cut and snipped until I was satisfied. There were pictures of the women both when they were alive and dead. I cut out the picture of a letter that had been sent into the Central News Agency. It had been named the Dear Boss Letter. In it the writer taunts the police. I put it next to the pictures of the victims.

I did not know why I held such a morbid fascination with these murders or what my reasoning was for doing this. The man responsible must be so very angry to be able to use such savagery on another human being; it would have to be someone who took great pleasure in inflicting pain upon another person.

An awful thought began to form in the back of my mind. I knew a man just like that all too well. He has the foulest of tempers and a terrible cruel streak, a man who has a penchant for brand new handkerchiefs. I knew I was being ridiculous but the thought would not leave my mind. I had to go to my writing desk to retrieve the diary I used to keep track of birthdays and important dates, and also Edward's visits home. I went through it and wrote down a list of the dates Edward had been home on a sheet of paper and then checked the dates of each murder. Edward had returned to London the day before each murder occurred and, to make it worse, the last few times he had been angry and upset with me when he had left.

A sickness began to fill my stomach which I could not blame on the baby growing inside me. For I think I know who this murderer is. I am too frightened to speak his name out loud. Not just for my own safety but that of everyone around me. I reread each article with a cold feeling of horror numbing my insides. It is quite clear the police have no idea what is happening nor who is responsible. There is so much written in all the newspapers about the murders it looks to me as if they are going around in circles. They have been inundated with so much information that it is preventing them from looking at it in a clear way.

I remembered the last time I went into his study and he pushed a piece of paper under the blotter on his desk and left the room, he was so angry with me. I looked at the letter again and studied the writing: it looked like Edward's. I had been so shocked by the contents I had not even considered the handwriting the first time I read it. I ran to the study and approached the desk, scared of what I might find. I lifted up the blotter and a sigh of relief escaped my lips when there was no letter under there. I then opened the drawers to look for his diary that I know he keeps for when he is at home. I could not find it in either of the two unlocked drawers, even though he normally keeps it in the first one, at hand should he need it. I pulled out the second one, which was full of blank sheets of writing paper. Then I took out each drawer from the desk in case it had fallen behind them and was trapped. I knelt down and bent my head and saw the familiar black book was fastened to the underside of the desk. With great care I removed it. I was so scared that Edward would walk in and catch me even though I know he is in London. After the last telephone conversation I would not be surprised if he turned up unannounced, but surely he would at least let Harold know, and I hope he would have the sense to forewarn me.

As I opened the book a single sheet of folded paper fluttered to the floor. I unfolded it to read the first line of the letter: 'Dear Boss'. I squirmed in horror and dropped it to the floor. I knew the only explanation for my husband to have a handwritten copy of a letter that had been sent to the newspaper was if he had written it himself: he wanted to taunt the police and the newspapers. Afraid now, I tucked it into the book and fastened it back where I had found it.

I still do not want to believe it to be true and I dare not tell anyone of my findings until I have firm proof of my beliefs. It could be a huge coincidence but in my heart I do not believe it. I made my decision that I would need to go down into the cellar and see exactly what it is he does down there for hours on end. If Edward is the monster all the newspapers are referring to as 'Jack the Ripper' then he must be stopped. I will need to make sure none of the staff are in when I go down there for I do not want them to be involved in this matter in any way. Oh, how I am terrified of that cellar and how I wish that Alfie was here to help me to be courageous and face whatever it is that I fear down there. I now realise that it is Edward who I have feared all along.

I went back to look at the grainy photographs of each woman. Polly Nichols drew my eye the most. When I look closely I can see the slightest resemblance between the two of us. Would I be so different if I did not have the luxury of beautiful

266

clothes and a maid to dress my hair each day? If I were dressed in my old maid's uniform I think there would be a striking resemblance. Does Edward truly hate me with so much passion that he would go out and take another woman's life because she reminded him of his wife? I fear the answer is yes, and if that is found to be true then those women have suffered the most awful fate imaginable because of me.

I could no longer look at the pictures, my hands were shaking so much. I went into the hall to telephone the police and lifted the receiver, but then I put it back down. What if it is all my overactive imagination? Edward would be arrested and publicly humiliated and then hanged, and I could not live with myself if it was not true no matter how much I dislike him. I felt so ill that I had to go and lie down for a while so I could gather my thoughts: my head was in a spin with it all. I went up the servants' stairs to my attic room. I did not want to look at the bedroom I shared with him. I took the cuttings with me in case any of the staff found them and, once inside, I pushed a chair against the handle just like I used to and cried myself to sleep.

11th November 1888

In my dreams I was chased through the dark cobbled streets of London by a man dressed in a black cloak and a deerstalker hat. He carried a long thin knife, which was dripping with blood. In the distance I could hear a telephone ringing and knew I should answer it in case it was Edward but I could not awaken from my nightmare. Instead I was running with bare feet as fast as I could. My pursuer was much faster and the gap between us was closing. I could feel the heat from his eyes burning through to the depths of my soul. I tripped and fell to the ground where I found myself entangled with the rotting corpse of Mary Kelly. My hands were warm and when I lifted them to my face they were stained bright red from her blood.

I must have screamed so loudly that I woke myself up. I blinked hard, feeling disorientated; it was daytime. The winter sun was shining through my tiny window and I was bathed in sweat. I felt exhausted, as if I had truly been running for my life through the streets of London. I got out of bed and stared at my dishevelled reflection in the cracked mirror above the washstand. My long dark hair was tangled and stuck to my face, my cheeks were flushed and the circles under my eyes were darker. I washed, dressed and went downstairs to a silent and empty house. Neither Cook nor Harold, or any of the others were anywhere to be seen. I remembered that Edward had given them all the day off. In a moment of rare kindness he had offered to pay for them all to go off on the steam train to Blackpool for the day. I remembered how excited Cook was and how I had laughed when she said how kind the master was – if only they knew the truth.

Today was the perfect day to go down into the cellar and find anything to prove that Edward is this fearful 'Jack'. My stomach ached just thinking about the cellar but I have little choice. I need to see what it is he does down there for hours. I hunted around in the pantry to find a candle and some matches. Then I went to the cellar door and stood in front of it. With trembling hands I reached out to touch the door, which was rough against my fingers. I had not been down there for a long time, but I thought about those poor women and realised that I had no choice. I slid the bolt across and pulled it but it wouldn't open, it had been locked. Frustrated, I knew that he would have the key with him; it was pointless searching for it and I did not know if there was a spare one. The only way I could gain entry was through one of the small windows at the back of the house. I would have to break one and get it repaired before Edward came home.

I opened the scullery door and went outside into the biting cold. I looked at the row of small windows; all of them were latched shut. I am small enough to climb through them, I just did not want to. Looking around for something to break the glass I spied the rockery which his Lordship had built. I prised one of the sandstone rocks away from the rest of them, grazing my fingers, but I was determined that I had to do this. It was heavy enough so I launched it at the window and shut my eyes. The noise of the glass shattering was so loud it echoed around the woods. I was thankful that there were only the birds to hear it. I wrapped my shawl around my hand and cleared the remaining pieces of jagged glass from the frame. I climbed through and found myself balancing on a rickety bookcase. It was so dark inside that I wanted to climb straight back out and go to the police, but the image of Mary Kelly in my dream last night would not let me. I owed it to her and the others to find out the truth about Edward and, if it was as bad as I expected, to put an end to it before he caused any more pain and suffering. I bent my legs and jumped down onto the floor. What little light came through the broken window gave me a small square of space to see. I took the candle and lit it with a match from my pocket. Standing there I looked around. The vast cellar was full of boxes and unused furniture. With the candle to light my way I cautiously ventured one step at a time through the cluttered dark space.

What was it that appealed so much to him down here? There must be something more than junk. As I got near the far wall the flame illuminated a small wooden door. A number of boxes were stacked against it along with two broken chairs. Intrigued, I set the candle down on one of the chairs and set about dragging the boxes away from the door. The only sound I could hear was the blood pounding in my brain. It masked the sound of the horse's heavy hooves trotting along the long drive through the woods to the front of the house. Breathing heavily I felt tired for I had not eaten since yesterday. When I had moved the boxes far enough away that I could open the door I was so focused on what this room contained that I never heard the front door open nor Edward call my name. I was scared of what may greet me on the other side. I tried the handle, not daring to believe it would turn and open so freely. Picking up the candle I stepped through the doorway into hell.

The walls were covered in the very same pictures and newspaper cuttings as the ones I had become obsessed with upstairs. In the far corner was a rocking chair. Next to that was a small table with Edward's deerstalker hat, which he wore to go hunting. I shivered at the thought. I turned away from the wall of horror and let out a small scream. There was a shelf on which a row of glass jars was placed. The jars were filled with a clear liquid but it was what was floating inside them that made me feel faint. I do not know much about human anatomy but I know enough to see that the things floating inside them belonged inside a person's body. My head began to feel muzzy and I had to tell myself that this was not the time or place to faint.

A loud noise as the cellar door opened cleared my head and my body became rigid. I could hear someone coming down the stairs into the darkness, and there was only one person I knew who had the key. I looked around for something to use to protect myself and saw one of Thomas's old garden spades leaning against the wall. I stepped towards it and then I heard his voice.

'Come out, come out wherever you are. I win because you are all alone.'

I knew this to be the absolute truth. This time there was no one around to hear me scream for help. The footsteps came closer until he was outside the door. My whole body trembled. I knew he was going to kill me and I did not want to die in this horrid room in the savage way that those other women had. I stepped closer to the spade, I had no idea what to do with it but it was something.

'Alice, I told you "no", I actually forbade you from coming down here and look what I have found: you in my room.'

I was so scared I could not find my voice to answer him back. Then he stepped into the doorway and blocked the only exit with his body. I knew that he would never let me leave and at that moment I realised that to protect the child inside me I would fight to the death. I would not be left down here where no person would ever find me. I was not about to become a memento of a sick and twisted man. I forced myself to take another step closer to the spade. As I made my decision the fear that I had felt moments ago left, and was replaced by a feeling of peace and calm. I thought about dear sweet Alfie and my baby: Edward was not taking me away from them. If the monster killed me then he would be free to continue killing innocent women and who would stop him? No other person in the whole of England knew of his dark secret, that Edward Heaton was the vilest man to ever walk the streets.

The voice that came from within me was strong and I did not recognise it. 'Edward, or would you prefer that I call you Jack? How could you? How could you murder those women? They never did anything to you.'

His laughter filled the room. 'Alice, that was the easy part. All I had to do was imagine they were you. My own mother preferred you, a servant, to her own flesh and blood. I loved the attention my mother would lavish on me until the day you arrived and stole her heart. All I ever wanted was her all to myself. Do you think I felt guilty when I pushed her down the stairs? A little, but then the feeling passed and I liked the fact that I was in control of who could live and die and that, Alice, is what started the fire within my soul. The first prostitute I killed cooled that fire for a little while but then it came back. Burning brighter and hotter than before. It is like a physical pain and it has taken me a while to finally realise that as long as you are alive I will never be able to extinguish it. I will tell you a little secret though: I like the killing far more than I ever anticipated. In fact, one could say that murder is becoming a bit of a bad habit.'

I watched his lips part and he smiled at me like a man gone mad. My hand was within reach of the spade but I had to be sure that I could move quick enough to hit him over the head with it. My palms were sticky with perspiration so I wiped them along my skirts. I had to stop him, he was insane.

'I thought you loved me, Edward. Am I so awful that you want me dead? Have you wanted nothing but to kill me for all the years I have known you? I never did anything to upset you and I loved your mother with all my heart. It is unfair for you to blame me for your own mistakes. You were the one who was so awful to me. She would never have noticed what a horrid person her son was if you had left me alone.'

He glared at me and I let out a loud sob and pretended to cry. I wanted him to think that I was weak and unable to defend myself. Like a predator he stepped closer and brought the hand out he had been hiding behind his back. The knife from my dream this morning glinted in the candlelight. I turned as if to try and run to the corner but my hands wrapped around the handle of the spade. I was terrified for I knew that my life depended upon this moment. If I died down here my soul would be doomed to wander this dark cellar for all eternity.

I screamed with fury and injustice and tightened my grip on the handle. Lifting it as high as I could I smashed it against the side of his head. Edward looked at me with surprise; he staggered to one side, dazed, so I drew back my arms and hit him again and again before he could lift that knife anywhere near to cut me. He fell to his knees and I hit him once more. I was not taking the chance he would get up. Finally he closed his eyes and collapsed onto the dirt floor, a steady flow of blood pouring from the wounds I had inflicted. I watched his chest rise and fall, praying that it would stop. I wanted his evil heart to stop pumping the blood around his body for ever. It slowed down and I did not dare to take my eyes away from him; the spade was poised in my hands ready to strike him should the need be. The knife had fallen from his grasp and was lying on the floor next to him. He didn't appear to be moving so I bent to pick it up.

His hand shot out and I screamed as he gripped my arm tight. I tried to pull away from him but he had such a tight hold on me it was impossible. His leg kicked my feet from underneath me and I fell onto the cold, damp earth. He sat astride me, his bodyweight making it difficult to breathe. Straddling me he took a handful of my hair and he pulled my head back so harshly that I could not see for the tears, which began to stream from my eyes. The pain was immense and I tensed as I waited for him to draw the knife along my throat. The very same knife that had killed so many women before me.

He bent close to my ear and whispered, 'Nice try.' His breath was hot against my cheek as he continued whispering what he was about to do to me into my ear.

It was then that I realised he did not have hold of the knife; for he was pulling my head back with one hand and the other was pressed hard into my ribcage. He continued to talk and I began to feel for the blade. He shifted his weight and my fingers stretched out a little more and found the cold hard handle of the knife. I gripped it hard. Edward bent down to kiss my forehead and say his goodbye and that was when I made my move. I lifted the knife and thrust it into his thigh, pushing with all my might until it was buried deep into his flesh. The grip on my hair released and he fell backwards, trying to free the blade, which was now embedded in his leg. As his weight lifted from my chest I crawled from underneath him.

Edward's hands were slick with the blood that was flowing from the wound, and he was unable to grasp the handle. I stood and watched as the colour drained from his face. He finally pulled the blade free and blood began to spurt from the wound in his leg. I stepped away so he could not reach out and grab me again.

He gasped. 'Alice.'

I stood my ground. He looked away from me and over to his wall of horror. A small smile played on his lips, his eyes began to glaze over, and that was how he died: lying on a cold earthen floor in a room he had made to house the memories of the murders he had committed. I stayed in the same place for what felt like hours unable to move. I had to make sure he was dead. He had got what he deserved and yet I still cried, and my heart filled with sorrow as I sank to the floor. When he had been still for a very long time and the pool of blood around him was huge I crawled over and shook his shoulder. He did not move but his body was still warm. I watched his chest to see if moved but it was still: he was dead. I had killed my husband and put an end to his reign of terror.

I stood on legs that did not want to hold my weight. I needed to go upstairs and call the police but something stopped me. My life would be finished. What would become of my baby? I would most likely hang for his murder and I would never know what it would be like to be with Alfie. Both of our lives would be ruined forever because of Edward.

It was then that the anger set in. I had never done anything to deserve this. I looked at the spade and decided I would bury him down here in his room full of trophies. He would be contained in this room for ever and I would be free to live the rest of my life, free to take care of those whom I love, and try to make amends for the evil deeds Edward has committed.

So I began to dig. I moved the rocking chair and table and started to do the hardest work I've ever done in my life. I was scared to turn my back on Edward, convinced that he may still wake up. By the time I had dug a hole big enough to drag his body into I was filthy, hot and smelt dreadful. It took what felt like forever. I looked at him. I did not want to touch his body so I had to summon up every ounce of strength that I possessed, for I had no other choice. I put my hands underneath his armpits and dragged him slowly to the edge of the hole. My arms were aching from the digging, and Edward was so heavy I felt as if I wanted to lie down and never wake up. But I would not let him win. With one final attempt I reached the edge of the shallow grave I had dug, and with a loud grunt I pushed with all my might and watched him tumble down into it. I kicked the wretched knife into the grave and it landed on his corpse. His black eyes were open, accusing me. I had to work quickly to cover his face so I would not have to look at it. He looked so handsome. Too young to be dead. I was overtaken by the pain of grief so immense I could not explain it.

When his body was covered in soil I pulled the chair and table back onto the uneven mound. I took one last look at the gallery of horror; no one would ever see this place or what it contained as long as I shall live. I did not want to touch the jars nor had I anywhere I could put them so I left them there. My body weary, I had suffered enough for one day, I walked from the room and shut the door. Dragging a bookcase over it I covered the doorway to the room that will haunt my dreams for the rest of my life. I then dragged the chairs and boxes over to make sure it was hidden from view if anyone should come down here snooping. I walked through the cellar and was no longer afraid. I knew it truly had been Edward all along who had scared me so. I made my way to the stairs. The door was open and the light which filtered through illuminated my way. With one final push I slammed the cellar door shut and smiled with relief to see he had left the key in the lock, for there was no way I could get it now if he had had it on him. I turned the key and pocketed it. I will hide it in a place that only I will ever know about.

I walked through the house to the drawing room and stared at my reflection in the mirror above the fireplace. It was hard to believe that it was me staring back for I looked so much older and very much like a street urchin. How I had aged in such a short space of time? My dress was filthy; covered in blood, soil and sweat. My hands were pitted with black soil underneath my fingernails and my hair was hanging loose around my face where Edward had pulled it almost from my scalp. I stopped at the sideboard where the decanters of whisky and brandy are kept on display and I uncorked the brandy, for the whisky was Edward's favourite, and then poured a large glass. I lifted my unsteady hands to my lips and then gulped. The first mouthful felt like a ball of flames rolling down my throat but it warmed my frozen body. I coughed and spluttered for a minute.

Once I had regained control of myself I picked up the crystal decanter and made my way to the stairs. The house was silent until the grandfather clock chimed the hour. I made the long ascent up to the safety of my attic room and shut the door behind me. I have no idea who or what I was hiding from; maybe I am hiding from myself. I just needed to be alone to grieve and to beg God for his forgiveness. I sat in front of the window, watching the rabbits play on the front lawn and I drank until I could not remember anything and the darkness took me to a peaceful slumber, where I dreamt that Alfie came to collect me and take me away from this house of horror.

CHAPTER 28

The persistent knocking on the door roused him from his sleep. It got louder and louder until he staggered off the bed and went downstairs to see who it was, hitting his shin on the hall table.

'I'm coming for Christ's Sake.' He saw Edith and Beryl, two of his mother's friends, peering through the glass in the front door. *Crap.* He opened it. 'Good afternoon, ladies, can I help you?'

Both women looked at each other, and then Edith stepped forward. 'Where's your mother? She knows we come around at three on a Wednesday.'

He grimaced at the thought of his mother's now frozen body stuffed into the freezer. 'Gone out.'

Beryl leant closer to him. '"Gone out"? What do you mean "gone out"? We've been coming here for the last ten years. The only time I've ever missed it was when my Frank passed away, God rest his soul, but I was back the next week. Your mother wouldn't just go out without letting one of us know.'

'You're right. I'm sorry, I meant she's gone away. My aunt in Blackpool took ill yesterday. She was rushed to hospital with a stroke and mother's gone to see her. I drove her to the station yesterday teatime to catch the five o'clock train. She said to apologise but she'll be back in a few days and will ring you then.'

Edith glared at him and he felt as if he had been interrogated by one of Hitler's henchmen. 'Make sure you tell her to ring me as soon as she's back. I'm very surprised she never rang me.'

They turned and walked back down the garden path, heads bent, muttering to one another. He shut the door and walked back into the hallway. He felt ill and barely made it to the sofa. He needed to think about what to do next. This murder business was exhausting. It wouldn't be long before the nosey old hags came back wanting to speak to his mother. He would only be able to put them off for a short time. He buried his head into his shaking hands.

**

Mike had pulled away from the tiny window, shocked by what he had just seen, but not that shocked he didn't realise he should be running as far away as possible. She had seen him but he didn't know if she had recognised him, it had been so brief. He was now sitting on a huge rock at the back of that creepy old house, panting like an old

282

man, he was so unfit. He hoped that they didn't come looking for him. He was disgusted with her but at the same time as horny as hell. She had never done anything like that with him. He was angry with them both and decided he would kill him, whoever he was; but that was probably a shite idea. He must be a copper but there was no uniform on the floor, so if he walked around in normal clothes then he must know how to handle himself because all the other pussies wore stab vests.

Mike walked into the woods. He didn't know what to do, and now he had seen his wife about to have sex with a total stranger he wanted her more than anything. He jumped when a man swinging a dog lead came around from the side of the house. The man whistled a couple of times.

'Lost your dog, mate?'

The man nodded. 'Every time I bring it up here it does a disappearing act.'

'Well, sorry to state the obvious, but why do you let it off the lead then?'

'Because it won't do its business while it's on the lead – likes a bit of freedom. I've a good mind to leave it but the wife would kill me if I went home without it.'

Mike sighed. 'Women, you can't live with them and you can't live without them.'

The stranger agreed and held out his hand. 'Henry.'

Mike grasped it and shook it up and down. 'Mike. Fed up and crapped on by my cheating wife.'

'Oh, that's really bad. How do you know she's cheating?'

Mike nodded in the direction of the farm. 'Because she's staying over there and I just caught her at it with some bloke.'

'Sorry to hear that. It's much worse than losing the dog. Although, to be honest, if it was my wife I'd be relieved she was going to make some other poor sod's life a misery. I think I'd shake his hand and wish him good luck.'

Mike smiled. It felt good to have someone to talk to. No need to tell his new friend that he'd knocked her senseless and almost killed her not long ago. 'I can help you look for your dog if you want.'

'That's very kind of you but I have an even better idea: if we don't find it we could go to the pub and get drunk, drown our sorrows.'

'Sounds like a perfect plan to me.'

They walked off into the woods looking for a nonexistent dog.

CHAPTER 29

Will came back inside. 'I couldn't see anyone. Are you sure you saw a face, it wasn't a shadow or something?'

She shook her head. It could have been a figment of her imagination or it could have been one of her newfound ghostly friends that seemed to keep appearing. 'It could have been. Maybe the excitement got too much for me.' She winked at him but the moment was lost.

'I'm sorry but I should really go. It's not that I'm rushing to get away, I just need to be there for the briefing.'

'It's fine. I know you do, Will. Someone has to put a stop to what's going on.' Annie was secretly relieved they hadn't managed to go any further. She knew she should be concentrating on herself and forgetting about men, but she couldn't help wondering if she would ever get the chance to make love to him, or whether fate would throw something in their way every time it got close.

'Come back when you get a chance. I'm missing you already.'

He ran his fingers through his hair then pulled her close and kissed her. She pushed him away.

'Get to work, Sergeant Ashworth. You're going to be late and I'll still be here when you finish, waiting for you.' She pushed him towards the door. 'Go and do some detecting.'

'Yes, boss. Don't go anywhere and keep the doors locked.'

She watched him jog over to his car and sighed. She was going to make the most of this even if it didn't last long. She deserved a little bit of happiness.

In the distance through the trees she saw two men. From behind one of them looked like Mike and she wondered if it was his face that had scared her minutes ago. She shut the door, locking it behind her. She was going to have a long soak in a hot bubble bath.

***

Henry was trying his best to keep calm but he was finding it hard. The woman at the farm was getting more exciting every day. He wasn't too keen on the thought of her having sex with the man, it tarnished his fantasy a bit. She had looked so helpless and innocent when all this time she had been the devil in disguise, trying to lead him astray. He smirked. No, that was definitely him and he was about to unleash all manner of hell.

After ten minutes of fruitless searching he turned to Mike who, underneath all the aftershave, smelt of stale alcohol. Henry sensed that he could be a big problem and one that needed taking care of. If he was hanging around it would spoil all of Henry's plans. What he needed to do was to dispose of him first. He had never killed a man before and Mike was a big guy, but he was pretty sure that if he got him drunk enough he would be able to take him out.

'Come on, this is a complete waste of time. Let's go to the pub.'

'I bet your dog is sitting outside your house wagging its tail by now anyway.'

Henry nodded in agreement and they headed off towards the pub a mile down the road.

***

Annie needed to know what had happened to Alice: when had she died and had she got to spend the rest of her life with Alfie? She had an urge to go to the cemetery and look for her grave. Annie hoped that she had finally been reunited with Alfie and lived to a ripe old age. She got dressed and shouted for Tess. If she couldn't walk around the woods she would take her to the cemetery with her.

It didn't take long to get there. She drove slowly past the crematorium from which a small number of people were trickling out, all wearing black and sniffling into handkerchiefs. She looked away, feeling guilty as if she had turned up to a wake wearing a low cut, bright red dress. She continued driving to where the really old graves were at the far end. The original chapel still stood at this end of the cemetery. It had high metal fencing around the outside but it was in an even worse state of disrepair than the mansion. An image of her wearing the most beautiful lace wedding dress flashed in front of her. She inhaled the sweet cloying smell of scented flowers which momentarily made her dizzy.

She stopped the car by a huge stone monument of an angel. She looked around at the others; this was the biggest one she could see. The smell disappeared when she got out of the car. Annie walked towards the seven-foot angel, which towered above the other graves in this part of the cemetery. It would have been beautiful once. Now it was covered in dark green moss and one of its wings was cracked and chipped. The angel was holding out its hands, beckoning Annie towards it. As she got closer a great feeling of sadness overwhelmed her. She blinked back tears as she read the inscription:

Here lies the blessed body of Alice Heaton. Wife of Edward, reunited with her son, James. Missed by all.

It was too much. Annie began to cry. Poor Alice had lost her son and she couldn't have made a new life with Alfie because, according to this, she was still married to Edward when she died. The grave was overgrown with no one to care for it. Annie felt devastated for the woman she had never met. Alice had stopped an evil killer on her own, she should be a local hero, not some long-forgotten person that nobody had ever heard of. She would come back and clean the grave and lay some fresh flowers on it. Annie would pay Alice the respect that she deserved. She bowed her head and said what she hoped was an acceptable prayer.

A cold hand squeezed her shoulder and she turned, expecting to see someone standing behind her; the place was deserted. She lifted her hand, placing it on top of the invisible one. The rain began to fall. It was time to go home and lockdown.

As she drove to the exit she glanced in the rear view mirror and saw a white figure disappear behind the monument. She needed to speak to Derek and try to find out what Alice so desperately wanted from her. She was glad that she wasn't mentally ill or brain-damaged but, then again, she wasn't sure if she liked this being able to see dead people stuff on top of everything else she had going on at the moment.

*****

The pub was empty, which made Henry a very happy man; the fewer people that saw him and Mike together the better. The barmaid was perched on a bar stool reading a magazine. She blew a huge bubble with her chewing gum and Henry frowned; he coughed.

'Yeah, what can I get you?' He looked to Mike who shrugged. He had sat on a stool at a table in the corner. 'Two pints of lager please.'

The barmaid still didn't look at Henry. She stood up, picked up two pint glasses and began pouring first one and then the other. He began drumming his fingers against the wooden bar. If there was one thing that really wound him up it was rudeness and she was just about the rudest person he had ever met.

She turned to look at him. 'Five pounds sixty please.'

He passed over a ten-pound note and held his hand out for his change. If she thought for one minute he was giving her a tip she could think again. He glared at her. *Did she just shiver?* He hoped she had. As he walked towards Mike she picked up the phone and began whispering to whoever was on the other end.

CHAPTER 30

Matt finished his second post mortem of the day and stripped his blood-covered gloves off and dropped them into the special waste bin; everyone else had gone for lunch. It seemed as if the whole town was dying. He had come into work this morning to three more bodies. His predecessor had never been one to rush anything, sometimes making relatives wait days before processing their loved ones. Matt didn't agree with that. The quicker he worked the faster the families could get the funeral arrangements sorted out. He had made a promise to himself when he took over as head pathologist for the South Lakes area that he would process his clients quickly, and as professionally as the circumstances allowed. Six months ago he had applied to go on the register of forensic pathologists for the Home Office, because sometimes it took days before one would be available to come down from the cities to carry out this work. It added to his caseload but he loved his job and was a workaholic.

He stared at the bank of fridges thinking about Emma Harvey. She wouldn't be out of here as fast as he would have liked. After stripping off his scrubs he made his way to the office. He had a mini fridge in there especially for his cans of diet Vimto and his cheese and onion sarnies. Taking out the plastic Chinese carton containing his sandwiches and a can of pop, he sat down at his desk. He began rifling through the pile of post on his desk, weeding out the junk mail from the ones that actually bore some importance.

His computer pinged and he opened up his emails. Giving them a cursory glance he leant forward: the address on the latest one was from a colleague who worked at the newly formed Institute for Forensic Science. The wound on Emma's neck had particles of blood and DNA along the cut and they were showing as a match for Jenna White's. He read further down the report, which said there were minute traces of dried blood found inside the wound. These had been run through the database. They were so old and deteriorated there was no match. His colleague hazarded a guess that those traces of blood were pre-Chernobyl, which meant that the sample had been somewhere that hadn't been exposed to any of the particles which could be found almost everywhere after the nuclear plant had a catastrophic accident in 1986, and they were probably a whole lot older than that. Matt scratched his head and stuffed the rest of his sandwich into his mouth. He put his feet on the desk and began to think about the possibilities of what it meant.

*

As Will arrived at the station he had a hunch that today was the day things were going to get better. Hopefully they would find some link which would help to locate Jenna. He walked past the community office to a lot of high-pitched squealing and laughter. Turning around he walked in to see what was happening.

'Now then, ladies, do you know that this is a place of work and it's against staff rules to be happy while carrying out your duties?'

Four faces smiled back at him. 'Morning, Will.'

'Come on then, what has tickled you lot so early in the morning?'

Sally stood up and walked over to switch the kettle on. 'It's disgusting, you wouldn't want to know, I didn't want to.'

He watched her open the fridge and begin to make him a coffee and for the first time ever he felt bad.

'Right then, you go and sit down. I'm going to make you all the best coffee you've ever had.'

Liz turned to look at him. 'Are you feeling OK, Will? Did you hit your head on the way in?'

He winked at her. 'Cheeky. I'll be back in a minute. Don't go anywhere.' He went off to his office to get the ground coffee and unused cafetière out of his bottom drawer. It was his Secret Santa gift last Christmas. He strode back around to the community office.

Sally looked at him. 'We were talking about our exciting sex lives, well, more the lack of it. Anyway why are you in such a good mood? Are you after something because we did loads of house to house for you yesterday? It took me twenty minutes to get the cow shit off my boots when I got home.'

Will gasped and clutched at his heart, doing his best to look hurt. 'Why don't you just stick the knife right in, go on push it harder? Do you lot honestly think I'm only nice when I want something?'

They all looked at each other and nodded.

He shook his head as he spooned the last of the coffee into the pot. 'I'm hurt. You know how much I adore you all and I never agree with anyone who gives you a hard time.'

Sally wandered over and squeezed his arm. 'Sorry, Will, we know you do and we love you really.'

He squeezed her arm back. 'I forgive you.'

He was the first one in the CID office and the pictures of Jenna and Emma both stared back at him from the whiteboard: Jenna, still breathing and full of life; Emma's lifeless white face, her lips tinged blue and a huge gash across her throat, her eyes glazed over. *I promise I'm going to catch him.* He walked closer to see if anything new had been added to the lists below each girl. The phone began ringing but he didn't answer it, then it stopped and started again.

'Good morning. CID. Will Ashworth speaking.'

The voice on the other end paused. 'Good morning, Detective Sergeant. It's Andrew Marshall. I'm taking over as the DCI and I've been reviewing our two cases. I just wanted to catch up with you and see how it's going.'

Will sat down. He had struggled running the cases for the few days while his boss had been off sick, but he knew they would send someone in to take over. It was all far too high profile to leave to him and his team.

'To be honest, boss, it's not going that well. We have a few leads as far as the murder victim Emma Harvey is concerned but nothing concrete. We also have a last confirmed sighting of Jenna White near to Abbey Wood, but as you will be aware it's a huge area to cover and we have search teams out again this morning.'

'Good. I take it we are assuming these cases are linked. When you say we have a few leads does one of them include a name for the offender?'

Will blew out his cheeks. 'No, we don't. It doesn't make sense at all: abducting one girl and then killing another. Leaving the body on show is quite unusual behaviour, but then again I can't say I've had much experience in this kind of situation.'

'Have you thought about consulting an external advisor, you know, a psychological profiler? If not, I have a very good friend in Manchester who would be willing to come down and take a look. Obviously it's your shout and I don't want to step on anyone's toes.'

Will tried hard to contain his excitement. 'Sir, I think it would be wonderful. If you could ask them to come down as soon as possible, because I'm afraid that time's running out for Jenna and the chances of finding her alive are very slim. I'll take all the help I can get.'

'Good, that's what I like to hear. No point being too proud to admit you could do with a helping hand, is there? Not when lives are at risk. I'll arrange it now. I spoke to her last night so she is aware and she should be with you by mid-afternoon. Her name is Grace Marshall. I'll tell her to report to the front desk.'

'Thank you, sir, I appreciate it.'

The voice on the other end erupted into a coughing fit and put the phone down. Will had thought today would be the day and he was right. He thought about how perfect it almost was with Annie yesterday and he was still grinning when Stu walked in, followed by Laura.

'Morning. What do you want: tea or coffee?'

They did a double take, confused. Will left to go and wash his coffee pot. Stu leant over and whispered in Laura's ear. 'He got a shag last night, that's why he's in such a good mood. I'll bet you a fiver.'

Laura glared at Stu and hissed. 'Not everything revolves around getting your end away, Stu. It's possible to be in a good mood for things other than sex.'

'I'm telling you when you're a bloke the only thing that puts you in a really good mood is having great sex, well, any sex, or watching re-runs of Doctor Who.'

'I worry about you. I don't know what's worse, the fact that now I know when you're in a good mood that you and Debs have been at it like rabbits, or that someone bought you the Doctor Who box set.'

'I wonder who it was then. First one to get it out of him gets a cream cake from that new bakery down the street.'

Laura considered it for a moment. 'You're off your head, Stu, but I'll do anything for a cream cake.'

Will walked back in. 'What are you two conspiring about?'

Laura smiled sweetly. 'Nothing in particular, just Stu's twisted take on life. Stu, why don't you tell Will what you just told me?'

Stu turned a vivid shade of red and spluttered, 'I was just explaining to Laura how great it is when you get a shag and how much it puts you in a good mood. Well, not just you, I more meant us, well, all men on the whole.'

Will scrunched up his face, trying to work out was Stu was saying, as Jake walked into the office.

'Ooh, serious conversation, what's up?'

Stu looked as if he wanted the floor to swallow him whole and Laura started to laugh.

'You lot are unbelievable, I'd rather have a bar of chocolate and a cup of coffee.'

The phone on Will's desk began to ring just as he'd shoved a slice of cake in his mouth.

Laura stepped forward. 'I suppose you want me to answer that?'

He gave Laura the thumbs up and she picked it up. Will got a whiff of her perfume and it smelt good.

'Good morning, CID, hang on he's here now that he's finished stuffing his face with Mars bar cake. I'll put him on.'

Will didn't know what was the matter with her lately. She was snappy and miserable and she looked like she'd lost a lot of weight. He would ask Stu later. Maybe she had boyfriend trouble although he wasn't even sure if she had one.

'Will speaking.'

'Hi, it's me, Matt. I just got some results back that were fast-tracked through to the lab from the wound on Emma Harvey's throat.'

'I'm listening.'

'The swabs showed two separate blood samples as well as our victim's. I'm afraid one is a match for Jenna White.'

'Shit.'

Everyone in the office stopped what they were doing to listen to Will's side of the conversation.

298

'I'm afraid so. Our suspect used a sharp knife to slit her throat. The only way to explain Jenna's blood being on that knife is that he used it to cut her before he used it on Emma.'

'You're sure about that? There's no chance the samples could have been contaminated or anything?' Will regretted the words as soon as he said them and Matt snapped back at him.

'Are you saying I'm an idiot who can't do his job properly?'

Will lowered his voice. 'No, I'm kind of wishing for Jenna White's sake that you're an idiot who can't do his job.'

The anger left Matt's voice. 'This is where it gets strange. The other sample is really old and there are only minute specks, but it's there, and a completely different blood type to the others. It looks like our killer favours antique knives as his weapon of choice and it looks like whoever owned it last time didn't clean it very well. There is some strange shit going on.'

Will was busy scribbling notes. 'Thanks, Matt.' He put down the phone and stood up. 'I take it you all got the gist of that conversation. The knife used to kill Emma had Jenna White's blood on it and another sample, which was really old. So while it's possible Jenna is lying somewhere injured we now have a firm connection between Jenna's abductor and Emma's killer. I am assuming the worst that Jenna was killed first. Laura, I want you to contact the White's Family Liaison Officer. Tell them to prepare the Whites for the worst. Not a word of this to the press, they are already printing utter bollocks and scaring everyone in a ten-mile radius, so let's not give them anything to go on. Stu, I want you to go around the secondhand shops and antique dealers, see if anyone has sold an old knife lately.' He glanced at Jenna's picture and clenched his knuckles into tight fists then left the room; he needed some air.

CHAPTER 31

Henry stopped the car outside his house. He looked at Mike who was leant over and slurring his words.

'Nice house, I always wanted a house with a garage but she wanted a conservatory. I think if I'd had a garage things would have been a lot different.'

Henry frowned, not wanting to enquire as to how a garage would make any difference to someone's marriage. But he nodded as if he agreed. Four pints of Stella had topped up whatever the loser had been drinking the night before. He had listened to him ramble on for the last hour, plying him with drink because Henry didn't know if he could overpower Mike unless he was drunk. The tales he had told him had made him wonder just how violent the man was, and he felt sorry for the woman who was married to him. He couldn't afford to have him turning up at the farm and spoiling everything so he'd come up with a plan.

Henry stepped out of the car and made his way down the garden path with Mike following behind.

He opened the door, expecting to be greeted by his mother's voice; instead he was greeted by silence. Mike tripped over the door and pushed into his back.

'Right, my man, where is that Jack Daniel's you were on about? I need to pee first though.'

Henry pointed up the stairs. 'Straight up, second door on the right.'

Mike walked up the stairs and Henry went into the kitchen. He could hear him moving around in the bathroom above him and took the hammer from out of the drawer. He thought about using the knife but it didn't seem right: that was for his girls. A couple of smacks over the head with the hammer would do the trick. He hadn't killed anyone with a hammer before so it was basically guesswork. His fingers closed around the shaft. The idiot upstairs was taking far too long; he hoped he wasn't being sick, Henry hated sick. He decided to go upstairs and see what he was doing.

Mike came out of the bathroom and fell against a door across the hall. As it opened so did his mouth. Staring back at him from the wall were lots of pictures: he knew that smile, he knew those dimples. He stepped inside the room, his eyes following a line of pictures up to the ceiling, and it was then that his legs began to tremble and he lifted his hand to his mouth. On the ceiling above the bed was a life-size picture of Annie, her black curly hair peeking out from underneath the blue woollen hat she wore when it was raining.

Mike's beer-soaked brain was trying to make sense of what was going on when the hammer connected with the back of his head. The first blow knocked him to his knees and the room began to swim. Mike winced at the taste of the stale lager and bile, which filled his mouth. The second blow was so hard it shattered his skull and a shard of it embedded itself into his brain, killing him instantly.

***

At the exact moment of Mike's death Annie felt a cold shiver go down her spine. She was driving back to the farm and trying to act as if everything was normal when really it was getting worse by the minute. She didn't know what to do.

When she got back she went straight into the house and locked up. The sky outside was growing darker, it looked as if another shower was on its way. Annie took out her phone and stood in the middle of the kitchen where she sometimes got a signal if she was lucky. She rang Will but it went straight to voicemail. She tried Derek but his was the same. She needed to do something so she began cleaning the kitchen, anything to keep her mind occupied. She contemplated ringing Jake but he was such a drama queen he would send a patrol car flying up to make sure she was OK, and technically she was, she just didn't know what was going on.

*

As Will walked past the sergeant's office he heard Kav call his name. 'Will, I think you should know, I've just taken a call from Carlisle bail hostel. Mike Graham left yesterday and hasn't been seen since. Jake informed me that you have taken it upon yourself to keep an eye on our Annie, which is very gentlemanly of you, so I thought you should know. Do you want me to tell her or will you?'

'Jesus. They only just decide to tell us this now, a day later. I'll ring her. Leave it with me.'

'I don't think he'd have the balls to go near her, not after his last ordeal before he got to custody. Mind you, he was a bit of a fighter, but no match for me and Jake.'

'I hope you're right Kav, I really do.'

Will left the station. He needed to go home and shower before the profiler arrived. He tried Annie again but still no joy so he left her a message. He really wanted to speak to her and hear her voice and he would keep trying.

***

Henry found it mildly disturbing that death didn't bother him anymore. He added the body count up on his fingers and he was up to four; five once he had the woman from the farm. He knew she would be the challenge. There was no way she would go down without a fight, not like the others. For some reason he knew that she was the one that could bring it all tumbling down, and somewhere inside him a tiny part wanted her to. He hadn't wanted any of this in the first place but he wasn't strong enough to fight against whatever it was that was driving him.

He looked down at the body on his bedroom floor. It didn't matter anymore, there was no point in hiding it. If by some miracle he killed the woman without getting caught he would think about what to do with the mounting number of bodies in his house.

He was washing the blood from his hands when the doorbell rang, followed by a loud *thud, thud* on the door. He froze and waited a minute, but whoever it was banged even harder on the glass. He stripped off his bloodstained shirt and dropped it into the washing basket then, splashing cold water over his hair and face he grabbed a towel and jogged down the stairs. Through the glass in the door he could see the outline of a huge police officer. The fluorescent yellow jacket filled the doorway. *It's over, Henry.*

Forcing himself to breathe slowly he opened the door. 'Sorry, officer, I was just getting out of the shower. Is there anything wrong?'

'Sorry to disturb you, sir, we had a call from a – ' He looked down at the name in his notebook ' – a Mrs Edith Wright. She is concerned about the welfare of your mother. She claims she hasn't seen her for a couple of days and it's very unlike her.'

'I'm sorry, officer, you've been misled and your time wasted. My aunt, who lives in Blackpool, was rushed to hospital. She has no family of her own so my mother has gone to visit her. I drove her to the station myself. Would you like to come in while I ring her and you can speak to her? But whatever you do don't tell her I haven't hoovered or polished.' He winked at Jake.

'Have you spoken to her today, sir?'

'About an hour ago. She rang to say she would be staying on a few more days.'

'That's fine. As long as you're not worried about her it's not a problem. Would you mind signing my notebook to say I've spoken with you and you're happy with everything?'

Henry turned to the side to wipe the sweat from the palm of his hand and noticed his mother's handbag on the floor by the side of the chair. His palms began to sweat even more and his stomach clenched so hard he thought he was going to throw up.

The copper looked at him. 'Everything all right? You don't look very well?'

Henry shook his head, signed the book and handed it back. 'Too much beer and a dodgy curry.'

Jake gave him a look of sympathy. 'Thanks for your time. I'll let Mrs Wright know that everything's fine. Take care.'

Henry stayed at the door to make sure he walked out of the gate and got back into the police car. He waved at him and shut the front door. He made it to the living room then fell onto the sofa, shutting his eyes as the room began to spin before it all went black.

CHAPTER 32

Jake drove back to the station. It was almost finishing time. That guy had been a bit odd but he wasn't going to argue with him. He should know the whereabouts of his own mother and he didn't seem a bit concerned. Jake updated the control room operator that everything was in order and that he'd update the informant himself. He went into the parade room and sat at the last empty desk. Picking up the phone he rang the number on the log and told the woman who called it in what he had found out.

'Did you go inside and check the house, officer?'

'No, I didn't. I believe that Mrs Smith's son had no reason to lie to me, therefore I had insufficient grounds to enter the property.'

'Well, young man, I don't know any woman who would leave town without their handbag. I saw it there when I peered through the window. It's still in the same place it was on Wednesday.'

Jake thought she had a point but it was five minutes past his finishing time and women normally had a lot more than one handbag. Plus Alex was cooking and they were going to open the expensive bottle of wine Annie had bought him for his birthday.

'Look, Mrs Wright, if you don't get in touch with your friend by tomorrow night I will go back and search the house myself.'

This calmed her down a little. 'Thank you, but I'm telling you something isn't right with this lot. I can feel it in my bones.'

Jake agreed with her.

*

Will made it back to the station in record time. Smelling of coffee and Chanel aftershave, he ignored the wolf whistle from Claire and Sally who were on their way out of the back yard, and dashed inside. He didn't want to miss the arrival of the profiler. As he walked past the front office the clerk, who he'd never seen before, asked him if he knew who DS Ashworth was. She blushed when he said 'me' and grinned.

'There's a Grace Marshall waiting for you.'

For the first time in a couple of days Annie faded from his mind as he thought about catching Emma Harvey's killer and bringing Jenna White home. He opened the door onto a bustling reception area, which was full of people that could have quite easily made the guest list for Jeremy Kyle. They all turned to look at him, hoping it was their name he was going to shout so they wouldn't be sitting there for hours. He surveyed the faces and settled on the twenty-something woman holding a briefcase on her lap: she was either Grace Marshall or someone's brief. He said her name and she moved so fast he almost missed it. She was obviously glad to be moving away from the kid next to her who was scratching at her head so much Will was surprised she still had some hair.

Grace followed him through the door, and once it had closed and the members of public couldn't hear him he spoke. 'It's a good job I didn't take too long or you would have got yourself a head full of nits.'

She tried to frown but smiled instead. 'Well, DS Ashworth, I would have passed them onto you for making me wait so long.'

He laughed and led the way around to his office. 'Welcome to hell, well sort of, it's not that bad when girls are not being murdered or going missing.'

'I was born and bred here, sergeant. I left to go to University then got a job working in a psychiatric unit in Salford with some of the more – how should I put it? – undesirable members of the public.'

Will held out his hand. 'Let's call a truce. I'm so glad you were able to come at such short notice. Things are happening which are out of our control and we need all the help we can get. There is one condition, though. Please call me Will: I hate all the DS crap.'

She held out her hand and shook his with the tightest grip he'd ever felt from a woman. They grinned at each other.

'Phew, I'm glad that's over with. Come on, I'll sort you out a desk and anything else that you might need. In fact, I can go one better than that, I can give you your own personal assistant.' He opened the office door and watched everyone stare at the new girl. Laura smiled at them then bent her head to continue typing. Will looked at Stu, who was staring at Grace with an awestruck expression. *Bugger, I can't let Stu work with her, he'll drool all over her.* He guided her over to his desk making the introductions as he went around the office. He paused when he got to Laura.

'Grace, Laura will assist you with anything you need if I get called away.'

Laura blushed but didn't seem too bothered by the babysitting duty.

Grace walked over to the whiteboards, opening her briefcase to search for a pen and notepad.

'I'll be fine for a couple of hours. I need to see everything you have up to now: case files, pictures, pathology reports, the whole lot. And then I'll need to go and visit the crime scenes.'

'Laura will sort that out for you. I just need to make a couple of calls.' He needed to see who he could send to keep an eye on Annie. She might think she was tough enough but he didn't think she was a match for the mad man of the Abbey.

311

CHAPTER 33

Henry found himself walking along the path to the woods. He couldn't remember how he had got this far but he headed towards the farmhouse. As he got close to the gate he could hear vacuuming inside so he jogged over to the hay barn and walked in, taking up his position in front of the window. He could see her flitting from room to room having a cleaning frenzy. It was tempting to go and knock on the door but he didn't think she would open it for him. He supposed he could try the missing dog routine one last time but if she phoned the police it would be over before it began.

While he sat dithering over what to do another man strolled up towards the gate. He hadn't seen this one before. How many men can one woman know? He watched, puzzled, as to who this one could be. He didn't know if he had the strength for many more murders in him, he was kind of all murdered out.

She had plenty of male friends but he hadn't seen any of the female kind. He wondered if she was lonely. He'd spent most of his life on his own and look where it had got him. The sound of the kitchen door being unbolted pushed all thoughts from his head. He watched as the man entered the house. He was quite old and he didn't think he would be much trouble in a fight. He listened for the sound of the bolt going across and smiled when it didn't. That was a very good sign: exactly what he had been waiting for. He stood and stretched. Five minutes and it would be chaos over there.

***

Annie was glad Derek was here. She felt like she was on the verge of breaking down, she was so worn out with it all.

'I got your message and came straight here. I've been thinking about the best way to get to the bottom of this, and the only thing I can think of is doing a séance in the house. That way I can get a feel for the place, ask some questions and hopefully get some answers. What do you think?'

Her mouth went dry and she couldn't get her tongue to move. 'I don't think I really want to. I don't like the thought of messing with anything like that, Derek, but do I have much choice?'

He peered outside. It was mid-afternoon and if the rain didn't start again it would be light for a couple of hours yet. Derek didn't want to be in that house in the dark either. 'No. I think we should do it now.'

Annie grabbed her jacket and the key for the house off the hook. 'Come on, if I think about it too hard I'll chicken out. Is there anything we need like a cross, holy water or maybe a couple of silver bullets?'

'A couple of cloves of garlic if you have them.'

The colour drained from her face, which stopped Derek from laughing out loud. 'I'm sorry, Annie, I was joking. I didn't realise you were being serious.'

She let out a huge sigh of relief. 'Phew, good, because I'm proper scared, my hands are shaking.'

He smiled and patted her arm. 'Well, then you're in luck because as it goes I'm one of the best in the business. We'll get this sorted out and put those ghosts to rest and have you back in time for tea. How does that sound?'

'Bloody wonderful, Derek. In fact, it would be amazing.'

She pulled her trainers on her feet just in case she needed to run.

'Ready when you are. I always did have a secret fantasy about being a Ghostbuster.' She winked at him but her voice trembled. Stepping outside she was followed by Derek who was followed by Tess. Annie ushered Tess back inside and locked up. Should she phone Will? She decided not to. It was time to take control of her life.

They set off towards the old house.

***

Henry had known his patience would pay off. He watched as they headed into the woods in the direction of the house. Perfect. He couldn't ask for anything more. He would give them a head start and follow them. The woods were so peaceful not even a bird was chirping. Thank God it wasn't the school holidays because then they would be full of screaming kids.

***

Edith could not settle. It wasn't right. In all the years she had been friends with Gladys she had never even mentioned having a sister, she may have said a distant relative but not a sister. Henry had looked different as well. When he opened the door his appearance had shocked her. He hadn't shaved for days and there were dark circles under his even darker eyes. Gladys had said she was worried about him and she could understand why.

Turning off her television Edith stood up. As she stretched the bones in her knees creaked. Shuffling over to the phone she rang Gladys again: it rang and rang, Edith knew she couldn't stand back and not do anything. Not when her friend might need her help. She knew where the spare key for Gladys's house was hidden so she phoned a taxi. She would ask the driver to wait for her while she checked the house. Never one to shy away from a fight in her younger days she knew that even if

315

Henry was inside she was going in regardless. What was the worst that could happen? He might call the police, but tough. If all policemen were as nice as the one she spoke to earlier it would brighten up her day.

CHAPTER 34

As they approached the entrance of the house Annie felt her body begin to buzz. It was as if there were some electrical current running through it.

Derek sensed her sudden wariness and reached out for her hand. 'It's OK, you are being bombarded with the memories of this place. Whoever lived here feels a strong connection with you. She trusts you and is trying to tell you something, although I don't understand why she has waited so long to start haunting someone.'

Annie shivered. She knew why. It all had something to do with the diary and the terrible secrets it revealed. She wanted to tell him about the diary and what she knew but she couldn't physically speak, something was stopping her.

Derek looked her in the eye. 'You will be fine my dear.'

She took the key from her jeans pocket, knowing that regardless of whether she was OK or not she had to go through with it for the sake of her sanity.

317

Derek stared at her. She looked different. Her face had taken on a slightly rounder shape and her eyes were focused on something that only she could see. He followed her as she pushed the front door open and stepped inside. The energy running through the house was so strong it made the hairs on the back of his neck prickle. Annie began humming and carried on walking through the big hall to the corridor.

'Come on.' She gave him a gentle smile, but it wasn't her usual one. They entered the kitchen; the smell of the damp and mould from the years of being empty turned his stomach.

Annie sniffed. 'Cook makes the best shortbread in the whole town and I'm so hungry.'

Derek took hold of her hand and led her to sit on the windowsill. 'Is Cook here now, Annie? What do you see?'

'I see Cook baking. There are trays of biscuits on the side ready for afternoon tea. If I'm good and get my chores done she will let me have one with a glass of milk. I must work hard and make sure they are all done before Edward comes to disturb me.'

The temperature in the room had dropped so much that when Derek spoke he could see clouds of his breath in front of him. 'Can you tell me about Edward. Why does he disrupt you, Annie?'

'Alice, my name is Alice, silly. You should stop calling me Annie, that is another girl. Edward is her ladyship's son and he doesn't like me very much. In fact, he hates me and I don't want to be here when he comes back because he is so mean to me.'

'Alice, how old are you?'

'I'm seventeen.'

'Alice, why do you keep talking to Annie? What is it that you want from her?'

'I think it is because she looks like me and I need her to help me: Edward has come back. He killed those poor women in London, you know: slaughtered and butchered them like animals and now he is back. I hear his voice whispering and his footsteps in the cellar. He wants blood, that is all he ever wanted.'

Derek was so absorbed in his conversation with Alice's spirit he never heard the footsteps creeping up behind him.

Annie's expression froze as she gasped, 'Edward.'

Derek turned to see a man standing behind him, a hammer in his hand. He swung towards Derek, hitting him on the head; his glasses fell off and he lost his balance. The hammer hit for a second time and Derek collapsed. Annie stood up from the windowsill and slipped in a pool of blood which was spilling from the side of Derek's head. As she felt the world turn black a pair of rough hands grabbed her.

'Well, well, it's been a long time, Alice. I never thought I would see you again.'

*

Edith got out of the taxi and stared at the house. It was in darkness. It was a relief that Henry was out, it made her feel a lot better about what she was about to do. She knocked on the driver's window.

'You wait there, young man. Keep the meter running. I don't want you to go dashing off and leaving me.' She walked up the garden path to the front door and looked for the plant pot with the shrivelled lavender plant inside. She bent down and lifted it up, and sure enough there in the plastic moneybag was the spare key. Her hands began to shake as she tried to put it into the lock. She had a bad feeling about this and was terrified about what she might find. But she had to do it for Gladys's sake: her friend may need her help.

As she stepped inside a strong smell like metal made her lift her hand to her nose. Her husband had been a sheet-metal worker in the shipyard, and the air smelt like his overalls did when he would bring them home every Friday to be washed. She went straight into the living room and picked up Gladys's handbag. Inside were her glasses, purse, phone and diary: all the things you wouldn't leave behind if you had to go away suddenly.

She put the bag down and went back into the hallway, shouting up the stairs, 'Gladys, it's Ethel. Are you there, love?' She was greeted by silence. Not wanting to risk going upstairs in the fading light she felt for the light switch and her hand touched something wet and sticky. As she bathed the hall with light she looked down at her fingers: they were covered in a dark red liquid. Lifting them to her nose she balked: blood.

Horrified, she stumbled outside to the waiting taxi. 'You have to phone the police, please tell them something bad has happened. There is blood on the light switch.'

The driver looked at her like she was a senile old bat. 'Now then, love, how do you know something bad has happened, did you see anything?'

Edith held up her blood-soaked fingers. 'Because, young man, I know what blood is. Now please call the police.'

He picked up his radio handset and asked the operator to get the police. Then he turned his meter off and muttered 'bollocks' under his breath.

Edith didn't know what to do for the best so she leaned against the car and waited.

*

Jake printed off the statement for a job he'd attended earlier, and was about to book off an hour later than he should have when a 999 shout came in for the house he'd attended earlier. He watched as the parade room emptied. He put his radio and CS gas into his locker and walked into Kav's office.

'Erm, Sarge, I went to a job at that address earlier and spoke to the bloke that lives there. He was a bit odd but everything seemed in order. Do you want me to go back out?'

Kav shook his head. 'Nah, get yourself home. It says on the log a taxi driver has reported it on behalf of his fare – some old bird called Edith Wright. She said there's blood on the light switch. It will be a load of old tosh, poor guy has probably cut himself shaving.'

Jake turned to leave, smiling to himself. That woman was a persistent customer if ever there was one.

CHAPTER 35

Will had gone through both cases with Grace who he found easy to talk to. She was blonde, tall, slender and very attractive – exactly his type – yet not once did he find himself imagining sleeping with her, which was a first for him. Instead he found that he could concentrate on the case and talk it through like a professional. The only woman who kept popping into his mind was Annie, and he couldn't wait until he was finished and could go and see her. His mother would be so proud of him.

He had shown Grace the crime scenes. He'd taken her to where Emma's body had been found and then to the Abbey museum. Along the way he pointed out where Jenna's last known sighting had been. The light had been fading rapidly and the Abbey ruins took on an eerie feel. He was tempted to ask if he could nip and check on Annie, but it was complicated and he didn't feel like telling Grace the entire history of his private life.

While Grace was pacing around and writing notes he tried to ring Annie again but it went straight to voicemail: he left another message. His chest began to burn and he rubbed it. He didn't have time to get heartburn now and he didn't have any Rennie® on him either. Grace finally returned to the car and asked to be driven back to the station.

When they had walked back into the office Stu gave Will the nod and he frowned at him. Laura caught the look between them and blushed. Grace had sat down at the desk with her notepad and was busy typing on her laptop. A little while later, when everyone else had gone home and Will was nodding off, Grace lifted her head.

'You can go home, Will. I'll carry on for a while yet. As soon as I have something you can work with I'll let you know.'

He was sorely tempted and stood up to stretch. 'I can't, sorry. I'm not allowed to leave you unsupervised in the station.'

'Ah, that's all right, I understand. I spent most of my childhood in and out of police stations.'

Will thought about it. She wouldn't be allowed to do her job if she had a criminal record.

'Let me rephrase that. I spent most of my younger days in them because of my dad. Oh God, that sounds even worse. I'm not a delinquent – my dad was a detective just like you, and a workaholic. I was always hanging around waiting for him, although I doubt it would be allowed these days, too many health and safety rules.'

Will relaxed a little, wondering if he knew her dad. He glanced at the name on the visitor's badge around her neck. The surname 'Marshall' glared back at him. 'You wouldn't be related to the Detective Inspector would you?'

Grace looked down at her hands and spoke much quieter. 'Yes, he's my dad.'

Will replayed every minute he'd spent with her wondering if he'd screwed up in any way; he didn't think that he had. 'Don't worry it's cool, and I won't hold it against you. To be honest I haven't met him. I just spoke to him on the phone but he seems like an all right kind of guy.'

She smiled, flashing him a perfect set of white teeth, and all he could think was how lucky it was he hadn't tried it on with her. She stood up. 'I have everything I need for now. I'll let you get home. Give me your number and I'll ring you if I come up with something you can use tonight. Otherwise I'll see you in the morning.'

Will recited his phone number and slipped his jacket on, excited to be able to finally go and see Annie.

Kav came puffing through the door like a stampeding bull. 'Murder, need you at the scene. It's a right fucking mess, so Smithy said. He went to an emergency concern for welfare some old dear rang in and he's only gone and found a body in the bedroom with the head caved in.'

'Female?'

'Nope, sorry mate, it's a male.'

Will looked over at Grace. 'How often do you get dead bodies piling up in this town? I know for a fact it's few and far between. It could be a coincidence but it could be our guy. Count me in,' she said.

***

Henry picked up the woman as if she weighed no more than a bag of flour. He threw her over his shoulder and surveyed the scene. The man was out cold, if not dying, on the floor. He would come back and sort him out later. His priority was Annie. He finally had a name for her as he'd listened to the conversation the two of them had before he so rudely interrupted. This time she would not get the better of him. It was only a matter of minutes before she would come round. He needed to get her into the cellar and into his little room. He carried her down the cellar steps to his trophy room. He needed no light; his feet could find the way unaided.

***

Kav, Will and Grace got into the unmarked car which was the only one left in the back yard. Kav drove fast and as they turned into the street they were greeted by chaos: three patrol cars with lights flashing illuminated the early evening sky; an ambulance pulled up behind them as they parked up. They could see a taxi driver arguing with Smithy about how much money he was losing while sitting there. Kav and Will got out of the car leaving Grace in the back. A silent look between them said it was the best place for her at the moment; she wouldn't be able to get out because of the child locks.

Will suited and booted for the second time this week and went into the house. He noted the blood on the light switch and followed a trail of it along the banister and up the stairs. He walked along the landing to the only room with an open door, keeping to the opposite side of the wall away from the banister, careful not to destroy any evidence. A noise behind him made him turn to see Kav.

'I couldn't let you have all the fun.'

Will stepped inside and stared at the pictures. It took a few seconds before they registered in his brain and his face went white. Kav stepped in behind him.

'Oh shit, what the fuck is Annie's husband doing in here?'

Will looked at Kav and then down at the body. He had never seen the man before but if it was Annie's husband then he had met his match. Kav looked around the room and sucked in his breath.

'I think we have a much bigger problem. Why is our Annie plastered all over the walls?'

They both looked up to the ceiling at the giant picture: Annie stared back at them smiling. Will turned and ran out of the house, his phone vibrated in his pocket. Tugging off his latex glove he answered to a frantic Jake.

'Have you spoken to Annie lately? I've been ringing her on and off for ages and can't get hold of her. If I hadn't had a couple of large glasses of wine I'd have driven up there but I thought you'd be there by now.'

Will had to concentrate to stop himself from throwing up all over the flower beds. 'Not since lunch, I've been busy. Jake, we've just come to a house and found her husband and he's dead. I'm going up there now.' He didn't have time to explain everything. He got back in the car, forgetting about Grace until she spoke.

'Is everything OK?'

'Not really. I can't get hold of my girlfriend and she is staying on her own in the woods behind the Abbey, and inside that house is her husband's dead body, lying in a room which is covered in pictures of her.'

'Go. Don't worry about me, get driving. I'll keep out of the way, but you might need me anyway.'

He knew this made sense but he couldn't think straight for the panic had taken over and a feeling of dread had settled in the pit of his stomach. Will had never suffered from anxiety or panic attacks, but he had a tight band squeezing his chest. He ignored it; he didn't have time to have a heart attack.

He drove into the rear yard of the station and dumped the car. He then ran inside to the sergeant's office taking the only set of van keys off the whiteboard and his radio and CS gas from his locker. He jogged back into the yard and let Grace out of the car. Swapping vehicles she climbed in beside him. It was years since he'd driven a van and it took him a moment of fiddling with the buttons to find the lights and sirens: he needed to get to the Abbey in record time.

He passed his phone to Grace. 'Please can you keep trying?'

She hit the call button and put it to her ear. 'Voicemail.' Grace had no idea who this Annie was but she was worried for her, so she kept on redialing. The phone beeped with an incoming call.

'Jake, should I answer it?'

Will nodded.

'Will's phone, he's driving can I help?'

Will could hear Jake's animated voice but couldn't make out what he was saying, 'OK, I'll tell him, we're almost there.' Grace repeated what she had just been told. 'Alex is driving him and he'll be here soon.'

'Good, if we need to split up we can. I just hope she's having a long soak in the bath and can't hear her phone.' He pulled up in front of the gates and swore; they were locked up tight. Jumping down from the van he felt in his trouser pocket for the key. 'Bloody hell, I went home to get changed and the key is in my other trousers in the washing basket.' He was furious with himself. Taking the huge Magnalite® torch from the footwell of the van he looked at Grace. 'I'm sorry to drag you into this. You can wait here if you want till Jake arrives. It's a bit of a trek through the woods but not that far.'

She snorted. 'Are you having a laugh? There's a man killing women on the loose and you want me to wait here like a sitting duck, no thanks. I'll follow you. I can handle a bit of exercise.'

Will smiled. She was growing on him by the minute. 'Thanks, but make sure you don't tell your dad that I made you do it.'

'You would be surprised at just how little I do tell my dad.'

They set off jogging along the path. Grace wasn't even breaking a sweat but Will was struggling to breathe. How he wished he'd joined a gym instead of talking about it. The band around his chest got tighter, squeezing that bit harder, and he had to start taking deep breaths in through his nose and out through his mouth.

He could see the outline of the farmhouse in the distance. There were no lights shining through the trees like every other time he'd been up here. Annie's car was parked outside, the dog began to bark as he pushed the door handle: it was locked. He peered through the glass, unable to make out much except the shape of the dog pacing up and down growling at him. He turned to check the barns just in case she'd hurt herself. He went into the hay barn first. He shone the powerful torch around until it reached the bales of hay by the window: they had been made into a makeshift seat. He looked at a dog lead on the floor next to it and his blood ran cold.

'She had an audience, Will.'

He looked out through the cracked glass and had a perfect view through the kitchen windows. Will took out his phone but there were no bars on the screen. Grace tried hers but it was the same.

'What about your radio?'

'It's in the van, shit. Why am I such an idiot?'

Grace looked around. 'The door is locked, her car is there and there is no sign of a struggle, so either she went with him of her own free will or – ' she paused and Will knew she was gauging his reaction to what she was about to say. He felt like shit and was trying to keep it together but he knew they were screwed. 'Or whoever it was took her by surprise coming out of the house. But unless he drugged her or knocked her out cold there would be some evidence of a struggle, wouldn't there?'

Will nodded as they left the barn. 'The only place within walking distance if you were carrying someone is the old house five minutes away.'

'Look, why don't I go back to the van for the radio. At least then you can let patrols know where we are and what's going on.'

Will was torn. He didn't want to let her wander off on her own with a maniac on the loose but he didn't have much choice. He couldn't waste time going back down there; he needed to get to the house.

Grace reached out and touched his arm. 'I'll be fine. I teach self-defence classes back in Manchester to the kids off an estate. I can handle myself and I'll be able to run down to the van and back in a couple of minutes.'

Will felt sick. If anything happened to her he didn't know what he'd do, but he had little other choice; he needed back-up and soon.

'Thanks, but promise me you'll scream as loud as you can if you so much as see a shadow.'

She nodded.

He passed her the keys and watched her set off running. Will turned the other way and headed towards the house. If anything happened to Grace he would never forgive himself, but Jake should arrive any minute and meet her half way. *Bloody hell, Jake in the dark is enough to make anyone scream, what was I thinking?* He rounded the final bend out of breath and paused to look at the mansion; it looked like every scary house in every horror film he'd watched. It was so creepy in the dark. He studied the upstairs windows for any moving torch beams but it was all pitch black.

Taking deep breaths to try and calm himself down he walked up to the front door. If he was going in there was no point in hiding; he may as well walk right in. He hoped the front door would be open and his prayers were answered when he cautiously pushed the heavy door and it moved. He had the gas in his pocket and some handcuffs on his belt and that was it. He never needed to carry a baton and he wasn't Taser trained. At this moment in time he would swap anything to have one or both of them. He stepped inside the entrance, leaving the door ajar, scared that if he closed it he wouldn't be able to get back out. He shivered. The atmosphere in here was awful. It was so cold he could see his breath every time he exhaled. Will stood very still and listened for any noise but there was none.

The only place he and Annie had never checked the other day was the cellar. Every old house this size had either a haunted attic or a demonic cellar so it had to be one of them, didn't it? He made his way through the house until he reached the kitchen. Shining his torch around the beam illuminated a pool of blood on the floor. Will couldn't breathe and the blood was pounding between his ears, he let out a sob and tried to tell himself that it didn't have to belong to Annie but it was fresh, it hadn't started to congeal; it was a big, wet pool. He shone the torch further and he could see drag marks leading into the next room; keeping away from them he followed, struggling to keep on his feet, his legs wanted to give way.

***

Henry had gone back up to check on the man. He didn't want him waking up and escaping. But he didn't need to worry. He was out cold and by the amount of blood on the floor he didn't think he would be waking up any time soon. He returned to the cellar to make his final preparations; he was almost ready.

This had been a very long time in coming. She had been his downfall once, but not this time. He would finally give her what was coming. She wouldn't leave his room alive this time.

He was no longer the quiet, reserved man who hadn't even got into a playground fight. He was a mighty killer who had been kept buried inside for so many years and it was good to be free at last. He would keep on killing because that was what he did. Images of his first victims flashed through his mind as if it was yesterday. He could see and hear them now, feel their blood and pain.

CHAPTER 36

Grace reached the van as a car pulled up in front of her and a huge man jumped out. She screamed and Jake threw his hands in the air, shocked at her reaction.

'Sorry, sorry, I'm Jake. Where's Will?'

She explained what she was doing rooting around in a police van and passed him the radio. 'I don't have a clue how to use it.'

Jake took it from her. '5129 to control. I'm off duty but been called out by the DS. We need patrols to the Abbey Wood. An officer has been taken by the suspect in the Emma Harvey murder.'

The radio crackled into life breaking the silence surrounding them. 'Say again 5129?'

Jake growled, the last thing he needed was someone on control who didn't have a clue. 'I need urgent assistance to the Abbey Woods. We need an armed response vehicle and is there a dog handler available?' He knew the chance of getting a dog was as good as getting six numbers on the lottery.

'Control to 5129 there is an ARV travelling as we speak. Jake, what's going on?'

'Can we get every available patrol here as soon as possible before there is another murder?' He put the radio in his pocket; he didn't want to waste any more time talking on it. He began to shake the gates as if the lock would magically fall off. Frustrated, he waved Alex to move the car out of the way and then he climbed into the van and reversed at speed. He revved the engine and floored the accelerator. Grace hid her face in her hands and Alex jumped out of the car screaming at him to stop. Jake didn't care, his two best friends were in those woods and he didn't want to think about what could be happening to them; the last thing on his mind was a bit of whiplash and a bollocking from the powers that be.

He sped forward and there was a terrific bang as the van hit the gates, which splintered easily. Bits of old and rotten wood flew everywhere. His head flew forward hitting the steering wheel and he slammed on the brakes. The front of the van had half a gate embedded in it, but at least they had access and the other police cars would be able to get in.

A patrol car sped up behind him, lights flashing. Jake shook his head, trying to clear the silver stars from of his vision, as he watched Kav get out of the patrol car. Alex was standing by the side of the road having a panic attack and Grace was trying to comfort him.

Kav marched over to the van and threw the door open. 'For fuck's sake, Jake, you're such a bloody drama queen, did you have to make such an entrance?'

Jake winced. 'Yes, I did, and I'm not letting anything happen to her this time, not if I can help it.'

Kav's face was grim. 'Good, I wouldn't expect anything less of you, son. I should have known Annie would be involved in this somehow, even when she's on the sick she's a bloody pain.' He winked at Jake. 'Right. Plan of action, what's happening?'

Jake lifted his arm and used his sleeve to brush away the trickle of blood running down his forehead. 'Will said the killer had pictures of Annie all over his room. Now we can't get hold of her. Will is up there looking for her in that massive old mansion.'

Kav tried to think clearly: it was so much harder when it was one of your own whose life was at stake. 'We need Task Force here with Tasers and guns. It's no good us steaming in without the right equipment. What have you got on you?'

'Nothing. Alex drove me here straight from home. I don't care, Kav, I'm not sitting here twiddling my thumbs waiting for the cavalry to arrive from bloody Ulverston or Kendal while my friends are being butchered in that house.'

'Ah, bollocks, you're right. I can't wait here either. I've got my gas, cuffs and harsh language.'

'And I've got my fists and a tyre iron in the boot. Alex, you wait here with Grace to send the patrols up to the house.'

Kav turned to Alex. 'Lock yourselves in the car. Task Force are travelling from Kendal so it may take them some time even though they are blue lighting it. Tell them from me there is no room for cock ups and to get to that house pronto.'

Alex nodded his head.

Jake took him firmly by the shoulders and pushed him towards the car. 'It's OK, I'll be back soon. Stay here and do exactly what Kav just said. If you see anyone acting weird run them over. At least then we might get put in a cell next to each other when all this is over.'

Alex nodded again and got into the car. 'Jake, please be careful.'

Jake winked at him. 'You know me, I always am.'

Kav pulled the remains of the gate from the van and they got inside.

Jake coughed. 'Is now the time to tell you I've had a bottle of wine?'

'You know, Jake, you never cease to amaze me. I never heard that. Just get driving.'

CHAPTER 37

Will didn't see the body until it was too late and he almost fell over it. Terrified it was Annie he held his breath and shone the torch down onto it. The relief when he saw it was male was overwhelming. He instantly recognised the man he had seen briefly on CCTV, the one who had come to the station looking for her. He bent down to feel for a pulse: there was a faint but steady one.

The man groaned and tried to open his eyes. Will took off his suit jacket and knelt down. He rolled it up and put it under the guy's head to try and stem the bleeding.

'It's OK, I'm a policeman. Help will be here soon. Don't try to move and we'll soon have you up at the hospital.'

As Will stood up a hand reached out for his wrist. 'Annie, she needs your help.'

Will choked, finding it hard to speak. 'I know, I'll find her.' He hoped that Grace had made it to the van and found the radio. But would she even know what to do with it? He walked towards the cellar door. His entire body felt as if it was dragging a lead weight and it was getting harder to breathe. He pulled the door with too much force and it opened, slamming against the wall.

***

Henry stopped; someone was here. That door was too heavy to blow open in a draught. He cocked his head to one side to listen. How many were there? The bottom step creaked once echoing throughout the cellar. Henry moved to the back of the room. On a box next to the door to his trophy room he lit a candle then backed into the shadows. The flame gave off a warm glow; he knew it would be the man and sure enough like a moth to a flame the candle drew him in. Henry looked down at the hammer in his hand. The wooden shaft was slick with blood. He wiped it onto his trouser leg so he could grip it tightly. He couldn't mess this one up. He was bound to be a fighter and wouldn't go down after just one smack.

***

Annie stirred. She opened her eyes. It was too dark to see anything but the smell told her where she was. She hadn't wanted to visit Edward's trophy room but here she was, and this was where he had hidden Jenna White because the smell of decomposing flesh was overpowering. Annie was lying on a damp earthen floor which she knew had at least one other body buried underneath it. At least she wasn't dead; there was still a fighting chance.

Panic began to fill her chest; she didn't want to be down here with a dead girl for company. Crawling to find the door her hands touched Jenna, her body was so cold and Annie felt bad; the poor kid must have been terrified to die down here all alone in this awful room.

She whispered, 'I'm taking you home Jenna, I promise.' She moved the other way, feeling in front of her until her fingers brushed against the rough, wooden door. Pressing her ear against it she listened. She could hear muffled footsteps on the other side. The flickering orange glow from a candle outside cast a tiny light underneath the gap in the door. She held her breath as the footsteps approached and then she heard Will's voice as he called her name.

'Will, I'm in here, I can't get out and Jenna's in here too, well I think it's her body, it's so dark.'

'Hang on, Annie, I'll try to open the door, are you hurt?'

Overwhelmed to hear his voice she fought back the tears. 'No, I'm fine, please just get me out.'

Will twisted the handle but it was locked. He turned to see if there was something he could use to break the door open with. A shadow stepped out of the darkness. He looked at the ordinary man standing in front of him; he didn't know what he had been expecting but not this. In Will's mind he was the epitome of evil. The man took another step forward and Will saw the blood-soaked hammer he was holding in his hand. Then Will ran for him. He swung his fist, which caught the man off guard as it connected with his chin. He was taller than Will but roughly the same build. The man swung the hammer at Will but he ducked and it whooshed through the air. Will lunged for him again, this time trying to punch him in the balls. He just needed to get him off his feet, and then Will knew he would take the hammer off him and use it to pound his sick head in: there would be no time to tell him to stop, he was under arrest and would he please come nicely, the look in his eyes said it all. This man had nothing to lose and would not blink at killing another person.

Will swung again but missed and got him in the stomach. The man shouted and lifted the hammer. Will ducked, expecting him to aim for his head, but instead it went much lower and he smashed it into his left kneecap. The pain was blinding – hot and white – and Will couldn't stop himself from falling to the floor. The man came at him again, and Will pulled the small black canister of gas from his pocket and aimed it at his eyes. He heard a loud yell and hoped he'd managed to blind him, but then the hammer swung down. He tried to roll but the pain in his leg was immense. The hammer connected with his temple and the world went black.

Henry smiled. This had been his biggest challenge and still he had managed to conquer it and take him out. The man's face was a grey mask covered with beads of perspiration, Henry leaned forward.

'She's all mine, you know. She always has been. You could never compare with me, and Alice knows that. She knew the day I set eyes on her that I would eventually own her. It was my choice to decide whether she lived or died.'

He unlocked the door and dragged the semi-conscious, blood-covered Will into the room.

'What have you done to him?'

Henry dropped Will and turned to her. 'Well, Alice, here we are again: same place, different time.'

The chair in the corner began to rock.

'I'm not your Alice, you stupid prick. I know who you are though. I've seen your little trophies. It's been a while. What took you so long?'

He was taken aback by her courage and found himself getting excited. He always had liked it when she put up a fight. For a moment he imagined what it would be like to take her right here in his little room with her boyfriend watching.

Annie whispered to Will, 'Stay with me. I love you and I promise we'll get out of here.' Annie's eyes filled with tears and she turned to face Henry, who was watching them with his arms crossed.

'Aww, that's so sweet. Are you two finished because I'm getting rather bored of this?'

Annie felt the rage and fury that had been building up inside her explode and she lunged for Henry. Hitting him with all her weight she took him down in a rugby tackle. They landed on the hard ground; it knocked the wind from them both. She didn't let it stop her and she lunged for his eyes. He caught her wrist and twisted it sharply behind her back. She tried not to yelp but he twisted it again so hard that Will heard the crack as the bone snapped. This time she screamed.

Will watched as Henry threw her to the side like a rag doll and then kicked her in the head for good measure. Annie felt herself losing consciousness, the darkness a welcome relief from the pulsating pain in her arm.

Henry looked at Will. 'It's such a shame you're going to die down here watching the woman you love being beaten and murdered by the greatest killer in the world.'

Will's eyelids fluttered. How pathetic. What he wanted to do was kill the bastard with his bare hands, but the room was swimming and he couldn't put any weight on his leg.

Henry walked out of the room, leaving them alone. Will tried to shuffle over to where Annie lay but the pain was so bad he slumped against the wall and tears of frustration and anger rolled down his cheeks. After a while he sensed movement, and opened one eye to see her crawling towards the chair. She started to dig in the soil with her good arm, her fingers frantically scraping away, looking for something.

Annie didn't know why she was doing this but Alice's voice had whispered for her to keep going and so she did. What else was there to do? Her fingers brushed against something cold and hard. She had no idea what it was but she struggled to work it free. Finally it gave and she rolled onto her back, exhausted. She looked at Will. His leg was bent at a funny angle and there was a steady stream of blood running down his head. He looked like a corpse. She lifted her hand to see what it was she was holding. It looked like a piece of dirty white bone the size of a small bread knife and she gasped, horrified and elated at the same time.

Shuffling back over to Will she leant back against the wall next to him and whispered, 'Hang on in there. I love you and I won't let either of us die down here.'

Will murmured his reply and he shoved his canister of CS gas into her hand. She smiled, then wiped the soil and sweat from her other hand and lifted the bone to look at it. She didn't like holding the thing and knew it was one of Edward's. She shivered. There was nothing else in the room she could use with one arm and she prayed she would be able to use the bloody thing to put an end to it all. Her arm throbbed and she shut her eyes, letting it all wash over her. An image of Alice with a dirty, tear-stained face holding a spade made her whisper, 'Same place, different time.' She tucked the bone under her leg and waited for Edward to come back. She knew exactly what she had to do.

CHAPTER 38

Jake made it to the grounds of the house without running the van off the steep track, down the embankment and into the river at the bottom.

Kav breathed a sigh of relief. 'I didn't doubt you for a minute. So now what? Do you want to split up or stick together?'

They got out of the van and walked up to the front of the house and the open door.

'Well, seeing as how neither of us has a clue I reckon we should stick together.'

'Not much of a plan but it will do for now, Jake.'

Jake walked into the darkness followed by Kav. They listened, but it was silent. Standing inside the hall Jake pointed to the stairs. Kav shook his head and pointed to the long corridor that led away from the hall. He began walking that way. Jake followed, terrified.

*

Henry leant against the other side of the door trying to compose himself. The bitch had taken him by surprise and hurt him with that little outburst. Who did she think she was? He couldn't let her think she'd almost got the better of him. It was quiet now. There had been some movement and whispering but it had stopped. He hoped the man was dead; it would serve her right knowing she was next.

It had all gone wrong and he had no choice but to go for his back-up plan. He had a petrol can hidden in the corner. The only thing he could do now was to burn the place to the ground with the bodies inside and hope that no one would be any the wiser. He unscrewed the cap and began splashing it around the cellar and a steady stream of it ran under the gap between the door and the floor.

Petrol fumes roused Annie from her semi-conscious state and she began to panic: fire was her worst fear. If he didn't come back inside the room they wouldn't stand a chance. The fumes were already overpowering, making her eyes water. Then the key turned in the lock. She tensed. This was it. She knew he was coming to kill her before setting them on fire. She reached out and squeezed Will's hand.

'We're not going to die in here, Will.' And then she shut her eyes. Let him come to her.

Henry walked in and smiled to himself as he placed the candle on the small table. Taking a final look around his room he strode over to Annie, bent down and pulled her head back to expose her throat. Annie didn't make a sound but lifted the gas, aimed it into his eyes and sprayed, blinding him. He cursed and released his grip on her a little. She felt underneath her thigh for the piece of bone and with as much force as possible drew it back, and then plunged it deep into the inside of his thigh. An invisible hand wrapped itself around hers, helping her to keep on pushing as far as it would go. He howled in pain and let go of her, stumbling back. Blood was gushing from the wound: she hoped she had got his femoral artery. She waited for his next attack but it didn't come. He deflated in front of her. All the fight had left his eyes. He stumbled backwards holding his leg. His legs gave way and on his way down he knocked the table and the candle to the floor.

Loud footsteps ran across the cellar towards the room and Annie tensed. *Please God don't let him have an accomplice. You can't let me think I'm going to live and then kill me anyway.* She dragged herself to her feet, one hand covered in his blood and the other dangling by her side. She sobbed as she saw the face that appeared through the doorway.

'Annie.' Jake stepped inside followed by Kav, whose face paled at the scene in front of him. He sniffed as the petrol fumes hit his nostrils.

'This place is going to go. We need to get out.'

Jake ran to Will. Dragging him up he threw him over his shoulder. Kav turned to help Annie.

'I'm OK, I can walk. You have to get Jenna out of here. We can't leave her, I promised I'd take her home.'

Kav winced. He was by no way squeamish but she had been dead a few days. Annie implored him with her eyes so he walked over, bent down and scooped her up into his arms.

They left the room as the candle flame ignited the petrol fumes. It was Kav who shouted, 'Run, or we're going to get cremated.' They ran as fast as they could to the cellar steps, carrying the wounded and the dead out of there.

Annie was terrified to look behind her. A wave of heat washed over them as they neared the top of the stairs. Still running, they made it to the front door.

Annie stopped. 'We can't leave Derek. It's my fault he's mixed up in this.' She turned and ran back to the scullery where he lay. Jake screamed at her but he couldn't do anything with Will over his shoulder; he needed to get him out to safety. Kav too was helpless, the body in his arms weighing heavy. They carried their loads out of the front door and down the steps to the overgrown, grassy lawn. Jake laid Will down and watched as Kav gently laid down the body of Jenna White. They turned and watched, relieved, as Annie stumbled out of the door, her good arm wrapped around Derek.

The woods behind them finally lit up with blue and white flashing lights. Jake dropped to the ground to begin his best attempt at CPR on Will.

He was unconscious and the same colour as the dead girl. Annie made her way across to them, standing next to Kav. He had never seen anything like it in his twenty-seven years as a serving police officer.

Annie collapsed on the ground next to Will, whispering in his ear, begging him to open his eyes. The paramedics arrived to take over and Jake, Kav and Annie huddled together.

Movement from the front of the building caught their eye and they watched, horrified, as the man Annie had stabbed fell onto the front steps, his hair on fire. Kav ran across and dragged him away from the burning building. Taking off his jacket he used it to extinguish the flames. Annie walked over to the man who had caused all of this pain and suffering; he didn't look so scary now. An orange glow filled the ground floor and she could feel the heat from the flames washing over them both. Bending down she wrapped her fingers around the bone protruding from his leg and yanked it free.

Kav squirmed. 'What are you doing, you need to leave that to the paramedics?'

She waved the piece of bone in the man's face and then walked up the steps and threw it into the flames where it belonged. *Burn in hell, you bastard.*

Another ambulance arrived and the paramedics ran to help the killer. Annie turned away in disgust. More police cars and two fire engines arrived. Annie walked to where Jenna's corpse lay on the grass and knelt down next to her.

'You're going home, sweetheart. I told you I'd make sure that you did.' And then she began to cry, real heart wrenching sobs.

Kav wrapped his arms around her. 'I don't know where to start. The main thing is you're OK, and Will, well he's in the best hands now. It might take a while but I'm sure he'll be fine.'

'I hope you're right, Kav, because my life had just taken a turn for the better and I don't want to lose him now.'

He looked at her arm. 'Come on, kid, I don't think your arm is supposed to hang down like that.'

At the mention of her arm pain shot through it up into her shoulder. 'Ouch, you've just reminded me how much it hurts.'

He walked her over to the ambulance they were loading Will into. 'Room for a little one?'

The paramedic nodded and Kav helped her in. 'You did great, Annie, it's just a shame you managed to burn the house down.' He winked at her and they both looked over to it. Orange flames were burning through the boarded-up windows, thick black smoke was filling the night sky; the whole of the ground floor was alight.

As she looked up she saw a familiar white figure at the attic window. Annie lifted her hand and waved, the figure waved back.

Kav shouted, 'There's a woman in there, top floor.'

Annie shook her head. 'No, it's the ghost of a woman who lived there a very long time ago.' They looked again but she had gone.

Kav stared at Annie. 'Jesus, this is getting worse by the minute. I don't understand.'

Annie leant her head back against the cold side of the ambulance. 'Me neither, but I'll explain it as best as I can later. My brother is going to bloody kill me; I was only supposed to be looking after the dog.'

Kav roared with laughter so loud that it echoed around the clearing. He slammed the ambulance door shut and watched as it slowly drove away.

*

The only sound in the hospital room was the steady beep from the monitors stuck to Will's chest. Annie had given her statement to Stu while her arm was being reset in the plaster room. She omitted the bit about what was in the room in the cellar and who was buried down there. No one needed to know; it was over.

The Accident and Emergency Department had been chaos with the arrival of her and Will, closely followed by Derek and then the man who had started it all. He was under police guard but the doctors had said his prognosis wasn't good. Jake had come to sit with her and after some dithering he had told her about finding the killer's house with two more bodies inside.

'Please tell me they weren't girls?'

Jake shook his head, pausing while trying to find the right words to say to her. 'No, they found his elderly mother stuffed into the chest freezer.'

'Who was the other one?'

Jake hadn't wanted to be the one to tell her but Kav had insisted it needed to come from a friend. 'Mike. They found Mike dead in the bedroom.'

'Mike who? Are you saying my Mike? Why would he be in some killer's house, isn't he supposed to be in Carlisle?'

Jake took hold of her hand. 'He did a runner from the bail hostel yesterday and they only told us this afternoon. Matt said he thought he had been killed this afternoon, and to let you know he will come and see you as soon as he can.'

Annie felt numb. What did she do now? After Jake left she went to the cubicle where a groggy Derek was waiting to go for a CT scan.

'I'm so sorry for getting you mixed up in all of this, Derek.'

He smiled at her. 'I knew you were trouble the minute I set eyes on you.' He winked at her and the porter came to wheel him away. She then walked down to the intensive care unit where they had moved Will an hour ago. The nurse had taken one look at her and wouldn't let her in because, in the nurse's words, 'You look like something from a bad horror movie, darling.' But seeing the pain in Annie's eyes she had melted and fetched a pair of blue scrubs from the linen cupboard, a towel and a plastic bag. 'You go into the disabled toilet over there; clean yourself up and then you can come and sit with him for a bit.'

Annie did as she was told. She carefully folded her clothes and put them into the evidence bags for Debs to analyse later. When she finally sat beside Will she tenderly picked up his hand and kissed it. Exhausted and broken, the painkillers began to kick in and she pulled her chair closer to his bed and shut her eyes.

EPILOGUE

Three Weeks Later

The winter sun was shining as they lowered Mike's coffin into the ground. It had been a small service as he had very few family and friends. The majority of people in attendance were police officers, and they were not there because of Mike but to show their support for Annie. Kav, Jake and Stu made a handsome trio in their black tunics. Will stood next to Annie wearing a black suit and leaning on a crutch. He looked much better but it would take a while before he would get back to normal. What mattered was that he was alive; they both were.

Annie didn't cry because she wasn't a hypocrite. Mike had become a stranger to her these last few years of their marriage and it was a relief to know he wouldn't be able to come back and hurt her ever again. She was with Will now, and in such a short space of time they had gone through more than what most couples face in a lifetime. She reached out for his hand. As the vicar said his parting words to Mike a huge weight lifted from her shoulders, and she threw a single yellow rose down onto his coffin.

Annie walked back to the funeral car and took out a beautiful bunch of white lilies. She began to walk in the direction of the old chapel. Will hobbled behind her at a much slower pace, keeping his distance. Jake, Kav and Stu watched her for a little while then turned away and began to talk about the latest football results. She finally reached Alice's grave; the angel smiled at her. Annie bent down and, laying the flowers at the foot of the monument, she whispered, 'Your secret is safe with me, Alice.' She stood up and blew a kiss to the angel then turned and walked back towards Will. He took Annie's hand and kissed her gently on the lips and they walked back towards the waiting car.

ACKNOWLEDGEMENT

This story is indeed a work of fiction and anything I have got wrong regarding forensics or police is entirely my doing and I have to admit I have used my creative licence to sometimes bend the truth a little. I would also like to state for the record that this book was plotted and my first draft written before I even applied to work for Cumbria Constabulary and therefore any similarities between my characters and colleagues are entirely by coincidence. None of the characters are based on any of the police officers or staff that I work with. On the other hand, however, I'm open to suggestions for my next book!

I would like to say a huge thank you to the Romantic Novelists Association and their New Writers Scheme. To Jan Jones for setting up a meeting with my editor, the lovely Anna Baggaley. To Anna for taking a chance and believing in me. To the wonderful team at Carina for everything. To the amazing Jayne Jakeman, who runs our local writing group and has spent so much time nurturing and showing me the error of my ways, and, of course, my amazing Roose Writers, who are such a talented, supportive bunch: Joan, Cathy, Anne, Pip, Luke, Jaz and Eddie—your turn next. And not forgetting Claire at Roose library for the support and supply of coffee. I would also like to thank my writing friend Bernadette O'Dwyer for all her wonderful support and, of course, my fellow blog members at TheWriteRomantics, you are all amazing.

A huge thank you goes to my friend John for allowing me to pick his brains concerning anything and everything. Caroline Kendall for being my very first reader and not telling me to find another hobby. My friends, colleagues and fellow PCSOs, especially Sam, Tracy, Tina and the late Cathy, who I miss so much, for their endless inspiration and laughter. Liz Gaskell for her graphic explanation of a post mortem. My brother Mark, his wife Christine and family for buying the most amazing house which inspired this book: I'm really sorry and I hope I haven't put you off living there.

Last but not least, my mam and dad for always being there, my husband, Steve, for his support and belief in me, and my children, Jessica, Joshua, Jerusha, Jaimea and Jeorgia for putting up with the microwave meals and unwashed towels— your mum loves you—really. xx

HELEN PHIFER—AUTHOR Q&A

The blend of crime and ghost story works beautifully in *The Ghost House*. What moved you to mix the two?

I have loved reading crime and ghost stories since I was a child. I would have to say that Enid Blyton probably inspired me to mix them both up. I was hooked on the Famous Five books and there was normally something criminal happening with a spooky story as a cover up. I loved it and couldn't get enough of them.

Do you write every day?

I try to, but I work full time and also have a large, busy family to look after. However, I find if I don't I get really cranky, so if I miss a day I make up for it the next.

What inspires you on a day-to-day basis when you're writing?

Anything and everything: a snippet of conversation, a byline in a newspaper. I've become addicted to Pinterest and have a board which is full of all sorts of spooky pictures. I think I have enough inspiration to write the next ten books.

You mentioned that this book was eight years in the making. What aspect of the story changed the most, from concept to final draft?

I would probably say the police parts. When I wrote the first draft, I had no inside knowledge of what it was like to work for the police. By the time I finished the first draft I had managed to pass all my interviews for my job in the police, so now I have plenty. I hope that it makes the story as authentic as possible.

When and where do you write?

The Ghost House and *The Secrets of the Shadows* were written tucked in a corner of my living room next to a huge television that never seems to get turned off. I'm very lucky that I can switch off and write wherever I need to. I don't have a set time when I write as I work shifts, so I just do it whenever I have a moment. I'm very proud to say that the bargain summerhouse my husband bought me two years ago has finally been totally rebuilt, had a new roof and been made fully waterproof. So, after years of dreaming about an office, I finally have one and it's great because it's halfway down the garden and the kids are too lazy to come looking for me.

Like Annie, you are a Police Community Support Officer. It's fascinating that you first took on the role for research. What was it like writing Annie's narrative, having that firsthand knowledge?

I was very lucky that I got my job; it was such a massive help in understanding what Annie's role was in the police. It was fascinating discovering how the police speak and deal with members of the public. It was also brilliant to become a part of the community team and make some truly amazing friends who helped me with any little question or research.

Nineteenth-century Alice, on the other hand, is completely different. But whose point of view did you enjoy writing more, Annie's or Alice's?

Ooh, that's a tough question. I really enjoyed writing both characters. I think Annie and Alice were both quite similar, as they were both strong women who ended up fighting for their lives, but if I had to choose I would probably say Annie, because I feel as if I know her inside and out.

What was your favourite part of the publishing process?

Seeing my book covers is always amazing, as they are so beautiful. It was a real moment for me to see the cover of *The Ghost House* on Amazon for the first time. I think it left me speechless for a whole hour.

There is a spine-tingling scene in which Alice realises that Edward is Jack the Ripper. What were the challenges of using such an infamous figure?

The research and making sure the timeline matched the dates

in the diary was pretty hard and time-consuming. Not to mention confusing at times. I've been fascinated by Jack the Ripper and what happened to him since I was a teenager. He was the first serial killer I ever learnt about and even more scary because he was never caught. I knew it would be a challenge, but I really enjoyed solving the mystery, even if it was all a figment of my imagination.

Which part of the book did you write first? Did it survive the edits?

Alice's story, because it came to me one day when I was walking my dog Tess in Abbotswood, where the story was set. By the time I'd reached the main gates and my car, my head was swimming with ideas that I had to write down. Yes, thankfully it did, although Henry Smith's introduction on the first page was a lot more gory and that didn't.

Which part did you save for the last?

The timeline in the diary where Alice was beginning to realise that Edward was perhaps not all that he seemed. I had to recheck the dates the original victims' murders had been released in the newspapers to make sure it was as authentic as possible.

Did you know the end before you wrote it?

Yes, for some bizarre reason I always know how I want the story to end before I sit down to write it.

The Ghost House contains ghosts, mediums and spiritualist churches. Do you personally believe in ghosts or the afterlife?

Yes, I have had a fair few spooky things happen and I know more people that have than haven't. It all depends on whether you believe or not. I think if you have an open mind you are more likely to experience things.

Which writers would you say have influenced you the most?

Enid Blyton, Stephen King and James Herbert have all had

a huge influence on me. I always wanted to be the female equivalent of Stephen King when I was younger.

The second book in the Annie Graham series, *The Secrets of the Shadows*, was released last year and the third book, *The Forgotten Cottage*, in October 2014. Has your writing process changed from when you wrote *The Ghost House*?

Well, I'm a lot quicker, that's for sure. It only took me four months to produce the first draft of *The Secrets of the Shadows*, which compared to eight years for *The Ghost House* is quite amazing.

Is there more in store for Annie's fans?

Lots. I get so many messages from readers of all ages wanting to know when the next book is out. What happened to Alice, did Henry die? Do Annie and Will get married? They make such a great couple I love writing about them and, with Annie's natural ability to attract every killer or ghost in a ten-mile radius, there are a lot more adventures in store for Annie, Will and Jake.

Loved The Ghost House*?*

*Turn the page for an exclusive extract from the second
book in the Annie Graham series:*

THE SECRETS OF THE SHADOWS

PROLOGUE

June 30th, 1984

Six-year-old Sean Black didn't like this house; it smelled funny and all the furniture was dark and old. He didn't like the man who walked around wearing the long black dress either. He knew that he was a priest because his mum had told him that he was; she'd also told him that they had to live in the presbytery next to the church, but he didn't know exactly what that meant. They had their own house two doors down from this one; it was much smaller, with three bedrooms and a tiny garden, but it was big enough to play in with his A-Team action figures. He wanted to go and dig out BA Baracus from underneath the rose bush in the front garden where he had buried him last week, before he got eaten by worms or went mouldy. His mum wouldn't let him; he had asked her this morning when he had finished his bowl of Snap Crackle and Pop. She had gone mad with him when he said he wanted to go and get his toys and would she take him, so there wasn't much choice. He was going to come up with a plan of his own—just like Hannibal always did—and go on a rescue mission. He would wait until his mum had a bath. She always spent hours in there and wouldn't notice that he had sneaked out of the door. He just hoped that the priest wasn't an enemy working for the other side and wouldn't drop him in it. His mum had been acting strange all week now and yesterday she hadn't let him go to his sister Sophie's funeral. Instead, she'd made him stay here, in this big smelly house with the woman the priest called his 'housekeeper'. He liked her because she baked nice cakes and would let him eat as many as he wanted when his mum wasn't looking.

Sean went upstairs to the room which had become his until he could go back to his own, with the Masters of the Universe and A-Team posters. The room had a big wooden cross on the wall and the only thing to read was a thick black book which had 'Bible' written in gold on the front. Sean had looked inside and then closed it again; the writing was so small it would take him forever to try and read it. He slumped on to the bed; it was boring here. At least when Sophie was alive he'd had her to play with—well, until she got poorly he did. It had started a couple of weeks ago, but a few days ago she'd got really poorly, saying words that he had never heard of and that were nothing like the French words they sometimes learnt in school. He didn't understand what was going on, but he knew it was something bad. Sophie had been screaming the day she'd died, really screaming, as if the priest and their mum were hurting her. It was so loud that he had crept from this bedroom to see if he could help her, but her bedroom door was locked. He had looked through the keyhole to see his sister on her bed with the man in the dress standing over her with a book like the one next to his bed. He was throwing water on to Sophie. Sean had watched as the priest had bent down and placed a wooden cross on to her forehead. He'd stared in horror as the cross burnt into her skin; the sizzling sound made him feel sick and he'd pushed himself away from the door. He thought he was going to puke all over the polished wooden floor.

Telling himself to be brave, he'd gone back to look through the keyhole again, to see Sophie thrashing around. She looked angry and hurt, then her eyes rolled to the back of her head until he could only see the whites of them. It was then that she began to choke. The priest was trying to lift her head and his mum was watching. Sean didn't understand why she didn't rush to help Sophie. He watched as his sister's face turned blue and, just like that, the noise stopped. It was over and Sophie was dead. The scream which came from his mum was far worse than seeing Sophie lying perfectly still, frozen in time. Sean scrambled to his feet and ran towards his room. Clutching a plastic toy to his chest, he fell to the floor and crawled under the bed, where he curled up in a ball and cried himself to sleep. He had stayed there, hidden from sight, until the priest came looking for him hours later. Father John had tried to talk him out, but Sean didn't want to leave his hiding place. The priest reached under to pull him out and Sean sank his teeth into his hand. There was a loud shout and a few bad words, but then the priest had lain flat on the floor so he could see Sean's face. 'Come on, son; you can't stay there all day. Let's go and get you something to eat.'

Sean shook his head, curling himself up even tighter. 'I want to see my mum… Where is she?'

'She's fast asleep at the moment; the doctor has been to visit Sophie and your mum. He had to give her some medicine.'

'What about Sophie—did he give her some medicine?'

'No, there is no medicine that will make your sister better, I'm very sorry to say.'

'I want to go and see Sophie then!'

'Are you sure? Sophie's soul has left this earth and gone to a much better place. All that's left is her body.'

Sean nodded; he needed to see if Sophie's face was still blue and if she had the mark of the cross burnt into her forehead. He crawled out and stood up. Father John reached out and took hold of his hand; as brave as Sean felt, he still grasped it and held tight. They walked to Sophie's room and Father John pulled a key from his pocket. Unlocking it, he turned to Sean. 'You're sure?'

Sean nodded and stepped forward, pushing the door open as he did so. His legs were shaking and he knew he had to be brave now, just like BA, so he held his head up and stepped into the room, which was much colder than the rest of the house. He walked across to the bed; Sophie looked as if she was asleep. Her long platinum-blonde hair was spread out on her pillow. Her blue eyes were closed and her face was a funny white colour, but it definitely wasn't blue. Her forehead didn't have a big mark on it and she looked like one of the dolls she played with all the time. Her lips were still pink and in her hand she had a cross and a bible. Sean pulled his spare Hannibal action figure from his trouser pocket and reached out to tuck it behind her fingers. He touched them and snatched his hand back—they were so cold. Reaching out, he tried again and this time he managed to tuck it behind her hands, shuddering as he did so. Then he ran away from Sophie, the priest and the end of his childhood to the empty room, where he scrambled back under the bed.

***

Sean wandered along the dark passage until he reached the bathroom, then pressed his ear against the door. He could hear his mum splashing in the water. Good, she would be in there for ages; she had the same long blonde hair as Sophie and it took her forever to wash it. He crept along to the huge oak staircase with the world's smallest carpet and ran down. So light on his feet the treads didn't creak once, he looked around the hallway—there was no sign of the housekeeper or the priest. He strode across to the front door as if he were allowed to be going outside and turned the handle. The door opened and he screwed up his eyes against the harsh sunlight. He grinned. Playing outside was his favourite; he hated being cooped up inside—especially in this house. Sean wanted to go home more than anything. He looked across the huge lawn over to the church. The door was shut, so if the priest was in there he wouldn't notice Sean sneaking out. The street was empty; he stepped out of the doorway and ran down the steps and across the lawn to the low wall which surrounded the front garden. He was on a mission now; it was important. He had to save BA's life—the A-Team couldn't survive with just the three of them; it had to be all four. He stopped outside his house and reached out to touch the gate; the metal was cold even though it was bathed in sunlight. He opened the gate, took three steps forward and then fell to his knees in front of the rose bush, where he began to dig in the soil with his fingers. Soon he felt the hard plastic of the figure he'd buried last week and smiled—he'd done it and saved the day. He stood up and went back out of the gate, closing it behind him. A shadow passed over the upstairs window, catching his eye. Lifting his head, he put his small hand to his forehead to shield his eyes from the burning sun, then looked up and squealed to see Sophie standing at the window staring down at him. He frantically waved his hand and grinned at her but, before she could wave back, a darker, much taller figure stepped behind her and pulled her away from the window.

Sean ran back to tell his mum that Sophie was in their house, he'd seen her and they could go home now. He ran into the presbytery and up the stairs to the bathroom, where he hammered on the door. 'Mum, Mum. You don't have to be sad now—Sophie's OK. I saw her looking out of your bedroom window. We can go home now.'

There was no sound of splashing water like there had

been earlier; there was no sound, apart from the steady drip of a tap which hadn't been turned off. Sean took hold of the door knob, twisting it until it turned and the door opened wide. That was when all the normal thoughts that a six-year-old boy should be thinking left him. He walked closer to the bath which contained his mother's lifeless body in a pool of bright red water. His stomach clenched and the voice in his head told him to run, but he carried on until he was close enough to reach out and touch her. Pushing her shoulder, her head lolled to the side and her glassy, open, dead eyes stared through him. Sean looked down into the bath and saw her arms and it was then that he opened his mouth and began to scream.

CHAPTER ONE

Annie Graham downed the tequila, then shuddered. She hated the stuff, but it got you drunk fast. Jake—fellow police officer and best friend—whose house they were in, laughed at the grimace on her face. 'You are such a girl, you know that, don't you?'

She squeezed her eyes shut. 'Yes, I'm a total girl and I'm not ashamed of it either; this stuff is bloody awful. I don't understand how you could even begin to actually enjoy it.'

Jake spluttered, managing to spit his tequila all over the black marble of the breakfast bar. 'Because I quite like the taste now I've got used to it and it does the job in half the time of six cans of lager. One more and then we'll be brave enough to go ghost-hunting.'

Annie giggled. 'I've had enough of that to last me a lifetime, thank you. After discovering I could see ghosts in a haunted house and being stalked by a serial killer six months ago, I'm quite happy *not* to go ghost-hunting. I can't believe you want to drag me to a cemetery when we're drunk. You'll be screaming at every shadow you see and then what happens if we actually do see something?'

'You're a wimp. I'm not going to be the one screaming and anyway don't you want to see if you can still see dead people or if it was all just a figment of your twisted imagination?' He managed to dodge the piece of chewed-up lime that she threw at his head. 'Sorry.'

Annie began to laugh so hard that she slid off the stool. 'I'm drunk and I don't think going to the cemetery in this state is going to be too productive. What if someone reports us and we end up getting arrested? There have been loads of metal thefts up there this month. Can you imagine the gossip that would spread around the station if we got caught in there?' Tears were rolling down her cheeks, smudging her mascara and leaving black trails.

Jake bent down; putting both of his hands under her armpits, he dragged her up from the floor. 'Nah, bollocks, we'll just tell them the truth. That we were ghost-hunting.'

'Your call, but if you insist—who am I to argue?'

He shrugged his huge shoulders and took hold of her hand. 'What the hell. Come on, if we get caught we'll say we were looking for vampires. I want to go now, before I chicken out. I've always wanted to do this, but never had anyone drunk or stupid enough to go with.'

They looked each other in the eye and nodded. Jake helped her into her coat and wrapped her scarf around her neck. His fingers brushed her thick black curls, which had grown back and now covered the scar that had once been on show. She looked so much happier and healthier now she didn't have Mike in her life. He bent down and planted a big wet kiss on her forehead and held her close. Annie wrapped her arms around him and whispered, 'Don't you go getting all soft on me, Jake. I'm OK now and I've never been happier. Everything that happened six months ago is done; life is getting better.'

Jake squeezed his friend even tighter. 'I'm not; I just hate what happened to you.' They pulled apart; Jake took hold of her hand and dragged her to the front door.

'Come on, there's no time like the present and, besides, your dream man Will might turn up soon and you know what a spoilsport he is. He'd never let you loose in a cemetery with your track record.'

They left the house holding hands and began the short walk to the cemetery gates.

'How are we going to get in if they're locked?' Annie asked.

'Sometimes you amaze me. You can climb walls, can't you? I'll give you a bunk up if you can't get those short legs up high enough.'

She slapped his hand in a half-hearted gesture; Jake squeezed hers back, a silent apology. Annie couldn't walk straight; her legs were wobbling as they approached the tall black cast-iron gates which loomed in the distance. Behind them was a blanket of pitch black which made her heart beat faster.

***

Will shivered. He hated cemeteries when the sun was shining and he could see everything around him, but to be here in the dark with no moonlight gave him the creeps. It didn't help that he was sitting in a car with Twit and Twat, the two specials who were very nice blokes but far too keen to get a piece of the action. They couldn't sit still and were talking utter crap. Every time a shout came over the radio the one sitting next to him would sit up, his body taut and his fists clenched, raring to get going. Will smiled to himself—at least he was getting a bit of fun out of it by torturing the pair of them; they needed to learn that police work wasn't all rescuing damsels in distress and blue-light jobs. As bored as he was, he really hoped that nothing would happen tonight with these two in tow, because it was all bound to go tits up in a big way. Two of his best detectives, Stu and Laura, were hiding behind some mausoleum near to the crematorium. He would rather have been with one of those two, but after the head injury and broken kneecap he'd got whilst trying to save Annie six months ago and the fact that it was freezing, he'd decided to pull rank for once and sit in the car.

He switched off from the two chattering voices and began to think about Annie. He was parked not too far away from her husband Mike's grave. He looked out of the side window and squinted; he could just make out the hilly mound of soil. Will would have loved to have given him what he deserved, but the town's first serial killer had beaten him to it. He had to admit that Annie was by far the best thing that had happened to him and he loved her more than he'd loved anyone, but he was still afraid of committing and, to be honest, she was still a mess. He hated the nightmares she had almost every night. She would brush them off as if nothing were wrong, but he had seen her pale face and eyes wide in horror as she crept out of the bed and into the bathroom. The first time he'd heard her stifling her sobs it had broken his heart and he had lain there dithering about whether to go and comfort her or give her some space. He'd opted to stay where he was, feeling useless. When she had finally come back to bed, he'd turned and wrapped his arms around her, holding her tight and stroking her hair until her breathing slowed and she fell back asleep. Tonight he'd left her at Jake and Alex's house; if his grave-robbers didn't turn up, he might go round for a coffee and see what they were up to.

***

Jake threaded his arm through Annie's and the pair of them weaved along the tree-lined road towards the cemetery. The blackness behind the gates looked ominous; she didn't want to do this. Why did she let Jake talk her into these things? She hadn't been here since Mike's funeral.

'We can't get in—it's all locked up.'

Jake looked at her in disbelief, 'Are you serious? You're a copper; you should know how to scale a fence.'

'Of course I know how to scale a fence, just not when I'm drunk. I don't want to land head first in someone's grave. I have a bit more respect than you do.'

'Wimp. Come on, I'll give you a bunk up.'

Annie ignored his offer of help and wobbled on ahead of him, scaling the gates before Jake could offer her his hand. She jumped off the other side and slipped. Jake bent over laughing.

'Come on then, big man, let's see if you can do any better.'

Jake took a run for the gate. For his size, he was surprisingly nimble and he managed to climb over it and land on his feet next to her. Annie tutted and began to walk away in the opposite direction to Mike's grave and Jake followed. She let out a loud scream at a statue in the distance and he started to laugh again. Her elbow landed sharply in his side and he stopped. She decided to walk up towards the old chapel, which was now boarded up and fenced off. Annie had been drawn towards it last year when she had come looking for Alice's grave—she had seen Alice's ghost in that area of the cemetery, so it was the logical place to go. Jake, who had finally stopped laughing, whispered in her ear, 'Come on; you're right, this is stupid. Let's go and order a Chinese.'

Stubborn as ever, she carried on walking. 'Now who's the wimp? You were the one who wanted to come here in the first place. I'm not leaving until we see a ghost; I'll prove to you I'm not full of crap.'

'I never said you were, but it is kind of hard to believe.'

Annie shook her head; it felt muzzy—too much tequila. She would pay for it in the morning, but maybe tonight when she finally made it to bed she wouldn't have any of those terrible nightmares about a secret room in a cellar with dead bodies inside.

***

Stu and Laura huddled together to try to keep warm. They couldn't really see the chapel from their position, but this was the only place where they could keep out of sight yet still be near enough to get there in a hurry. Will's voice echoed through their earpieces. 'Two people just climbed over the gate and are heading your way up towards the chapel. It looks like a man and a woman but hard to tell from here.' Stu crept to the side of the wall; straining his eyes, he could make out a tall man and a much shorter woman who were stumbling hand in hand. Laura popped her head around to take a look and rolled her eyes at Stu. 'I can't see those two getting up to anything other than a quickie, that's if he can get it up. Those two are hammered and I'm freezing in a bloody cemetery of all places. How do we get roped into these crappy jobs? Join CID, become a detective, solve serious crime. Yes, right, what a load of rubbish.'

They watched as the dark figures finally reached the chapel and then the taller one bent down to give the shorter one a bunk up the fence. Will's voice echoed in their ears. *'Go, go, go.'*

Jake's hand pushed Annie and she grabbed hold of the top of the fence just as two figures came hurtling up the path, followed by a car with headlights on full beam, blinding them. Jake landed on the ground with a loud thud as someone rugby-tackled him. He landed on his back with some bloke on top of him. Annie, blinded by the light, began to shout, lost her grip on the fence and then slipped to the ground. She landed next to Jake and whispered, 'We are so fucked.'

The car stopped in front of them and a familiar figure climbed out, shouting, 'Police, don't move.' Laura slapped a pair of handcuffs on Annie whilst Stu cuffed Jake. Annie took one look at Jake's shocked expression and began laughing. Will stepped closer to take a look, pushing Twit and Twat out of the way, who were standing with batons and CS gas drawn, ready for battle. 'Jesus.'

Jake grinned at him, 'All right, Will; fancy meeting you here.'

'Would you like to tell me exactly what you two are doing in here at this time of night?'

Annie was speechless, her laughter getting more hysterical by the second. Composing herself as best as she could, she screeched. 'Sorry, officers, whatever it was, it was me.'

Will clenched his fists in anger. Annie hiccuped so loud it echoed around the graves. 'Sorry, Will. Jake and I decided to do a spot of ghost-hunting.'

Will's voice shook as he barked at Stu and Laura to uncuff them. His cheeks were flushed red and he leant down to grab Annie's arm. 'Jesus Christ, I can't leave you two alone for five minutes; you are a bloody liability.'

Jake had sobered up remarkably well compared to Annie, who was trying to stifle her laughter and not doing it very well. Jake looked at Will. 'Sorry, it's my fault. I begged her to come with me.'

Will shook his head and grabbed Annie's arm much more roughly than he'd intended, instantly regretting it as her face became a mask of fear. She pulled away from his grip. 'I can manage on my own.' Annie sobered instantly; she knew that Will would never mean to harm her, not like Mike used to, but still, her feelings were hurt.

'Sorry to interrupt your little party, sir.' She spat the words out. 'Come on, Jake, let's go back to your house and finish that tequila. Oh, and Will, don't bother coming round after you finish whatever it is you're doing in here. I'll be far too busy holding a séance.' She stormed off, making Jake jog to catch up with her. Neither of them spoke until they reached the gates, where they looked at each other and started laughing once more. The wind carried the sound up to the chapel, where Will was standing shaking his head and trying to figure out what had just happened.

Stu and Laura waited for Will to tell them what to do. 'Right, since those two have almost certainly messed up any chance of catching our grave-robbers tonight, I think we should leave. I can't see anyone coming in here now after all that racket.'

The two specials looked relieved to be able to escape the boredom; they wanted to be out where the action was, although, judging by what jobs had been passed over the radio in the last hour—a group of kids throwing stones at a taxi and a pensioner who had fallen out of bed—they wouldn't get much excitement working 'response' either. Will was just glad to get rid of them; he'd had enough for tonight. He waited for them to get in the car and then muttered, 'Come on, first round's on me. If I get drunk I may just find all of this slightly amusing.'

Stu smirked. 'It was kind of funny, Will. What are the odds on those two deciding to give *Most Haunted* a run for their money while we were on observations in here?'

Laura laughed; she agreed with Stu. They got into the car and Will drove down to the gates, where Jake was trying to give Annie a bunk up. Jake turned and saluted them. Will passed the keys to the gate to Stu. 'Open the gates and let the stupid buggers out and don't say a word. I'm really not in the mood.'

Stu got out and opened the gates. Will watched as Jake and Annie giggled at something Stu had said to them. It would be all around the station tomorrow, but it wouldn't be his fault; they only had themselves to blame. He waited for Annie to turn and look at him so he could smile, but she didn't. Instead, she clutched hold of Jake and stumbled off in the direction of his house.

Laura had been watching Will; she had seen the look in his eyes when Annie had marched off. He wouldn't admit it but he was upset. Laura had never met a woman with so much baggage and even more bad luck. Fingers crossed Stu would be his normal wimpy self and leave them after half a pint of lager to get home to his wife. For all his bravado, he was nothing more than a henpecked husband; it would be nice to be alone with Will in the pub. She'd had a thing for him for the past twelve months, yet he'd not once looked at her in anything other than a professional capacity. She grinned to herself at the thought of what she could do for him if she were given the chance. Stu looked at her and whispered, 'Never in a thousand years; he's in love.'

Laura shook her head. 'Twenty quid says I at least get a kiss off him.'

Stu growled, 'For twenty quid I'd want a blow job, not a kiss. Tenner and you're on.' Laura smiled sweetly and nodded in agreement.

June 25th, 1984

Sophie and Sean were playing hide and seek upstairs. Sean wasn't very good at it because he was too small to climb up into any of the cupboards, which meant that Sophie always found him. She had laughed at him last time she found him behind their mum's bedroom door, hiding underneath her long fluffy dressing gown. This was his favourite hiding place and he felt safe there because it smelled of coconut shampoo and his mum's perfume. He buried his head into the soft robe to stifle a giggle when he heard Sophie shouting, 'Fee-fi-fo-fum, I smell the blood of an Englishman.'

He could hear her footsteps as she ran along the landing, the creak of the bathroom door as she looked inside and the bang as she slammed it shut again and ran to the next bedroom. He was too young to understand that she was making a fuss so as not to make him feel bad about being too little to find a good hiding place — she was kind like that. She could be horrible to him, especially if he had taken one of her Sindy dolls for his A-Team men to rescue, but most of the time she was nice. He heard her footsteps as she ran closer to his hiding place. He was staring down at his feet, so he didn't see the dark shadow that walked past the door, but he shivered and felt his teeth begin to chatter. It was so cold; he hugged the robe tighter to him to keep warm. He sniffed and then gagged; there was an awful smell in the room—a bit like when his mum made veg for dinner and they didn't eat it all because it was horrible. She would forget and leave the pan on the cooker for days. He wondered if his mum was cooking veg for tea and he pulled a face. He didn't like any of it except for the green peas and he only liked them because they made good ammunition for the A-Team to flick at the bad guys. The light left the room and Sean felt the hairs on the back of his neck begin to prickle. It was sunny outside so he didn't understand why the room had gone so dark. He wanted to peek out from his hiding place, but his Hannibal voice was telling him, 'No'. He had to stay hidden, then he would be safe. Sophie had stopped running about and he heard her make a funny high-pitched noise. It wasn't very loud at first, but then she let out a really loud screech which made him jump with fright. There was a loud thud, which was followed by more screaming. Sean was scared, but he had to go and see what was wrong with his sister, so he ignored Hannibal and ran from the room on to the landing, where Sophie was curled into a ball screaming. He didn't know what to do, but then his mum came running up the stairs and bent down to see what was wrong with her. He had never seen anyone with a face as white as Sophie's and he was afraid for her.

'What's wrong, Sophie? Tell me what happened!' Sophie stared at their mum and shook her head. 'There was a man…he was all black and he smelled really bad.'

She let out a sob and began crying.

'What man—where did he go? Did he hurt you?'

Sean began to feel scared; he had smelled that bad smell but hadn't seen any man. He turned his head to look around and make sure that the man wasn't behind them. Sophie nodded and Sean watched his mum's face turn the same colour as Sophie's. 'He pushed me over and told me to get out.'

Sean felt his knees begin to shake; he was so scared and he needed to pee really badly.

'Sophie, where did he go—is he still in here?'

His mum pulled Sophie up from the floor and then she grabbed him by the shoulder and pushed both of them behind her. She picked up a vase of flowers off the small table, discarding the flowers and dropping them to the floor.

'Sophie, I need you to tell me where he is—which room did he go in?'

'I don't know, Mummy. I think he's gone. He walked into the wall.'

She lifted a shaking finger and pointed at the wall opposite them and whispered, 'He went through there, but I think he will be coming back…he doesn't like me.'

Sean watched his mum put the vase back on the table and then she turned to face both of them. 'Sophie, if you are telling me lies you will be in trouble, young lady. No one can walk through walls. Now, do you want to tell me what really happened or are you going to continue telling fibs?'

Sean wanted to tell her that there was a man who had smelled bad, but he didn't want to make his mum even angrier, so he kept quiet and didn't look at Sophie. He felt sorry for her and she would be angry with him if he knew and didn't speak up. But then his mum picked up the vase again and walked into each bedroom to look under the beds and in the wardrobes. Sophie and Sean followed her. She even checked the cupboard in the bathroom where the hot water tank was, but the only things in there were piles of towels. The only place his mum didn't check was the attic, but since there was no ladder he reasoned that the man couldn't be hiding up there, not unless he had superpowers and could fly like Superman. He felt Sophie's hot breath as she let out a sigh of relief; she was standing so close to him, clutching his arm so hard he couldn't move it. Their mum turned to them both. 'Now, I don't know what game you were playing or why you are telling lies, Sophie, but you mustn't do that ever again. You nearly gave me a heart attack; I thought someone had attacked you.'

Sophie bent her head as big teardrops fell from her eyes on to the floor. Sean reached out his hand and curled his chubby fingers around Sophie's cold, much more slender ones, then squeezed hard—he believed her. Their mum went downstairs and they followed her, neither of them wanting to be upstairs without her in case the bad-smelling man came back through the wall.